I looked back into my book and saw black and white photos of

girls standing in a courtyard, all wearing the same gray frocks and the

same short haircuts with bangs, hanging sheets for miles. Blank stares

on their faces and slumped shoulders made each girl a shell carbon-

copy of the next. There were always two or three nuns, in old-

fashioned long white habits and white skirts, off to the side, watching

with carved scowls and judging eyes.

INISH CLARE
The Pirate Queen: Book Two

CITY OWL PRESS
www.cityowlpress.com

Cover Design by Tina Moss. Map Design by Jake Peterson. All stock photos licensed appropriately.

Edited by Amanda Roberts.

For information on subsidiary rights, please contact the publisher at info@cityowlpress.com.

Print Edition ISBN: 978-1-944728-51-9

Digital Edition ISBN: 978-1-944728-52-6

Printed in the United States of America

INISH CLARE

Jennifer Rose McMahon

CITY OWL
PRESS

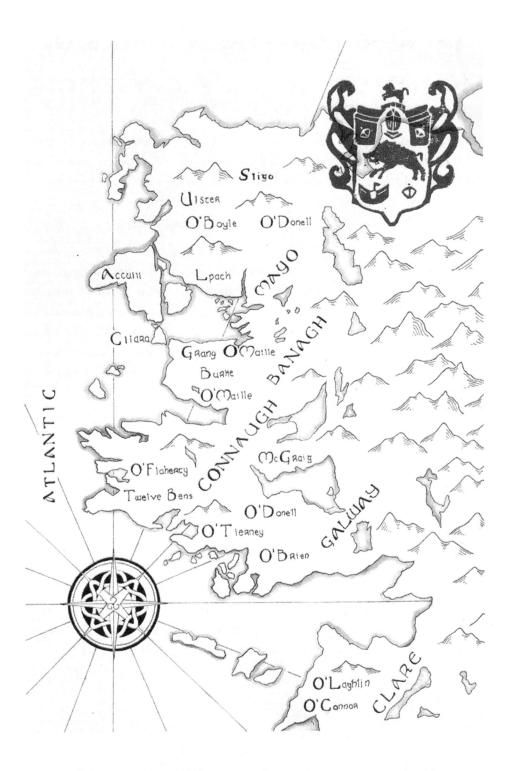

ATLANTIC

Sligo

Ulster

O'Boyle   O'Donell

Accuill

Lpach

Giiara

MAYO

Grang O'Maille

Buake

O'Maille

CONNAUGH BANAGH

O'Flaherty

Twelve Bens

McGraig

O'Donell

GALWAY

O'Tieaney

O'Brien

O'Laghlin

O'Connor

CLARE

PRAISE FOR THE WORKS OF JENNIFER ROSE McMAHON

"McMahon's excellent debut, BOHERMORE, makes a contemporary paranormal mystery feel cozy and romantic... The slowly unfurling romance doesn't go in obvious directions, which adds to the story's allure. Teen and adult readers alike will be clamoring for the sequel."

- Publishers Weekly Starred Review

"Engaging, beautifully written scenes, and idyllic descriptions of Ireland and lyrical dialogue keep the tale of the Pirate Queen moving at a quick pace. The characters are engaging and they draw a person in to this tale of adventure and intrigue...Adrenaline-fueled action and enough twists and turns to keep even the most astute readers on their toes, this is a captivating story with a heroine who is forcefully engaging."

- L. Kane, InD'tale Magazine

"Jennifer's novel captures the connection with the past which we treasure in Ireland. The Irish landscape, contemporary social life, the Irish language and romance are woven into this fantasy story. I am certainly looking forward to the sequel."

- Sarah Kelly, O'Malley Clan Chieftain

"This book was so interesting. It was romantic, there was mystery and the imagery was phenomenal. Once I began reading it, I could not put it down and actually sighed out loud when I read the especially sweet aspects of the book...all while I was reading it on the beach"

- Reviewer

To the O'Malley Clan

"Terra Marique Potens"

Powerful by Land and Sea

Chapter One
Return to Grace

Scrambling over shifting stones of the ancient rock wall, laid by hands of countless generations, I cursed the stinging Irish nettles as I vanished into my family cemetery. Every inch of the hallowed space was familiar, from the oldest tombstones with weathered medieval carvings to the "newer" centuries-old gravestones—Celtic crosses that were cracked, tilted, or fallen. The decrepit O'Malley boneyard was in the same state of time-crushed ruin as last winter when I'd almost lost my life there.

Cloaked by heavy spruce boughs laden with hanging ivy, the silent stillness of the graveyard was ethereal, isolated from the outside world. Mist stirred like thick smoke around the foundation of each tipped cross or limestone slab as I moved deeper into the solemn sanctuary. My curiosity drew me in farther as thoughts of my haunting visions swirled in my head.

Tracking my ghostly hunter was my primary focus, because I was growing weary of the torment of forever being stalked. I had new information now that made me stronger, smarter. I intended to end the curse before it ended me and any future I might have.

The raw scar on my chest burned back to life as I crept close enough to read the gravestone epitaphs. My hand jumped to the ancient ring hanging from my necklace and closed around it with a fist as I looked back for Paul.

Thoughts of my grandmother placing the relic around my neck

sent chills through me. It had only been a few months since her passing, back in Boston. She'd died two months after my grandfather. Of a lonely broken heart, I was sure. My return to Ireland after their deaths was an easy choice for me. My family was gone. Ireland was where I felt most at home now. For many reasons—my roots especially. Rebuilding my life here made sense.

I released the heavy ring and it dropped back to its rightful spot, nestling into the scarred burn as a micro-pulsing of molten intensity returned. The rising discomfort, then pain, sharpened my senses, reminding me of the other ancient relic in my jacket. My hand moved to my pocket by instinct and pressed around the outline of the contents to be sure the leather parcel was still there.

"Come on," I whispered like a sneaking child and waved for Paul to catch up. "What are you doing?" My eyebrows scrunched as I watched his paranoid gaze scan the perimeter of lumbering trees that dated to far before my grandparents ever left Ireland. I peeked back over my shoulder in the direction he was perusing, half expecting to see a spook.

"Wait, Maeve. Somethin's different." His brogue thickened and his head tilted as he froze, listening.

"No. It's exactly the same." My classic impatience poked at him. "Just like when we flew out of here last time. Look." I pointed. "That's the ivy that snagged my foot as we ran from her and the…." My eyes moved to the tomb mound and I fell silent. The danger of our last visit brewed in my muscles and turned my bones soft. Fear crept back in, once again, to curtail my plans.

The heat generated from my pounding heart turned me to rubber as I moved from confident explorer to skittish quarry.

"Aren't we safe this time? I have her ring…." My words faded into the mist, losing any promise they may have held.

Facing my ancestor from five hundred years ago, the great pirate queen Gráinne Ní Mháille, shot fear through my soul. The medieval legends of Grace O'Malley told tales of piracy, battle, and revenge.

I'd always believed she was responsible somehow for my mother's death, and for the centuries-old curse that had plagued generations of the O'Malley women. I needed to end it if I was going to have any semblance of a normal life and any hopes of a future for the women of my family. If any were left.

"Shh." Paul's finger went up to freeze time and he moved his palm across the air as if to detect any disturbance. "We're not alone."

My ears flinched, like a deer sensing its hunter.

"What?" My quivering feet carried me to him in a millisecond and I grabbed his arm, turning then to see his view. I watched and listened. "Do you think it's *her?*"

The wind hadn't whipped up yet. The blasts and the terror hadn't come. All the wrath and vengeance of her soul, ready to attack. But nothing happened. How could she be near without the terrifying accompanying wind, violent bursts, and screams?

The screaming.

The blood.

My body shuddered at the memory of my visions.

Every muscle in my body tensed around my bones, turning me to a rigid statue where only my eyes could move.

She would come for the ring.

I was sure of it.

That was why I brought it back.

It was like it connected me to her, somehow, and I would use this to my advantage.

My hand wrapped around the ring on my necklace again, feeling its heat and vibrating anticipation. It was the ring from her true love, Hugh, given to her over five hundred years ago before he was murdered by the rival MacMahon Clan. Visions of the brutal slaying replayed in my mind as I recalled the vivid details of my horrific nightmare that played out the devastating historical event.

I swallowed hard and wondered if I was playing with fire. My impulsive nature always got the best of me and somehow landed me in situations like this—in a cemetery with the ring of the wrathful pirate queen. My second thoughts crashed in on me, making my knees tremble.

My grandmother had protected the ring for years, back home in Boston. It had been passed down and kept safe for generations, but now I'd brought it back. Back to Ireland's legendary chieftain, the pirate queen. She'd been hunting me my entire life, in my strange visions—my awake dreams. All for this. I squeezed the heirloom, feeling its centuries of suffering.

I opened my hand and looked at the ring. The ornate Celtic designs swirled in my eyes and the heavy gemstone protruded among the mythical beasts and spirals, holding secrets of medieval times. This ring could be Grace's direct connection to Hugh. Maybe it held the power to heal her eternal suffering and grief... to settle her tormented soul.

All I knew was that the power of the ring was strong enough to cause my grandfather's mother to send her eldest son away to America to hide the ring and never come back. Thoughts of Joey leaving his Irish home to protect his family filled my heart with sadness.

I missed my grandfather and hoped my final hours with him back in Boston, telling him every detail of my original trip to his homeland, the discovery of Grace, and my hopes to end the curse, were enough to bring peace to his soul. A part of me knew I had come back to Ireland for him. My Irish roots ran deep, especially through my grandfather. Patrick Joseph O'Malley. My Joey.

I figured I could use the power of the ring to stop Grace from hunting and terrorizing me. And future generations of O'Malley women, like all those from the past who suffered the same visions and stalking. Many losing their lives to it in one way or another, including my own mother. I had to end it. Confronting Gráinne Ní Mháille and offering her ring back seemed to be my only option for a resolution.

I looked at Paul's face and traced his stubbled jaw, chiseled with clenched focus, but his warm blue eyes softened with caution and concern. Guilt washed over me as I worried about putting him in harm's way... *again*.

Grace attacked us here last winter, with clear intent to kill, and there was no certainty that she wouldn't try again. But she had recognized him then, right before attempting to strike him with her sword. She looked straight into his soul, like she knew him, and dropped her sword in the ivy. She fell to her knees and buried her face in her hands.

The memory of her grieving form constricted my throat.

A glint of light flashed in my eyes and my head twitched in its direction. Paul's chin jumped toward it at the same time.

His wide eyes turned to mine and I met them with equal hope.

The sword!

It visited my dreams again and again, glinting its vibrant light at me, luring me back to Ireland from its ivy-covered bed.

I squeezed Paul's hand. "Oh my god! It's her sword. Do you think it's the sword?" My nerves bounced me in my shoes. "Come on."

I pulled on him to follow me as my other hand held the ring at my chest. The scarred spot where it burned me months ago was throbbing to a point of warning and hysteria.

Paul's hand tightened on mine.

"Don't move. There's someone here." He stopped short.

Blood drained from my head, leaving me dizzy at the thought that he might be right. Though he was no longer my professor, thank god, I still knew enough to believe his every word.

Crack. Snap.

At the edge of the trees. Motion.

A dark figure lurked in the shadows of the gloom. It moved like fluid away from the far edge and into the maze of gravestones. My feet stepped backward along with Paul's, though I didn't take my eyes off the... person.

His tall frame, masculine in its size and stature, was covered in a dark brown cloak. The oversize hood draped over his bowed head, concealing any features. Only his hands remained exposed in a creepy, prayer-like position. He continued to move toward us, as if he were gliding across the ground.

"Let's get out of here." My whisper caught in my tight throat.

"Come on." Paul turned with me and moved in a determined gait, heading toward the bright light of day radiating just outside the sallow shelter of the graveyard.

Following his steady pull, I turned back to the ghostly figure and let out a yelp as I saw his form moving toward us at a sprinter's pace, hands extended forward, palms facing each other, beating up and down for stealth speed.

My head spun back toward the light of day.

"Run!" I screamed.

I pulled on Paul in a panic and before he had a full view of our attacker, his pace amped up to full sprint as he yelled, "Jazus! What the…."

He raced with me toward the ancient stonewall—the border between our ghostly world and the real one. I fell in sync with his strides as my ears filled with a blood-curdling growl from behind us.

It started out low and grew into a complex sound of a runaway freight train or an evil boar possessed by the devil himself. The terrifying sound shattered my mind as it pushed through my hair and coated my skin, proving he was nearly upon us.

We flew over the wall, slipping on damp moss and knocking loose a top stone that rolled past my feet, tripping me up. Paul gripped my elbow in a steel lock, steadying me as we ran for the car, stumbling on rocks and gravel.

I looked back over my shoulder, expecting to be grabbed any second by terror in human form, but the cloaked stranger was nowhere to be seen.

Paul fumbled for his keys as my eyes darted all around.

"Hurry up!" The shake in my voice worsened with every quake of my body.

The engine revved to life and Paul threw it in reverse and blasted us backward down the lane as I watched the graveyard move farther and farther away from us.

Regret brewed in my stomach as the desire to go back overtook me immediately.

"Wait. We didn't get to…." My words of longing to go back for the sword were cut short as my eyes jumped to the tall figure standing rigid on the stonewall, watching us pull away. His hands interlaced again in a prayer position and his head tipped down, allowing the hood of the cloak to flop over it.

He remained motionless as we drove away.

***

"In here, in here." I pointed to the parking lot near Warde's Pub. My hands rubbed my knees until they were hot. "We can't just go home after that. We need answers," I panted. "Let's find Padraic." I brushed my messy hair away from my face. "He knows a lot about my family… and Brigid."

My defeat at the cemetery turned to determination in a heartbeat.

Paul turned to me with tight lips, then parked the car. "Fine. It's worth a shot."

Our stools in Warde's Pub beckoned us back since our last visit months ago, and Padraic welcomed us as he wiped the counter and set our square napkins in place.

Though it was just a couple miles from the O'Malley graveyard, the safety of the pub made it feel like light years away.

"Ach, sure, was wonderin' when I'd see ye again. Back for more, are ya?" Padraic snapped his towel at me.

I leaned forward to get a look down the length of the bar, hoping Donal might still be at the back of the pub, dwelling in the shadows. Stories of my distant cousin Brigid began with these men in Warde's. Tales of a possessed girl with visions. Not unlike me, really, which made it even more disturbing.

Their tales said she was taken away from the O'Malley farm when she was eighteen and sent to the Magdalene laundries. My eyes closed to clear the haunting thoughts. I could have ended up just like her—committed, institutionalized in an asylum, and forgotten.

I looked at Padraic, still unsure how to feel about him. He had been the bearer of bad news about the laundries last time we were here, but shooting the messenger wasn't going to help. "They was a cursed family, them O'Malleys," he said last winter with little empathy or filter. "The women had all gone stark ravin' mad."

My mouth pressed into a frown remembering his crass words. I shook it off with a twitch of my shoulders. I knew different. I had the same visions as Brigid, of the pirate queen, and knew Gráinne Ní Mháille wouldn't stop tracking the O'Malley women until she got what she wanted. The ring.

If I could just throw the ring at the vision of Grace O'Malley and have it all poof into oblivion, I would. I'd throw it and run. But there was more to it. I was certain. The unfortunate nagging in my gut told me the ring needed to be passed, directly and cautiously, at just the right moment, like a sacred ritual. My lip curled up in disgust and self-loathing, wishing I didn't have to take it all so seriously, but I knew I was right.

Facing her was my plan, and not a pleasant one. She scared the crap out of me and worse, she had the power to end me.

"Yeah, back for more. I guess you could say that." I huffed at his comment. "It all feels very unfinished." I tipped my head at Padraic. "Like the O'Malleys just disappeared from their homeland and no one knows what happened to all of them... particularly Brigid. Where could she *be* now?"

I wrapped my hands around my coffee mug, searching for warmth, wondering where all the local O'Malleys had gone.

"Ach, lassie, 'tis all but legend now, fadin' into the mist of time." Padraic moved down the bar, wiping in a rhythm of decades of similar strokes. "The O'Malleys dispersed. Lost their land through the ancient Brehon Law and moved on. Shame 'tis." His voice faded as he went farther down the bar. "'Twill always be their land, though."

I turned to Paul and raised my eyebrows in question. "What's Brehon Law?"

He nodded, as if in agreement with Padraic, absorbing what he said.

"It's ancient Celtic ruling, from medieval times. Governed the people through laws that were actually quite modern for their time." He looked down the bar toward Padraic. "He must be referring to its property laws, which basically granted ownership of 'property in question' for a fixed amount of time. Generations, really."

"Fixed amount of time?" My eyebrows scrunched, narrowing my eyes.

"Basically giving the original owners time to prove their rights to the land. Once the deadline hit, though, Brehon Law would grant the land to the current holders, if the original landholders couldn't prove their claim, that is."

My eyes widened. "That's a bit harsh. Isn't it?"

"It's actually quite fair. Particularly since the deadlines are generally set for hundreds of years." He flipped his hair away from his face. His windblown look sent tingles into my belly and warmed me.

It was much more than legend though, as Padraic called it, with a flick of his rag. Paul and I knew there was more to it. I had her ring. And in my pocket, the leather satchel held promises beyond imagination—an ancient tomb key.

My grandfather kept the medieval key back in Boston, hidden safe in his garden with St. Brendan the Navigator as its protector. The iconic statue in the backyard held the secret within its stony base, behind a camouflaged mysterious little hatch, for countless years. And now the key was back here in Ireland, right in my pocket.

My smile quivered as my throat tightened. I missed him. Every day. I missed Gram and my mother too. The hollow emptiness of grief carved out my heart each day. Feeling alone and lost, my love for them had nowhere to go. It festered in me, trapped. My journey back here, to Ireland, was the best way for me to stay connected to them in some way.

And Gráinne Ní Mháille, Grace O'Malley, she was my family too. And my hunter. My sixteenth great-grandmother. She'd been terrorizing me my entire life, and even worse, I knew she had something to do with my mother's untimely death. I was sure Mom's "heart condition" had a direct link to Grace's tortured soul and broken heart. It made sense. I reached for my own heart to be sure it held its steady beat.

I ran my hands through my hair, pondering the enormity of the task in front of me. I was determined to break the cycle that plagued the O'Malley women and get my life back and would let nothing stop me.

Paul reached under the bar and took my hand, reminding me of the other reason I'd returned to Ireland. He ran his fingers through mine, sending chills all the way to the ends of my hair. He bent his head to look into my face.

"Maeve, this isn't going to be as easy as we thought," he said with gentle raised eyebrows.

My response to his touch distracted me from his words as I focused only on his mouth. He'd turned my world upside down in every imaginable way. And I just wanted to devour him every minute.

I blinked into his wide pupils and reached for his windblown hair, attempting to control it a bit, then flashed back to the ominous figure in the cemetery.

"Who the hell was that anyway? Or *what* was that?" My hands slapped down on my lap.

My teeth clenched in annoyed distraction.

I wanted to find Grace's sword. I wanted to see if the tomb key was a match to the ancient mound in the cemetery. Its capstone read G R A, 1500-something. Even if it was a match, though, I had no idea what I would do next. It's not like opening a burial crypt like a grave robber was something I could actually do.

My head tipped and I stared into space for a minute.

No. No way.

I pushed on my temples and looked straight into Paul's eyes.

"I want to go back to the cemetery. We have to." My eyes begged his.

He shook his head and rubbed his scruffy chin.

"I don't know. It's dangerous." He pressed his lips together. "I know it's important to you, but I'm not going to put you in harm's way again. We need a better plan." He glanced down the bar. "We need to be prepared for anything, everything."

Paul cracked his knuckles in thought. He looked back into my eyes and hesitated.

My eyebrows shot up.

"We need Brigid," I said.

A chill shuddered through my body.

My lost cousin Brigid was the missing link. She was the only person on this planet who had the same visions as me, the same violent assaults that interrupted our lives and made us freaks. Brigid could have answers.

I nodded my head at Paul as our next moves fell into place through our connected eyes.

"Padraic. Two pints."

Paul bought more conversation time with Padraic as the stout took its own sweet time settling in the glasses before being topped off.

"So, Padraic," Paul continued, "the laundries… which one would they send the girls to from around here?"

Padraic's back stiffened.

The laundries were an unspoken topic, one of disgrace. If they weren't discussed, then maybe they never existed.

The shadow of shame that washed over Padraic's face was a national reaction to the matter.

Paul had done his graduate studies on Irish history and the Magdalene Laundries were a vague part of it, always shrouded in mystery, but enough for him to be able to enlighten me. I remembered his stories of the laundries, all disbanded now—institutions for "fallen women" where young girls were sent if they became unwed mothers or if they showed promiscuity or any signs of mental illness. Ireland's religious laws were rigid and these "physical and mental" conditions were considered unholy. The nuns would come and the girls would never be heard from again.

My pint sloshed in the glass as my shaking hands struggled to remain steady, making it worse, but my visceral response to the idea of the laundries couldn't be controlled. My lips pressed together in loud silence.

"Ya should'na be askin' about the laundries. They're gone now." Padraic eyeballed Paul like a criminal.

Paul adjusted himself on his stool and cleared his throat.

"Understood. But you remember, Padraic, Maeve's cousin was sent to one." He gestured his head toward me. "Brigid. We aim to find 'er."

"Right. Right. I know, lassie." Padraic's head hung and he nodded to me. "God bless 'er soul."

"She's my only family, Padraic. I need to find her. To tell her she's not alone. That she's not crazy."

My heart tore at the thought of Brigid spending all those years thinking she was insane or possessed from the visions. She must be somewhere around fifty by now—tormented her entire life without any explanation. The intense visions started with her at eighteen, same as me. And then she was gone. Taken away.

"I'm sorry. You're a fine pair with good hearts. But it's a dead end fer ya."

Padraic stopped his serving and wiping and looked straight at me, as if it were my final hour.

My heart skipped a beat as his sympathetic gaze shot fear into me, like he knew something.

"How so?" Paul grew impatient.

"She was sent to the House of Tears, I reckon." His eyes avoided ours. "St. Mary's. In Tuam. 'Twas where all them girls from around here was sent."

Paul jolted back as if he'd been punched.

"St. Mary's? The Tuam babies?" Paul gasped.

Padraic nodded.

"I've been studying the excavation. Christ." Paul shook his head and looked down into his pint glass, into oblivion.

"*What?*" My voice pierced the air.

Had they forgotten I was even here?

Padraic moved away from us to attend to other patrons, who seemed all set to me.

"I know where St. Mary's is. They might know about Brigid." Paul's lips turned up in a fake half-smile, but his worried eyes gave him away.

"House of Tears? What is that place?" I asked in a revolting tone, pulling away from him.

It sounded to me like a made-up horror movie script. My imagination spun evil scene after evil scene as sickness soured my mouth.

"The laundries," Paul admitted with flat affect.

Chapter Two

Forbidden

Dodging big, wet rain drops, Paul and I ran for my blue door. His arm sheltered me as I crouched from the drops, forever trying to stay dry in the wettest part of Ireland, the west.

"How'ya Miss O'Malley. Master McGratt." Mr. Flaherty, my landlord, nodded at us from his shelter of the overhang from his paint shop sign. His heavy brogue made it nearly impossible to understand him.

He'd welcomed me back after my grandparents passed away and rented me my flat again. 122 Bohermore. But he still always looked at me through sideways, squinted eyes, as if he were trying to figure me out, or worse, like he saw something in me no one else could see.

His gaze followed us as we pushed through the blue door into my alleyway, leading to the entry to my flat, and then he headed back into his paint shop flapping his rag into the air.

Paul and I raced up the stairs and into the kitchen, slipping on the shiny black and white tile, all the way to the sink to shake off and drip dry. Paul pressed against me as he shook his hands through my hair, pushing wet bits off my face. The pressure of his body on mine sent my mind spiraling.

He had been my college professor, when I first came to Ireland last September. Untouchable. Forbidden. But now, here in my kitchen, he was just Paul. Well, not just.

He leaned in and ran his lips across my jawline, inhaling deeply.

"You smell like the rain." He pulled back and gazed into my eyes.

Tempted to fall into the warm depths of his stare, I dropped my eyes to the floor instead—thinking about Brigid and how to find her.

Paul reached for a tea towel and dried the ends of my hair with it.

"What are you thinking about? I can see the wheels turning." He gave a gentle smile.

"Sorry. I can't help it." I took his hand and squeezed it. "I need to start at the library." My mind raced ahead of me. "To look up St. Mary's and the laundries. To find out what happened to the women who were sent there."

I tipped my head at Paul as his eyes stared out the window, distracted.

"What?" I asked.

"Sorry. No, I agree." He shook his head. "I just couldn't help thinking about your landlord, there. He's an odd character." He smirked. "I'm not sure Ol' Mr. Flaherty likes me much. He's a bit protective of you, I'd say."

"Of course he likes you," I replied as my brows scrunched in question.

"Nah. He looks at me funny. Like he can see right through me or somethin'." He shot an exaggerated shiver through his shoulders. "Ya haven't told him about us, have you? Ya know, our whole *history* thing?"

I shook my head fast.

"No. Never. He'd think I was crazy." I wrapped my arms around his ribs. "But you're right. It's not just you. He looks at me funny too, like he's spooked. Like he knows something."

If Mr. Flaherty had any idea of what we'd been through together, he'd probably evict me like I was a possessed witch.

I squeezed Paul closer to me, thinking of the time we had to spend apart while I was back in Boston. So much had happened and then I had to leave so abruptly, like we were torn apart. It felt good to be with him again.

"I'm so glad to be back here with you," I whispered in his ear. Just the thought of him patched my heavy heart. "You make me feel like I'm home."

He smoothed my hair back.

"When you left me, I thought m' heart had been ripped out." He stroked my cheek, remembering our painful goodbye. We'd hardly had a moment to even think about it since I'd returned. "But now, it's like I can breathe again."

His head fell as he held his cheek against mine, moving his hand around the back of my neck.

"You knew I'd come back," I whispered. "You set me up with that book. Left me no choice." I smirked and pushed him away.

He came right back to me like a magnet.

"I'm sorry. That was the only way I knew how to tell you. On your own time, your own pace." He smirked at his effective ploy. "My mind was blown too. Sure, 'destined to be together' seemed a little heavy for parting words." He huffed. "Plus, I wasn't sure if it could hurt us in some way."

I thought of the book he gave me as I boarded my flight home last winter. It was of his family heritage and held incredible information of his lineage—direct connections to Grace. To me.

"How could it hurt us?" My eyebrows shot up.

Paul stepped back and ran his hand through his hair. His shirt rode up enough to expose the skin over the waist of his pants. My eyes lingered there.

"I don't know. It didn't end well for them, you know, Grace and Hugh." He grimaced. "So finding out I was a descendant of Hugh DeLacy kind of scared the crap out of me. I mean, you're connected to her. I'm connected to him. And the dreams…."

He burst his fingers at his head, as if it were exploding.

"Right. The dreams don't end well for you typically." I curled my lip in disgust, thinking of how he had similar dreams to my visions, only he died in his. Every time.

"That's an understatement."

"Well, I kinda see it as a sign that we were meant to be together." I smiled and glanced at him sideways as I pulled him closer to me. "It takes the guesswork out of it, right?"

I breathed in his fresh-air, woodsy scent and laced my fingers in the belt loops of his pants.

He had a powerful way of making my festering grief have someplace safe to go. Someplace happier and whole. Providing relief from the pain. And I trusted him for that.

His arms wrapped around me, arching my back, and I lifted my face to his. He dropped his head down, burying it in my shoulder, and whispered in my ear.

"I just don't know what I would do if something ever happened to ya. I couldn't bear it." He inhaled, breathing in my hair and my face. "Never leave me again, Maeve. I can't be apart from you ever again. Promise me."

His words softened my muscles as tingling desire coursed through me.

His smoldering eyes moved from mine, down the lines of my body and back to my mouth. His breath quickened as he pulled my body against his.

"Maeve. What are you doing to me?"

He brushed my hair from my face as he gazed into my eyes. He moved his mouth closer to mine and his breath tickled my lips. He pulled my hips against his and kissed me. His soft lips searched mine, pressing them open, kissing me deeper. His hunger excited me and I kissed him back with a passion that left me panting.

His hands ran down my back and up along my ribs, brushing the sides of my breasts. My breath sucked in as I ran my hands over his strong shoulders and down his arms. His toned muscles sent craving through me. His arm held my back as his other hand ran down the middle of my chest. My back arched in response to his touch.

His hand rested in the center of my chest bone and he kissed me again.

Buzz! Buzz!

I jumped as my heart skipped a beat. I couldn't shake the scandalous jitters that lingered from when he was my teacher, always fearing being caught together.

"Dammit! Who is that?" I barked at the old-fashioned buzz of the doorbell.

"Jazus. What I could do to you…," he whispered and shook his head at me and then at the buzzer. "You have me completely bewitched, Maeve O'Malley."

He tucked the bottom on his clean oxford into the waist of his pants.

Oh my god.

I licked my lips, dreaming of more time with him.

With obvious reluctance, Paul released me and the warmth of his body left me, replaced with a chill of emptiness. I craved his closeness instantly.

I thumped down each stair with a heavy step and moved through the alley-like corridor toward my blue door. The buzz from the doorbell continued in the back of my mind, incessantly buzzing. I pulled on the swollen door until it gave way.

"Don't you ever answer your texts? What the hell!" Michelle blasted at me.

She pushed past me into the narrow breezeway.

She'd stayed in Galway all this time, ever since we first arrived together on the same flight last September, and had actually decided to stay indefinitely. Her boyfriend Declan had something to do with *that* decision, for sure.

"What?" I checked my empty pockets for my phone. "What texts?"

"You promised a girl's night out when you got back from Claremorris. Soooooo, ready?" She tapped her foot and checked the time on her phone. The frizz of her windblown hair left zero evidence of her preppy, perfectly straightened bob when we first met. She'd left the designer labels and personal primping far behind.

My thoughts jumped to Paul, waiting in my kitchen, and I ached to be with him. My head fell back as I flashed to the lost moments.

"Thought it might be you." Paul's voice caught me by surprise as he approached from behind. "How're things, Michelle?"

His warm voice proved his affection for her, but the hidden tone of disappointment didn't go unnoticed by me.

"Oops, I get it." Michelle's face reddened and her hands shot up in defense. "Didn't mean to interrupt anything." Her sarcastic, drawn-out tone poked fun at us.

"No worries," Paul said. "I was just leaving. Maeve could use a friendly distraction for a bit."

He leaned in and kissed me, lingering for a moment longer than necessary, reminding me of what I was missing. "Meet you at the library tomorrow?"

Awesome. He was going to join me at the library tomorrow. Perfect.

I needed his help researching St. Mary's and the laundries and what became of the women who stayed there.

"Definitely. That would be great." I smiled to hide my disappointed eyes, wishing he would stay. "See you tomorrow."

I watched him leave out the blue door and onto Bohermore. And then he was gone.

Before I could fully wallow in the void of his leaving, Michelle stole my attention, pulling me up the stairs to get ready for our night out.

***

"So what'd you find at the cemetery? Anything good?" Michelle tried on a pink lipstick and smacked her lips in the mirror over my dresser. "Your curse is alive and well, I assume."

"Actually, yes. About the cursed part." I shot her a sideways grimace. "There was some creepy dude in a brown cloak, trying to scare us away."

A chill ran through me as the vision of the cloaked figure haunted me again.

"Seriously. Probably Fergal. What a freak." Her stiff tone emphasized her disdain for Fergal. "He's always getting in the way of your dream quest. Dick."

She jabbed me with her elbow and snickered.

"Hmm. Maybe." I considered if it could really have been Fergal. He *was* from a rival clan of the O'Malleys, the one likely responsible for the murder of Hugh. But was Fergal capable of masterminding… well, anything?

"He'd make a good villain for my book though," she interjected. "I'm gonna tell Declan about this. We need some extra layers for the project. An unexpected antagonist."

Her level businesslike tone made Fergal seem less dangerous or not real, but that didn't change anything.

"Don't even say his name," I whined. "He's like that nightmare dude, where if you think or say his name he materializes! And then you're dead!"

I punched her arm to stifle her.

"Oh my god! That's good stuff!" She bounced like I was the best muse a friend could have. "Just no wells! Those creep me out too much!"

I pulled on my favorite jeans and a cute top that hung a little off one shoulder, almost by accident, showing my tank top, and darted into the bathroom to make an attempt at fixing my hair.

"Come on. You're fine."

Michelle yanked me toward the door as I reached for my phone and wristlet purse. I stumbled and dragged my feet, feeling like I'd rather stay home. With Paul.

But going out with Michelle was important too. She was my ballast. A reminder of how totally crazy everything was, but how perfectly normal at the same time.

"Michelle?" I slowed my pace following her and she turned to me.

"Yeah?"

"I'm a little scared." My eyebrows rose as my eyes misted.

She stopped short.

"What do you mean?"

"I don't know. I feel like something big is happening. Like I'm about to change or something. And I don't want to change. I want to stay me."

"Maeve, you'll always be you. Nothing and no one can change that."

She reached for my bent arm, weaving hers into it, and pulled me along, arm in arm, toward our evening out.

Her words hit me deep. "I'll always be me."

That was good because I was heading into some uncharted territory and had to wonder if I would come out on the other side unscathed. I seemed to have a habit of jumping in head first with things here in Ireland without really thinking about consequences.

I just didn't want to jump too deep into trouble I couldn't get out of.

***

Flying past Eyre Square and bouncing down Shop Street, I struggled to keep up with Michelle. She was homed in on a secret destination she refused to reveal and swerved through the busy cobblestone road.

Summer in Galway brought the crowds and the evening sky stayed bright until practically eleven o'clock, giving the feel and energy of mid-day.

Giggling the entire way, she took my hand and swung my arm in smug knowingness. Then, without question, I heard it. The deep bass vibrations first, then the smooth sounds of rhythm and blues.

Mojo.

I stopped short.

"No!" I stared at Michelle with pure terror bolting out of my pupils. "I can't!"

"Oh, yes, you can. And you will! He'll die when he sees you." She was giddy like a schoolgirl.

"Michelle! You're evil." I combed my hair with my fingers and straightened my top. "I hate you." I pressed my lips together, confirming the presence of subtle lip gloss. "Do I look okay?"

What was wrong with me? The thought of seeing Rory again sent me to Crazyville. Particularly while playing in the band, and same pub, where I'd first fallen for him.

"You're gorgeous, as always! Now, come on." She yanked me into the hidden, arched doorway of Lynch's Pub.

It was packed tight as usual with the local crowd. Pints and chatter filled the space and the music topped it up to overflowing. Hearing the familiar sound of Mojo spread a huge smile across my face and I stretched on tiptoes to try for a glimpse of Rory.

He was my first... love, I guess. I'd met him when I'd just arrived in Ireland last fall, right here in Lynch's. Somehow, though, it was not meant to be.

His future was rocky and unstable, until right before I had to leave. Then he seemed more focused, ready to take the first steps toward accepting his role as chieftain of his clan, something I knew nothing about but which impressed me anyway.

I sucked in a deep breath as I glanced around the pub. The thought of seeing Rory again was exciting. Maybe too exciting. I bared my teeth at my own thoughts, then bit my lip.

We squeezed through the crowd, forging our way to our favorite bench against the wall with a clear view of the band. It was the same scene, just different faces. Girls squished together in front of the lead singer, Finn, vying for his attention while Rory, the guitar player, sheltered himself behind the shadow of his amp.

My heart jumped into my throat when I caught sight of his silhouette.

"Paul would kill you right now if he knew you brought me here!" I yelled above the music.

"I know! But I couldn't resist!" She craned her neck and wove through the crowd to see if she could get a look at Rory. "There he is!" She pointed, taunting me, knowing he would create a rise in me of some kind. "It just seems like he was the start to everything. You know, when we first got to Ireland. I just had to bring you back here!"

My breathing slowed as I soaked in his form. Our memories flooded me like a tide of raw emotion. He was the first boy I'd ever kissed and I figured that must be why I was reacting to him like this. He'd told me to get in touch when I returned....

Rory stepped out of the shadows and led the band with a guitar solo that pierced through my soul. It echoed in my chest with a sultry rhythm and I begged for him to notice me.

As if I willed it, his eyes turned to meet mine and my blood pressure plummeted in his gaze. His mouth opened, like a gasp, and his playing faltered. The music lost time and missed a couple beats as he stared into my face, taking in every feature. I smiled at him and then lost sight as a big guy moved in front of me, pushing toward the bar.

I heard Rory's playing regain its pace and the music tightened up again. I strained to get him back into my view.

Just as the guy moved away, I caught sight of Rory again, still looking my way. Only this time, it wasn't a gaze of fond recognition and longing, but a glare of loathing hatred.

His eyes bored into mine and I recoiled in shock. His gaze

penetrated into my soul with judgment and threat. My heart lurched, nearly coming up my throat as my flight response kicked in.

I grabbed Michelle and pulled her through a wall of people, forcing our way to the door.

"Let's get out of here!" I begged.

We flew down Shop Street, searching for a safe pub to hide in, and jumped into The Quay's. I pulled Michelle to the back of the pub and fell into a corner nook.

"What. The hell. Was that?" she said with her lips curled back and eyebrow raised.

A shudder ran through me, like I'd just heard my final judgment.

"Holy crap. He hates me."

***

Flipping through an Irish history book at the university library while Paul googled information on St. Mary's, I felt a twang of guilt for seeing Rory last night. It wasn't my idea, but still, I went along with it without much resistance.

Michelle was laden with guilt too and spent hours replaying it, trying to figure out what was wrong with him—why he'd been so aggressive. She begged for my forgiveness for the setup. A true romantic, she was shaken that she didn't get to witness a love-struck Rory pining for her "untouchable" best friend. I could kill her.

I guess *my* guilt came from the way he made me feel, at first. Butterflies. But it was his glare of daggers that truly disrupted my soul.

What the hell was that?

 I looked down at the pages again, seeing nothing.

Rory had distracted me, yet again.

How did he do that? Every time.

"I went back to the cemetery last night," Paul stated, staring down at his computer.

"What? Why would you do that without me?" I gawked at him. "Paul!"

I wasn't sure if my reaction was from the betrayal of him going without me or fear of him going without me.

"I had to. I didn't want to bring you back there in case there was trouble. I had to check it out for myself." He looked straight into my eyes.

"Okay, fine. So what happened?"

He pressed his lips together.

"I snuck along the border and observed. Just ta see if the cloaked arse-hole was still there. To see if we could go back without him interferin' again."

"Yeah?" I leaned in, eyes wide.

"He was there. Just gliding around among the stones and mostly around the burial mound. Like he was guardin' it or something."

A shudder ran through me.

"No! That's so creepy. Crap!" My head shook from the thought of being held away from the cemetery. "Who the hell is that guy?"

"I have no idea. But for now, we need to stay away from there. Until he's gone, anyway." He scrolled through his computer, changing the subject with his actions.

"You shouldn't go there without me." My annoyance rang in my high pitch. "Or at least give me the option. I could have helped if something went wrong. Don't do that, okay?"

I reached for his arm and squeezed his wrist.

He nodded and gave a half-smirk.

"So, apparently, St. Mary's has a log of all the names of girls who were sent there and whatever became of them." Paul spoke aloud as he stared into his computer. "Sounds like it might have accuracy issues, but it's definitely worth checkin' out."

The unwavering commitment in his steady voice convinced me this was our next move.

I looked back into my book and saw black and white photos of girls standing in a courtyard, all wearing the same gray frocks and the same short haircuts with bangs, hanging sheets for miles. Blank stares on their faces and slumped shoulders made each girl a shell carbon-copy of the next. There were always two or three nuns, in old-fashioned long white habits and white skirts, off to the side, watching with carved scowls and judging eyes.

My eyes lifted to Paul's as fear crept into me, wondering about the fate of Brigid. If I couldn't find her, I might never get another person's perspective on the visions and basically, the curse of Grace

O'Malley.

I needed her. I needed her to confirm the visions were real. That she saw the same things and knew Grace was in search of help... or something. Anything.

Maybe she would have details or information on what to do or where to look next. Without Brigid, I was on my own.

Paul's screen had newspaper clippings pulled up from images. They showed a convent-like structure with a big cross at the front gate. It was St. Mary's. The photos gave it an eerie sense of foreboding, like a "do not enter" warning and a chill shook through me in response.

"We're going there?" I asked, baring my teeth in apprehension.

"Yep." Paul clicked on more images.

Excavation photos showed dug up areas outside of the convent, or "Home for Mothers and Babies," as some captions referred to it. Others used the spine-chilling title, "House of Tears." One of the headlines said, "800 Babies."

"What's that?" I pointed at his screen.

He slapped his laptop closed and turned to me, ashen.

"Babies?" I prodded.

"They found a mass grave there." He spoke down toward his lap.

I swallowed hard.

He continued, "Our timing is probably not ideal. And they say St. Mary's will likely be shut down altogether."

"We still need to go. Especially now. They can't hold their secrets there anymore. They have to give up *one* more, to us."

I imagined finding Brigid. Was it even possible? I wondered if she would have answers about Grace O'Malley and the curse that plagued our family. Maybe she would have clues for me, information to help me find Grace, to reunite her with Hugh, or at least somewhere to begin.

If I could confirm the final resting place of Grace O'Malley, I could return her ring in hopes of reconnecting her to Hugh. That would settle her soul. It felt like the right thing. And for Grace to see Paul and me together, that would bring peace to her, too.

It had to. Because I couldn't spend the rest of my life running from a ghost.

"Paul, what will we say to Brigid? If we find her." I bit my thumbnail to the quick.

"No idea." He stared past my shoulder in thought. "Maybe she could tell us about her visions. She may have more details, different from yours." He focused on me. "She could know something important and not even realize it."

"I don't want to waste another minute. Let's just *do* this," I decided.

I stood up and pressed my hands on the table in determination.

"We're going to the House of Tears," I stated.

Chapter Three
House of Tears

My nerves caused me to fumble as I packed my cinch sack for the trip to St. Mary's—the House of Tears. A jacket, water, tissues maybe?

It was all moving so quickly. I'd only been back in Ireland for a few weeks and any warmth left of July in Boston was quickly dissipating in the mellow chill of the late Irish summer.

I threw notebooks and pens from my bag into a pile on the floor to make room for my things for the trip. My class schedule for the fall lay crumpled on top of the pile. The full list of courses made my stomach turn as I wondered if I had taken on too much. Archaeology, Celtic Mythology, History of the Druids—all classes I was sure Paul would not be teaching. That was Rule One, from now on.

My phone chirped. Paul's name lit up.

On my way

Butterflies fluttered in my belly, searching for their way out. I wasn't sure if it was nerves for the trip to St. Mary's or Paul's effect on me. Both?

I waited outside my blue door, pacing off my nervous energy. The Celtic crosses up the road in Bohermore Cemetery watched me with curiosity, always tilting their gaze in wonder.

"You look more than ready," Paul jeered through the open window. "Hop in, me lady."

He pushed the door open and held a coffee out to me as I got in. His warm smile soothed my twitching nerves.

"I'm kind of freaking out right now," I stated. "This is by far the craziest thing we've done. I mean, tracking a pirate queen ghost is one thing, but searching for a lost cousin who was sent to the laundries when she was young… now, that's crazy!"

I dug at my thumb cuticle until it bled.

"You're cute when you're scared," Paul teased. "Come here."

He unbuckled his seatbelt and reached for me.

I moved over to him, careful not to spill our coffees as he pulled me right into his arms and held me. He brushed my hair out of my face.

"You make *me* crazy," he mumbled.

And he kissed me.

His summer stubble and smell of outdoors thrilled me as my mind swam in color swirls and glowing light. The wetness of his lips made me want more.

"You're me heart, Maeve Grace O'Malley. I'd do anything fer ya."

He helped me back into my seat and buckled my seatbelt for me.

As he pulled into the traffic on Bohermore, I watched him. I soaked in his angular features, his cheekbones and lashes. His flannel shirt and khakis. His hair, a little past its trimming date, and his lips. Full and warm.

"What?" He shot a look at me.

Shit! Caught in my eternal Paul McGratt love gaze again!

"Nothing. Just liking you." I smiled a guilty smile.

"Good. Keep doing that."

He kept his eyes on the road as he picked up speed on the N17.

Destination Tuam.

***

The white sign with black borders was in the shape of an arrow and read TUAM 5km.

My breath sucked in.

Hedgerows flew by, so close to the car they scraped it. The narrow road was a death trap if there was any oncoming traffic. Paul slowed and pressed to the side each time a car headed our way.

"That didn't take long." My apprehension oozed from my words.

"It's basically halfway between Galway and Claremorris," Paul said, keeping to the facts, probably so I wouldn't start to fidget.

Once we were in the small town, we followed the GPS as far as it could take us, but then fell off the grid into uncharted green zone. Kind of like when you're on a ferry and all around is just blue. This time, all around was just green.

One lonely green road led us to St. Mary's.

Paul parked the car along the empty roadside, bordered by stone walls and ivy, and we walked the short way toward the complex. We passed a few scattered bungalow homes, all white with red doors, children playing in the yards, and dogs roaming freely.

Curious eyes watched us with precision as we moved closer to our destination, as if protecting what they felt was theirs—sheltering the secrets they lived next to and the sacred lands their children played upon.

Unsettled, I looked away. We didn't belong here. This wasn't ours to see. I kept my eyes down and continued to move forward, remembering my cousin, Brigid. Then, remembering the babies, I held Paul's hand like a vice grip. He kept his steady gait and moved me along through my insecurity.

"There it is." His flat voice stopped me in my tracks.

I stared at the large white cross on the front gate, warding me off like every other ogler, rather than welcoming me in. It led into a high-walled yard, sparse of any landscaping. A shiny black granite plaque drew my eye. It marked the nearby area in memory of the babies buried there, and sent an icy shudder through my spine.

High up, beyond the grassy yard stood the structure referred to as "the home" by locals. *Shutter Island* came to mind as I surveyed the gray walls of the building and its uniform tall, narrow windows, dark gray roof, and lack of any other notable features. Stark and bare. Just gray.

Off to the side, hidden in overgrowth, was a statue of Jesus in a long robe, reaching out with his open palm, blessing the area. My lips pursed to the side at the contradiction.

Paul pushed the rickety, squeaky gate open and we took our first steps onto the long, black drive leading up to the institution. A solemn darkness hung over the building, and its still silence added to its creepiness. I couldn't be sure if anyone was even inside.

A white door in the middle was the only visible access and "decorative" steel bars covered all the lower level windows giving an actual appearance of security restraints. *One Flew Over the Cuckoo's Nest?* I reached for the aged buzzer and hesitated, having hoped for a more appealing novel reference, like *Gone with the Wind*.

"Go on." Paul nudged me with his chin.

I pressed the doorbell and flinched from the loud, angry clanging it created inside.

I looked at Paul with worry, praying no one was home. The seconds dragged by raising my hopes with each measurement of time.

A moment later, the door pulled open, causing my heart to flip.

"Can I help ya?"

An older woman, thin but with strong posture, maybe sixty-five, held the door and waited for our response with a pinched face. Her solid stance filled the doorway, blocking our view, as if she protected what was held within.

My words were lost in panic as she sized us up and prepared to close the door in response to our silence. I bit my lip and stepped forward to address her.

"Hi. I'm sorry to bother you. I'm looking for someone." I choked back tears that threatened to interrupt my voice. "I'm Maeve O'Malley and this is my friend, Paul McGratt. We're looking for my cousin."

The woman looked us up and down with one eye squinting and her lips pressed together in a white line, like we were stupid.

"There's no one here anymore. Are ya daft? Good day." She moved to close the door.

"Wait. Please. Her name is Brigid. Brigid O'Malley. I need to know where she went. What happened to her. Please." The crack in my voice exposed my desperation.

The woman hesitated. She opened the door again and poked out with narrowed eyes. "Who are you?"

"Maeve O'Malley. My grandfather left Ireland for Boston when he was eighteen. I've just learned of his niece, Brigid. She was sent here long ago, when she was a teenager." My rambling threatened to close the door again. "Maybe forty years ago. I need to find her."

"Why? What business have ye?" The door closed a little more.

"I want her to know she has family. Me. And I have something important to tell her. Something she *needs* to know." I stepped closer, as a strange confidence rose within me. "Do you have any information on her? A register or log book. Anything that might lead me to her?"

The door opened a little wider, then stopped. Then it opened fully as she took another close look at us.

"Cup a' tea?" she asked through a sideways glance.

"Yes. Yes, please. Thank you," I stammered.

She stepped to the side, allowing us full entry into the foyer.

The stark emptiness was disrupted only by an enormous crucifix on the wall, full of graphic detail and suffering. Thorns, bleeding puncture wounds, despair, and pain. My eyes grew wide with concern and I peered at Paul. His smile proved he was holding back a chuckle from my unsettled response to Jesus on the cross.

We followed her to the back into an industrial kitchen. Shiny stainless steel counters and island, deep sink with huge spray hose, and an ancient stove that she lighted with a match. We sat on metal chairs at a wooden table and watched her move about the kitchen.

The windows opened out to an inner courtyard that had a kitchen garden with rows of potatoes, herbs, and lettuce. I recognized them all from my grandparent's garden back home.

"You have a lovely garden. You grow your own vegetables?" I asked.

"Hmm? Yes. Not many of us left here for such a large facility. The few of us keep it going for now. The garden keeps us busy. 'Til they shut us down, anyway."

She filled a silver pot with tea bags and hot water and brought it to the table. I helped her bring the mugs over.

"The history of this place has it tainted, ya see," she added. "I think the people just want to see it gone. And take any bad memories wit' it."

Paul nodded while I sat silent. It was all so new to me that I hadn't formed an opinion yet.

The woman's sideways glance looked as if it were searching me for an impression, or a judgment, maybe.

"Sure, we'll be out on our ears by year's end, so we're told," she continued. "Nowhere to go. Who'd want us?" She paused, then reanimated. "Milk?"

She poured some into the creamer from a large glass bottle. A line of solid white at the top stopped the pour at first. The cream had risen. I wondered if the cow was anywhere nearby.

She poured the tea and sat in awkward silence. I looked around the room, anywhere but at her.

Finally, she spoke.

"I'm Mary. Head of household. I'm pleased to make your acquaintance." She nodded at both of us. "We don't get many visitors, mind you. Just gawkers. Hoodlums and the like."

She looked into her tea.

"Thank you for meeting with us, Mary. It means a lot," Paul said.

"Ah, sure, yer Irish. Figured you for a Yank as well." Mary smiled for the first time. "Sounds like a Dublin accent." She tilted her head.

"'Tis."

"I come from Bray me-self. Used to run up Bray Head as a girleen." Her eyes twinkled when she looked at Paul.

"I've done the cliff walk there. Beautiful place." He shook his head, remembering it fondly.

"Ah, sure. So you know it." Her smile took her back to her youth.

She topped up our cups with hot tea.

"Tell me now, Miss O'Malley, about your cousin, Brigid." She crossed her hands on the table and leaned in to me. "Whatcha want to know?"

On the spot, I had no idea what I wanted to know. Everything, I supposed. I wanted to know if she was okay. Was she treated well? Did they think she was crazy? What did they do with her? Was she alive? Where was she? Was she here? My mind raced with questions.

"I want to know if… if she survived all the… the crazy. I need to meet her. To tell her she wasn't alone with her… troubles. Do you know where she might be?"

My direct tone must have been off-putting but I couldn't help it. Desperation was rising in me.

"Now, I'm not sure how much you know about this place. Much

of it has been soiled with ugly lies and exaggerations. But much of it is also true. You will latch on to the bits you choose to believe. Much like everyone else." Mary seemed well used to judgment.

"Do you have a registry? Or a book of some kind that kept information on the girls?" I ignored my tea and only stared at Mary.

"Yes. I think I can help you, Miss O'Malley. But I need a moment. Will you give me a sec to have a look-see?"

She stood and straightened her apron, wiping her hands down its faded gray and white checkering.

"Of course. Yes, yes. Thank you." I nearly fell out of my seat.

She left the kitchen through a small passage at the back, behind the industrial-sized fridge.

I turned to Paul with my hands pressed into my lap, nearly bouncing in my seat. His expression didn't match mine and he continued to look at the passage she left through.

"What?" I asked.

"It's like time is standing still right now. We have no idea what information she'll come back with. It could be good news. It may be bad. We have to be prepared for anything." He took my hands in my lap and held them tight. "Are you ready for this?"

"I always think yes, then crazy wind comes or screaming pirate queens, so maybe this time I'll say no. No, I'm not ready for this, but here goes anyway." My attitude gave me power and strengthened my focus.

I smiled at Paul.

"Okay. Deep breath," he said.

Time crawled. Tea grew cold. Daylight began to wane. Paul's fidgeting bugged me and I'd picked my cuticle to the bone.

Then, footsteps.

Mary was coming back.

Paul and I stood at the same time and waited at full attention for her report.

Mary stood in the passageway before entering into the kitchen. We watched her every movement.

"Maeve. Paul. I would like you to meet Brigid O'Malley from the O'Malley farm on the Drumlin Road."

Mary stepped into the kitchen leading a sallow, withdrawn woman into the room. Her oversize gray sweater swallowed her up and the heavy dark shawl finished her off.

My breath sucked in sharply, making a sound I couldn't hide. My hand flew to my mouth to stop it as I stared at Brigid.

Her eyes glued themselves to the floor and she slouched enough to make it look like she wanted to *be* the floor. Her appearance made her look as if she were ninety years old.

"Oh my god. Brigid." My words took on their own life. "Mary. Thank you."

Mary reached for Brigid to encourage her farther into the room.

"She's a shy one, aren't ya, Brid?" She nudged Brigid farther. "Go on now, go see your cousin from America. Come a long way to see ya now."

Brigid shuffled her slippers across the floor without allowing any space between her sole and the tile. Mary brought her to the table and sat her down.

"There now. I'll make fresh tea and we'll all get acquainted." Mary smoothed her apron again and went to light the stove.

Paul rubbed my knee as we sat too.

"Hi, Brigid." I bit my lip. "I'm Maeve. From Boston. I've been dying to meet you."

Brigid continued to stare at the table top while rubbing her hands on her thighs.

"My grandfather was your father's big brother. He left Ireland when your father was sixteen. Told me he was a big man, learning the ways of the farm."

Brigid snuck a peek at me with one eye as Mary stepped out into the kitchen garden.

"Then I learned about you from some men in Warde's Pub. They remembered you."

"Who?" Her head jerked up and the question hit me like a stone.

Her voice was rough and jagged.

"Um, Padraic, the pub owner, and another man from the bar. Donal, I think. He remembered you well."

I watched her shoulders relax and her breathing slowed.

"I remember Donal. Took me to a dance. Didn't speak a word the entire night." She smirked and looked at me for the first time. "What do you want?"

Her question was as direct as an arrow.

"Well, I wanted to meet you. I don't have much family. And you're part of my family." I swallowed. "I guess I wanted you to know that you have some family too."

"No."

Her word carried more weight than a full dissertation.

"What?"

"No. You want something. You came for something. What do you want?"

She stared into my eyes as if looking straight through me. Like she had me figured out. The transfer of power was dizzying.

I turned to Paul, lost at how to answer. I was still unsure about her sanity, basically, and needed to know more about her.

She started to get up.

"No, wait. Please. Okay," I begged her to stay.

I watched her sit back down and stare straight at me, waiting.

"Okay. So, I have these strange visions. Like dreams, while I'm awake. There's wind, fear, screaming…." I watched her for a reaction, but saw nothing. "There's a pirate queen. Grace O'Malley. Do you know of her?"

Brigid didn't move. Her face reddened. Then went purple. She pounded her fists on the table and hollered, "Mary!"

Her response made me jump in my seat and Paul sat back like a blast of wind shot through him.

"Mary! Mary! Mary! Mary!" She screamed while smacking her hands on the table and shaking her head.

Mary flew in from the garden with pure alarm splashed over her face and dropped her herb cuttings.

"What is it, Brigid? What is it?" Mary took Brigid's hands to try to soothe her. "Come on, Brigid. Everything's okay. No need to be upset." She put her hands on Brigid's shoulders. "Let's get you to bed. Time for a rest, honey."

Mary helped Brigid stand.

Paul and I continued to stare in frozen bewilderment.

"I'm sorry." Mary turned to us. "It's best you be takin' your leave now. Brigid's had enough." She couldn't hide her displeasure with us in her scowl. "See yourselves out, will ya now?"

And they disappeared through the passage.

I sank in my seat.

"What? That's it?" My hands went up in question.

I looked at Paul for an answer. He was writing something on a torn piece of paper bag.

"What's that?" I leaned in for a closer look.

"I'm leaving our mobile numbers in case they need to reach us. For anything."

I watched him finish his writing and then pulled myself out of my seat.

"Let's get out of here," I murmured.

From deep within the home, Brigid's muffled wails permeated through every wall.

"No! Mary! Help me!"

I covered my ears and raced past Jesus on the cross and burst out the door, as if I would have lost my mind if I stayed in there for another second.

Chapter Four

Blown to Bits

The silence in the car was deafening.

Flattened by the disappointment of Brigid shutting down, I clung to the miracle that she was even found. I had to admit that it wasn't really a shock that she freaked out at my mention of the pirate queen. I mean, that's not normal, right?

I looked out the window as the home faded from sight.

But it was normal for Brigid. And for me.

"So now what?" I pouted. "That's it?"

I looked at my phone. Michelle had texted me.

Sooooo is she freaky like u

I shook my head and smiled as I typed back.

No quite normal actually

Brigid's response couldn't be used against her, really. How else was she supposed to respond to someone who wanted to talk about pirate queens and basically the worst part of her life out of the blue? *I* probably sounded like the crazy one.

"Back to square one, I guess," Paul said in a slow exhale.

His words flattened me. Square one offered nothing. I was in the dark again.

My phone rang. I figured it was Michelle, but it was an unknown number.

"Hello?" I asked cautiously.

"Maeve?"

"Yes."

Silence.

"Hello?" I said again.

"It's Brigid."

I froze and turned to Paul. My panicked expression lightened his foot on the gas pedal.

"Come back." Her voice sounded miles away, lost deep inside her head.

"Okay. Um. I can come back. Like, now?" I looked at Paul, and he was already turning the car around.

"Yes."

Click.

My heart rate hit high gear in two beats.

"Oh my god. She wants me to come back. Holy crap!"

My hands shook as I wriggled in my seat. She had really freaked me out screaming Mary's name like that. I had no idea now what to expect.

"This is it, Maeve. She's ready. She's gonna talk to you." He nodded with raised eyebrows.

I blew my breath out through pursed lips, contemplating what I would say to her. I rehearsed different scenarios and brought myself to a frothing frenzy before realizing I just had to be honest and be myself. I had nothing to lose.

We parked closer to the gate with the white cross, but still far enough away to be respectful of the hallowed grounds, and walked up the black drive to "the home." The white door was open before we reached it.

Mary greeted us with a smile.

"Thanks for comin' back. Brigid's calm now. I think you just surprised her. No one has ever asked her such questions. And so directly, mind you." Mary looked down at her wringing hands. "She's been... programmed, you could say, about her mental illness. She believes her visions are a sickness she should never speak of. Your questions frightened her."

Mary led us into the kitchen. I scanned the room for Brigid, half-expecting her to jump out from behind the fridge, trilling a high-pitched wild woman call.

"She's been here most of her life, as ya know." Mary looked around the space to show us the small world Brigid has existed in. "And it was not always pleasant, ya see."

"Did you work here back then? Did you know Brigid early on?" I wondered if Mary cared for Brigid. If they'd been here together for... a while.

"I knew her. We were sent to the laundries 'round the same time. We've been here together ever since." She reached down to straighten her already-smooth apron.

My throat constricted making it impossible to speak. I attempted to swallow the tension only for it to get stuck and squeak as it moved down.

How could Mary be sent to the laundries? "Promiscuity" maybe. It was so unfair. Every girl had the same curiosities about intimacy as every boy, yet they were punished for it.

Paul jumped in. "I'm sure you've both got stories to last a lifetime."

"Ach. We do. And then some." She looked out to the kitchen garden. "But we have each other now. And a few of the other girls. The ones who couldn't leave. Didn't know how to or had nowhere to go." She wrung her hands. "Sure, I'm most worried for Brigid. You know, for when they shut us down and drive us out of this place. Might sound funny, but it's home to us."

Mary reached for my arm and placed her hand on it.

"She's out there in the garden waiting for ya. It's best Paul stay in here for a fine cuppa tea. She's not all that comfortable 'round men. Hasn't seen many of 'em in her time here."

I moved toward the door, looking back at Paul with my eyebrows pulled up in the middle with worry. He nodded for me to go.

"I'll be here by the window if you need me. Just gimme a holler." He smiled and turned his attention to Mary.

The two of them would chatter endlessly about Dublin and Bray for starters. Mary had a twinkle in her eye for him.

I walked out onto the main path in the garden and moved through the various sections of vegetables, flowers, and shrubbery. Past the simple topiaries, Brigid sat on a stone bench with her hands folded between her knees, rocking.

She glanced up at me and looked down again, avoiding my eyes.

"It's okay, Brigid. I'm not surprised you reacted that way. It's my fault. I said too much too fast. I'm sorry."

She peered up again like a scolded child, as if making sure I wasn't angry with her.

"Can I sit with you?" I asked.

She scooched over, leaving plenty of room for me on the bench.

We gazed out at the garden and back toward the house. Paul's tall form filled the window and moved in animated conversation. I imagined Mary's big smile and jolly laughs, absorbing every word.

"So, you wanted me to come back?"

I'd let her be the first to mention Grace this time.

"You scared me," she whispered.

"I know. I'm sorry. I didn't mean to." I angled my body toward her.

"I've seen the pirate queen." She bit her lips with a small yelp and tightened her fists between her clenched knees.

"I know." I'd figured that out from Donal's stories of her visions.

Brigid's entire body tensed and her head shook back and forth in small twitches. "You've seen her too?"

She looked up with one eye, waiting a safe distance for my reply.

"Yes. Many times." I nodded. "It's not pleasant. She frightens me."

"Me too!" Her head picked up and she looked directly at me. "She scares me. Terribly." Her volume grew louder with each word. "I can't hide from her. I'm not even safe *here*. She's going to get me, you know. She's going to kill me."

Her eyes darted around the garden as if Grace were lurking there.

"I thought that too, Brigid. For a long time." My tone remained steady and calm. "But I think I've learned some things about her that will help stop her."

My wide eyes begged her to believe me.

"Stop her? How?" Brigid's hands worked the fabric of her pants like dough.

"She wants something. She's been hunting for it through generations of O'Malley women. I think if I can return it to her, she'll be able to rest and move out of the in-between." My head nodded in hopeful acceptance.

Brigid's brow scrunched together. "What are you talking about?"

"Her ring. The ring of the pirate queen. I think it has the power to reunite her with her lost love. And to stop all of this." My eyes brightened.

Brigid straightened her spine and became rigid.

"That ring is cursed. I heard it was sent away. Lost forever. Cursed." She pushed herself farther from me across the bench. "What do you know of the ring?"

"I want to confront her and stop her. With the ring." I turned to face her. "Then she'll leave us alone. So we can have normal lives."

"But she's not real." She shook her head and squinted her eyes at me. "They told me she was just in my head. I made her up. And then they sent me away."

She was teetering on the edge of the bench now, shimmying one inch at a time away from me.

"Why are you here?" Her voice reached a new high pitch.

"You didn't make her up, Brigid. And you're not the only O'Malley woman to be stalked by her."

I thought of my mother and her visions. She never really told me much about them. She hid them, really. But they consumed her.

"She's real. And you're not alone." I pressed my hands into the stone bench, feeling the rough surface grind into my fingertips. "I'll stop her, okay? Everything will be better. I promise."

"How?" Her short reply held a child-like tone as her posture curled to pouting. "How can you stop her?" Her head shook in denial. "She'll kill you."

I reached into my shirt and found the ring settled into my chest. I pulled it out by the chain and let is twirl freely in the open air.

"With her ring," I stated.

Brigid jumped away like I'd pulled a venomous snake out and she fell off the bench. She kicked away from me as if being attacked.

"It's okay, Brigid. It's not going to hurt you." My tone remained steady, though a shake was threatening it as my panic rose from her reaction.

"You!" She pointed a shaking finger at me. "It's you!"

She scrambled to her feet and circled me in surveillance.

"I knew you'd come for me!" Her voice reached shrill.

"Brigid, it's okay. There's nothing to…."

"You! Demon! You are *her*." Her face grimaced. "You're her!" Her finger pointed at me, all over.

"What? Who? What are you talking about?"

"The lost daughter! Maeve Grace O'Malley. The lost daughter of the pirate queen. You've returned."

Her shouting reached scream levels and the back of my mind heard the kitchen door burst open.

"You're a witch! You tried to trick me! To make me join ya. Get out!" Her eyes flashed red with pressure and intensity as spit flew from her mouth. "Get out! Get *out!*"

Paul grabbed me and pulled me away. Mary wrapped her arms around Brigid and moved her through the garden toward the kitchen door, swinging her arm and pointing around the house for us to leave that way.

Paul held his arm tight around my shoulders and led me around the building, past the blessing hand of Jesus reaching out from the overgrown bushes and around to the front. We raced past the sacred baby grounds and into the safety of the car.

The darkness of night cloaked "the home" and only a few dim lights illuminated some of the windows. I was sure I heard the wailing of a thousand souls. Was it Brigid?

"What the hell was that?" Paul pulled the car around and sent gravel flying in his hasty acceleration.

"Holy crap!" I panted into my hands. "When I showed her the ring, she freaked. Accusing me. Calling me a witch. Trying to get her." I shook my head to release the images of her attack. I rubbed my temples. "She called me the lost daughter."

Paul stopped the car, knocking me forward, then back in my seat, and turned to me.

"*What* did you say?"

"The lost daughter," I repeated as I leaned in to watch his expression.

He stared ahead at the road, eyes narrowed as if confused.

"What?" I flinched, then crossed my arms.

I looked over my shoulder, back toward the House of Tears.

He cleared his throat.

"I'm not sure. I need to look into it more, but I've heard something about that." He rubbed the back of his neck and kept his eyes forward.

I dropped my face into my hands and my mouth went dry. So many unanswered questions. Instead of answers, I was only left with more questions.

"Rockfleet. I need to go there." I spoke through sweaty palms on my face.

Thoughts of Grace O'Malley's castle loomed in my head. It was nearby and maybe, I don't know, maybe Grace would be there. I could confront her. Maybe get some answers or somehow just end it all.

Urgency ran through my veins like adrenaline.

"What? Now?" His pitch rose as his body went rigid.

"We're already halfway there." The beg in my voice almost whined. "I don't know. The things Brigid said. I feel like I can't stop now. Can we just check it out? See if there's anything there?"

"I don't know. It's late." He glanced at the glowing numbers of the clock on his dash.

He was right. It was late.

But I couldn't stop now. Brigid had said too much. Knew too much. My head shook in confusion from all her accusations.

My fingers tapped on my knees. "It doesn't make sense to go home now. Not without answers."

"Tell me what she said about the lost daughter." He grew impatient from my scattered thoughts.

"She went nuts when she saw the ring, then she called me the lost daughter. Said I'd come back, like from the dead or something." My voice went quiet and my head fell.

I leaned my head against the window and melted into the door as I watched the street lights fade in the distance and the dark expanse overtake the view.

"It's like she thought I was a ghost." I sank in my seat and closed my eyes, thinking of her insinuations.

She said I'd come for her. Like I was the evil one. Like I was part of her visions. My mind went numb and I focused on my breathing.

Paul's voice shocked me back.

"There it is."

He slowed the car and the sound of the gravel road under the tires filled my ears to full volume.

"Stop here," I said in shock. Stunned we had arrived at all.

I gazed at the dark, brooding castle—a black hole cut in the evening canvas of hills and sea. Its stony walls rose high from its square foundation and the pointed top jabbed into the heavens.

"So you want to tell me why we're here?" Paul's voice oozed of impatience. "We're not going in there, you know. Not in the dark anyway."

His eyebrows rose as he stared at me and his lips pressed together.

I opened my door and stepped my left leg out. Paul's hand held my shoulder back.

"Hey." His hand held firm.

I reached my foot out farther and his grip tightened.

"Hey! What the hell are you doing? You're not going in there." His voice cracked as he lost hold of me.

I pulled myself out of the car and looked back at him.

"Okay. I just want to walk over there and look around." I flashed innocent eyes at him.

Paul left the engine running and the headlights on as he jumped out of the car.

He mumbled under his breath, "Jazus Christ, flippin' middle a nowhere, feckin' middle a' the night... just after gettin' attacked by yer crazy cousin...."

He came around and took me by my shoulders.

"We can't go puttin' ourselves in danger. Ya can't just go lookin' fer trouble. We need to plan and use caution. Okay?"

"I know. I'm sorry. But those things she said. She knew things," I mumbled as I moved closer to the fortress.

I gazed at the castle, steadfast in its foundation. I shrank from it, feeling the strength and permanency of the pirate queen. The thought of her hunting me my entire life terrified me. And what about my own family some day? If I ever had a daughter, she would be doomed too.

"Brigid's not right in her head. She's been too long there. Institutionalized. Her mind's had too much time to play tricks on her." He shook his head and exhaled. "Terrible shame, really."

"No. She knew stuff. She called me a demon. And a witch." I looked to the ground and bit my lip. I walked closer to the castle and Paul stayed by my side. "And she said I was *her*, the lost daughter. What the hell does that *mean?*"

"Nothing. She's delusional." Paul slowed and reached for my arm. "Hang on."

I stopped and listened with him.

"What?" My impatience made me fidget.

"This is just a bad idea. I have no idea how I let you talk me into—"

Whoosh! Bam!

A burst of air blasted us right off our feet and we fell back onto the road with a splat. My palms burned from the scratches left by jagged gravel. I rubbed them together and watched Paul pull himself up.

He moved in slow motion and shouted words of caution but his voice trailed off into the night air and morphed into a cool breeze. I watched the sound move across the green expanse and out to sea.

Dark greens, browns, and black swirled around the castle as sounds of an unknown language filled my skull. The language of the ancient Celts. I'd heard it before. Now it whispered to me.

"*Méabh.*" My name whirled around me and through me. "*Méabh Gráinne Ní Mháille, Tá tú taisech. Ceart na héagóracha na céadta bliain.*"

The words danced around me with sounds from centuries past. My head dropped back as they blanketed me. Every nerve in my body tingled and sent bolts of energy through me, creating an urge to take action.

I followed the sounds, absorbing them into the depths of my

being and allowed them to shape me from within. My bones tightened and became stronger, holding me more solidly upright. My muscles lengthened and twitched as new energy moved through them. My thoughts sorted and a clarity settled my racing mind as my eyes opened wider than ever before.

I turned my head toward the pounding and throbbing. The melted scenery took on cleaner edges and the colors separated, forming defined shapes. The sounds moved from musical to choppy as my eyes focused on Paul.

"Maeve! Maeve! Let's get out of here! Come on."

He pulled me but I was stuck solid and couldn't move with him.

I turned from his tug to look at my other hand. It was clasped around the heavy metal ring of the ominous black door of Rockfleet Castle. Pulled in both directions, my fingers clenched like a vice on the ring.

Words formed in my mouth and I spat them out.

"My hand is stuck!"

I yanked and pulled.

Paul pried each finger open until my hand released the ring.

We raced to the car, blinded by the beaming headlights. It was impossible to know what we were heading into, adding to my disorientation. Was someone there… or something—hiding in the brightness of the lights?

Paul pulled me to his door and shoved me in from his side. I wiggled over the shift and into my seat, peeking out my window expecting to see a ghoul staring in. His door slammed shut and gravel shot out in all directions as he left donuts carved in the dirt and clouds of dust in our wake.

"For the love o' Christ!" His foot laid heavy on the gas. "God dammit!"

His anger had little effect on me. I knew I shouldn't have gone there. I knew it was dangerous. But I couldn't help it. I was drawn there. By something bigger than me.

And they spoke to me. Voices actually spoke to me.

"Something's happening." I studied my hands like they were new to my body.

The ancient words cloaked me in new skin.

Paul stared straight out at the road, jaw clenched.

"I'm changing." I spoke into the night.

Maybe this was what enlightenment was.

My thoughts had moved past my personal identity and took on a higher level of thinking. Beyond myself. Like a floating dream, my mind traveled across the green expanse, searching for my people.

His foot lightened off the gas and the car returned to a steady speed. He turned to me.

"What are you talking about?" His voice carried a curt tone of annoyance.

"They spoke to me."

He turned his gaze back to the road and floored it.

Chapter Five

Celtic Cross

I dropped down on my favorite bench at the Spanish Arch and searched for insomniac swans, particularly the black one people had been talking about. Paul hovered by the side of the bench, shifting his weight from one foot to the other.

"I just can't go home yet," I spoke into the crisp night air. "It's like my whole world is changing in the span of one night. I feel different."

It was like I had a new responsibility, not only to myself, but to every O'Malley and the land that was theirs. But I was still powerless in my heart. What authority did I have to do anything about any of this? My mind shifted back to the ring.

It always came back to the ring.

Paul sat down on the edge of the bench with his hands on his knees, looking out toward the water.

"I should get you home."

My eyebrows pinched together as I looked sideways at him.

"I feel like I could sit here all night," I prodded to get a reaction.

I watched him more closely. He hadn't looked at me since the car. And his words trailed out anywhere but at me, as if he were detached or even asleep.

But I felt so awake, more than ever before.

My senses sharpened as I heard distant sounds of car engines, boat horns, and dishes clanging and was surrounded by a complex mixture of scents. I smelled my grandfather's gardening jacket, my mother's house sweater, and the inside of Paul's car.

I rubbed my eyes and pressed my fingers across my eyebrows, then blinked across the river at the twinkling lights of a housing estate.

I turned again to face Paul, wondering what was bothering him, but my words stuck in the back of my mouth from his brazen stare. It was as if he were looking at a stranger, someone who scared him. As soon as my eyes met his, he darted his gaze out to the river. And then out to the sea.

It was too late though. I saw his thoughts in his eyes. It was as if he didn't know me anymore.

Like taking a punch to the gut, I reached for my chest and sucked in air. Something spooked him, beyond the usual. Something he heard at the castle or maybe the lost daughter stuff.

"Did you hear the voices?" I asked.

He pursed his lips. "Yes."

Relief washed over me. It *was* real. He heard them too. But that also might explain his distance.

"Did you understand the language? Do you know what they were saying?"

He looked out to the water.

"Yes."

I nodded my head and pressed my lips to the side. "Thought so."

I knew it. He heard something in the voices that scared him.

He turned to me.

"Did *you* understand them?"

I shrugged my shoulders. "No, not the actual words or language. But I knew what they meant. So, I guess, yes."

The voices anointed me in a way. As the chosen one. Paul knew this too. It scared the crap out of me, so I could only imagine how it made him feel. But he shouldn't be pulling away from me at a time like this.

I needed him to talk to me. Tell me what was bothering him.

A giant splash from the river wall sent spray up on us. A wet slosh ran down my face and made me squeal. I jumped up and ran to the river's edge to look in. Paul was by my side in an instant, looking across the ripples and waves.

"There!" He pointed toward the bridge. "It's a seal. He's gone the wrong way."

The seal flopped its massive form near the wall again, sending a thunderous wave of water up and over. He redirected himself and we watched him glide his way back out into the bay again.

"Whoa! He was huge! I've never seen one that close before in the wild." My breath was taken away by the sight and sheer power of the creature.

I looked back at the area he last struggled and sloshed, by the bridge. In the heavy darkness over the bridge I noticed a lone figure that nearly blended in with its surroundings.

"Paul, someone's there." I pointed to the middle of the bridge.

The person's head lifted from the sound of our voices, revealing his oversize hood and cloaked shoulders. A gasp escaped my lips as I recognized him as the figure from the cemetery. My heart stopped from the thought that he'd followed us and knew how to find us. His determination to derail me made my knees weak.

"The monk," I whispered to Paul. I didn't know what else to call him. "The same guy, in the dark cloak."

I reached for his arm as he straightened and pulled myself close to him.

"What the hell...." Paul squinted into the darkness for a better look.

In the same blink, the monk moved away across the bridge to the far side.

My breath exhaled as he left our sight and my tight grip loosened on Paul's arm.

My first instinct was to get out of there. Get to the car and go home to hide behind locked doors. But my next inhale brought with it courage and curiosity. A primal urge grew in me to protect and persevere—protect myself and Paul, but to also end the threat. A threat that seemed to be against something much bigger than us.

"Come on! Let's go after him," I yanked on Paul's arm. "It's gotta be Fergal. He's following us!" I dropped Paul's resisting arm and took a few steps toward the bridge. "Come on. You *know* he's stalking us. I need to find out why. He knows something about all of this."

"No." Paul turned back toward his parked car.

His refusal to jump to action rattled me.

"What?" I looked back across the bridge hoping to catch a glimpse of the stranger. He was gone. "We can't stop now."

My eyes darted from Paul to the far side of the bridge and back again. My hands went up with my shoulders in puzzlement.

"I mean, I don't know what's going on either, but I need to face this, Paul. You know that, right?" My plan formed itself through my spoken words. "I'm going back to Rockfleet. And to the cemetery. All of it. Until I find Grace."

My adamant tone pressed on him to join me in taking action.

I was determined to pursue every angle. Paul needed to know this. There was no turning back now. Not ever.

Paul's new reluctance was killing me. I wanted to punch him in the face. To wake him up and get him back in the game. The sick feeling of grief returned to my once-stronger heart and weakened it. I couldn't bear it if Paul became guarded around me. Or worse.

Paul's head hung and he stared at his feet.

"I'm sorry, Maeve. It's too much. Too fast. It's just not...." He followed the sound of a distant horn and took a deep inhale. "It's getting too big. I feel like I'm going to lose you to it all. Or, like, you're not going to need me, or want me, anymore. I just need time to think."

"Do you think I don't have the same fears? Look at what's happening to me. But I need you to stay with me. Completely. Don't pull away from me. Please." My eyes begged him more than my words. Despair poured out of my pupils.

Paul's eyes remained fixed to the ground and I squinted in pain as my world imploded into me.

My vision blurred and my hearing squeezed into a vacuum until they both synchronized onto a single point of focus—Paul. It was too much for him. He couldn't do it anymore.

"Take me home now. Please."

Paul was bailing on me. It was written all over his face. His eyes were wide with fear and his furrowed brow was layered with line after line of doubt.

I hadn't seen it coming though. He'd been by my side from the start. From discovering Grace O'Malley as the source of my horrible visions and then learning she was my family. And Paul, he was the descendant of Grace's lost love, Hugh.

It was perfect, Paul and me. It made perfect sense. We had each other and could put an end to all of this together.

The thought of him pulling away was more than I could bear. A sense of abandonment hollowed me out, making me sick. I swallowed to hold down a retch as nausea twisted my face into a grimace.

My thoughts raced for an explanation.

What turned him so suddenly? Brigid? The voices?

My lips pursed as anger replaced my grief. Paul was my match. He was the other half of me. It wasn't right for him to do this.

Paul pulled up to my blue door at 122 Bohermore. I unbuckled my seat belt and shifted in my seat to face him.

"What turned you?" The betrayal in my voice made it sound like an accusation.

"Jesus, Maeve. I'm not turnin' on ya."

"Yes. You are. I felt the shift. It's done."

The resolve in my words turned sharply in the air and pierced my heart. Saying the words out loud confirmed my worst fear. Losing Paul.

I reached for the ring hanging from my necklace and held it for security as my knuckles rubbed the tightness in my chest. Our future wasn't clear to me anymore and I turned my gaze away from him.

"No. I just…." He pursed his lips, hardening his words.

"What is it? What's wrong?" I turned back to him and pushed his arm in frustration from his evasiveness.

His eyes glared into mine.

"The voices. What they were sayin'."

I knew it. The voices freaked him out. But why?

"They want me to lead something, right? It was like, encouragement, like I was on the right track." I searched his face for answers.

He nodded his head, but there was more. His downward glance and tight lips proved it.

"It's too dangerous. We need to stop. It needs to stop here." He stared out across the glowing light beams from his headlights. "You need to rest. We just need to slow it down a little, okay? Can we do that? Just to catch our breath?"

My head exploded and all senses left my brain. How could I slow down now? It was time to keep plowing forward.

What was his problem?

I glared at him as if he was the enemy.

"Who's the defector now?" My eyes narrowed with each word.

His face fell, like he'd taken a bullet.

All I wanted was to jump into his lap and kiss him better. For him to hold me with his unwavering affection and desire.

"Come in. I'm sorry." I reached for his hand.

This argument was dumb. We couldn't let this tear us apart.

"I can't. Not tonight." He kept his gaze forward.

I stared at his unmoving position and reeled back in surprise. Then I bolted out of the car and pushed through my door without looking back.

I leaned on the inside of my blue door, listening for the sound of his car pulling away. The sound of silence chilled me. After a breath, I inched the door back open and peeked out.

His car was gone. The dim street lights of Bohermore reflected off the shiny wet streets and sent long shadows along the lane toward Bohermore Cemetery.

I peered to catch a glimpse of the Celtic cross monuments that seemed to always keep an eye on me. They were cloaked in the slumber of darkness. I glanced down the other direction of Bohermore, toward the city center, and squinted into the sudden blast of misty sea air. I blinked to clear my vision and pulled strands of hair out of mouth.

The next burst left no question.

The wind was coming.

Memories of my last awake dream flooded my mind. Grace, in the O'Malley cemetery, attacking Paul and me with her sword and her mask of vengeance and grief. We ran and….

Whoosh!

The wind blasted me back inside the blue door into my alleyway. The space that led to the door of my flat swirled with mist and dust. I fumbled along the length of the way, feeling for my door, craving for the safety and shelter of my home.

The expanse ran longer than seemed possible, and I groped and pushed through the whipping gusts. I crouched and angled for a better look through the wind. Up ahead, a break in the storm opened the view. On my hands and knees I moved to it, gasping short breaths as the air was pulled out of me by the forceful gale.

If this was Grace… If she was coming… I would throw the ring at her. Without Paul, she wouldn't see the eternal love of her bond with Hugh living on in us. To rest her soul at peace. But that didn't matter anymore. Without Paul, I just wanted to end it in the quickest way possible.

Panting, I pulled myself into the stillness of the void. On my knees, I caught my breath. Light opened the space, revealing a winding road through thick tall trees. The gnawing in my gut told me there was someone lurking, someone following.

I moved along the winding road that quickly opened up to a rolling green expanse leading up to a manor. The huge estate was grand, like a sprawling English castle you'd see on a postcard. Nothing like the stout stronghold of Rockfleet Castle, but more elaborate.

I moved across the lawn, passing crafted topiaries and garden statues. The darkness lingered, making it difficult to see the manor's details. I moved close to a tall evergreen, probably twelve feet high, carved in the shape of a four-sided pyramid. I leaned into it for shelter as I looked at the distance between me and the immense front door.

Vulnerability coursed through me as I felt alone and unprotected. Deep in my soul, I was exposed and had lost my armor somewhere along the way. I froze, rooted to my spot, blinking non-stop. It was up to me to get to safety. To protect myself from harm.

As I gauged my next move, I heard a rustle behind me and was reminded of the ominous feeling of being followed. Or stalked. Or lured?

My breathing accelerated and burst in and out of me.

I turned my head against all resistance of my body and focused on any possible movement behind me. My heart lurched into my throat when I caught sight of the brown-cloaked man moving across the great lawn directly toward me at an effortless speed.

Terror filled my every muscle as I blasted from my topiary toward the entrance of the great manor. With no clue on how I would get the doors open or get inside, I raced toward them as if they were my savior.

Pumping my arms for extra speed, I looked back as my legs carried me forward. The monk was nowhere. He must have hidden behind the lawn trees.

I flew up the stone terrace and smashed into the enormous wooden doors. They met in the middle with two massive brass pulls. I reached my hands through them and heaved with my entire weight. They bulged out from my efforts but fell back securely.

I looked back over my shoulder, terrified of what I might see, what might be right behind me.

As my eyes focused around me, I saw movement from the pyramid bush. The brown hooded cloak glided from behind the greenery and moved toward me in an unreal gait that lumbered in size and weight, yet gained ground effortlessly. His heavy frame was unmistakable but his agility was haunting.

I turned back to the door and gave another heave. This time knowing my life depended on it. The doors groaned open, enough for me to squeeze in. I swung around to close them tight as the monk leapt onto the terrace and barreled toward the doors.

He reached them just as the gap came together between them. With one final pull, I looked through the crack and his bloodshot eyes pierced mine just as I sealed it shut.

I knew those maniacal eyes.

Fergal.

My shriek was drowned out by the sound of the doors slamming shut. I pulled them in tight and twisted the brass fixture to lock them. My breath raced out of control as my eyes darted around the dark, centuries old space.

Not a sound came from the other side of the doors and I backed away from them with light, silent steps. My eyes adjusted to the new light inside the aged manor and I moved farther in, drawn deeper by my fear of my outside attacker but also by the mysterious décor.

The Victorian-era furniture and tapestries created a haunting, regal feel. The glow of the fireplace pulled me farther in and I tip-toed across the foyer into the great room. My breathing steadied as my eyes darted around, taking in every details of the space and searching for clues of any inhabitants.

I warmed my hands by the glowing embers in the fireplace and looked at the crest above. The boar and galley jumped out at me first. It was the crest of the O'Malley clan, crossed by two medieval swords.

My heart raced as I moved around the room. Generations of family portraits covered the walls, giving the feeling of a reunion or important family meeting. I searched for one that depicted Grace O'Malley. One that portrayed her in her true likeness.

I wanted, more than anything, to see her. To see anything that would help me. I yearned for something to make sense. To give me confidence that I was on the right track.

My shoulders slumped as I saw nothing that resembled Grace. But it felt as if she were here, or could be here. Her presence was all around me.

Lost in confusion, I searched the portraits for familiar names or a family resemblance and found only unknowns. My arms hung by my sides and my posture slouched as I backed away. Heat grew behind my eyelids as my throat tightened.

But then, in a blink, I was drawn to one portrait in particular across the room. A life-size painting of a young woman, masterfully done, with lace details in the fabric of her dress and fine lines on her knuckles. I focused on her clothing and her necklace and followed the ends of her long hair all the way up to her face.

I looked straight into her eyes and gasped as my hands flew to my mouth. I stepped back, shaking my head, moving away from the portrait.

How could it be?

I dropped my eyes to the ground in hopes it would go away. Maybe I'd seen it wrong.

With my head still down, I raised my eyes, just enough to sneak a second peek, and regretted it in an instant.

Her face was identical to mine.

Like looking into a mirror. Every feature. Her long brown hair. The distant look in her sea-green eyes. Lips at-the-ready to purse to the side in cynical judgment.

And her necklace. I recognized the chain. I reached for it, hanging from my own neck.

I grasped the ring dangling at my chest from the strong chain, certain the same ring hung from *her* necklace, hidden under her blouse in the painting. They were a perfect match.

I backed out of the room hoping to remain unnoticed, feeling the eyes of every portrait upon me, tilting their heads and watching… knowing I'd made a discovery.

As I stepped back, I bumped into a rock-solid object as big as me. I swung around and came face to face with a Celtic cross monument. My senses cleared from the fresh breeze that washed across my face. The darkness sent a shudder through me as I gazed upon monument after monument. A sea of Celtic cross gravestones.

I was in the Bohermore Cemetery.

I took one look around me and darted for the exit, sure the undead would be reaching for my ankles to trip me up. Rows of ancient stones moved with the shadows as I whirred past them, generating a level of fear in me that nearly forced a guttural scream. I flew toward the metal archway of the graveyard and burst through it out onto Bohermore.

My feet didn't stop pounding the sidewalk until they reached 122. Through my blue door, down the alleyway, and into the white door leading into my flat, I held my breath the entire way. I leapt up the steps, into my room, and dove under my covers.

My body quaked with massive shivers as I lay motionless in my bed, praying nothing and nobody would sense my presence or existence.

***

"I can't do this." I spoke to the mascara stains on my pillow.

Somehow I'd slept after my strange sleepwalking encounter in Bohermore Cemetery. Though it all began with the wind. The lines were blurred between what was real and what was more real.

The truth in the things I saw left no doubt in my mind.

It was all real.

And now, I didn't want it. I wasn't enough. Not brave enough. Not strong enough. Just, not enough.

I dragged myself through my morning routine and left the safety of my flat for NUIG. The university library mocked me with its knowledge and information. Tempting me with tidbits yet holding the most important details just out of my reach.

I was afraid.

Brigid scared me. The voices at Rockfleet scared me. Not because they were odd or haunting, but because of their truths. I was next in line. Somehow, it worked its way down to me. If I traced the family tree closely enough, it would all lead directly to me. I had no doubt.

But the tree had broken branches. Its inner rings represented years of struggle or years of prosper. I googled Grace O'Malley a million times and flipped through the big weathered book of Irish chieftains even more.

The rightful chieftain to the O'Malley Clan seemed to fall into years of darkness and uncertainty in some centuries. Information of land treaties and deeds muddied the waters.

I thought back to the historical meeting of Grace O'Malley and Queen Elizabeth I, remembered as the meeting of the Pirate Queen and the Virgin Queen. Queen Elizabeth granted Grace's land in the west of Ireland back to her from Sir Bingham's clutches. Grace defended her land valiantly her entire life. It was uncertain what became of it all after that.

I slammed the heavy cover of the chieftain book shut. A dizzying amount of detail swam in my head, causing vertigo.

I needed Paul.

I needed his love and support. And I needed his expertise. He could help me sort through the historical accounts, the family tree, deeds, and treaties. But something spooked him. More than what he said. It was like he had a greater understanding of what the voices at the castle were saying but wouldn't tell me. What could get to him worse than what we'd already been up against?

I shoved my stuff into my backpack and swung it over my shoulder. The waft of dark roast tempted me toward Smokey Joe's and I made a beeline for the coffee shop.

***

My hands clutched the warm cup as I scanned the tables of the campus coffee shop for familiar faces. Most tables were empty, not surprising in summer, so I drew a bead straight to the cozy area overlooking the River Corrib.

My phone buzzed in my pocket. It was Michelle.

Girl where r u?

Crap. I was supposed to meet Michelle at Griffin's Bakery. I totally forgot.

I scrambled to gather my things and saw him out of the corner of my eye. His slightly overgrown hair, his strong shoulders and stark white oxford, his attaché bag slung casually over his shoulder.

It was Paul.

My heart flipped and butterflies took full flight. I grabbed my pack and threw my coffee cup at the barrel, ready to race over to him.

Then she turned the corner after him.

Patricia.

He ordered two coffees and they sat at a table by the exit.

The blow left me breathless and heaving for oxygen. The punch to my face busted my nose and crushed my skull. I imploded. It took every ounce of energy to not fall on the floor in a puddle.

I slunk my head as deep into my shoulders as it would go and headed for the exit.

Please don't look up. Please don't look up. Please don't look up.

I passed his table with as much distance as possible and kept my eyes on the exit.

Stealth.

He was in conversation with her as I passed without notice. I picked my head up and just as I allowed myself to begin to fall apart, I heard my name.

"Maeve. Hey, Maeve."

I turned back and across Smokey Joe's. It was Harry. He had his hand up in a wave.

I hadn't seen him since I left last January. He was one of my closest friends at NUIG. My heart jumped from the sight of his smiling face, but just as I reached to wave back, Paul looked up. He saw Harry. Then he turned and saw me.

His face fell and turned all shades of white.

I spun on my heels and bolted.

With my head down, I speed-walked right off campus, past the Cathedral, and into the city center.

Harry must have still been standing in the same spot looking at the exit wondering if he'd seen a ghost. I'd explain later. Or maybe that wouldn't be necessary. I'm sure he saw Paul there. And then Patricia. He wasn't stupid.

***

The warm, flaky scent of sausage rolls wafted along the cobblestone streets and led me straight into Griffin's Bakery.

"This is my third one." Michelle looked up from her plate with a guilty smile. Flakes of pastry from her sausage roll clung to her lips. "It's your fault, you know."

She licked her lip and enjoyed the buttery crumbs.

I dropped down into my chair and collapsed into a pile of mush.

"Give me a chance to catch up. It's already looking like a four-sausage-roll morning for *me*." I plopped my arms onto the table.

"Okay. Spill."

A slow inhale pulled the last twenty-four hours together into a fairy tale, or ghostly legend rather, and I poured it over Michelle.

Her jaw hit the table early on, around the "Brigid rant at St. Mary's" part, and it never pulled up after that, until my final words and the "Patricia" part.

Michelle smacked her lips a couple times, realigning her slackened jaw and took a slow sip of her coffee.

"My head hurts." She rubbed her temples and sat back in her chair surveying me in a new light.

"Yeah, I know. Mine too." I half-smiled. "And I'm tired."

She scratched her head. "What are you going to do?"

"I have no idea. My plan seemed so clear when I came back here. But it's a total mess now." I looked into my coffee. "I think I'm done.

It's too much."

Hopelessness carved out my inner strength and left me feeling broken and weak. I didn't know if I had the strength to keep going any more. Alone.

Everything had changed. Paul was my soul mate, I had thought. And *that* was a huge part of our journey to bringing Grace to a place of rest. Now, it seemed I was on my own.

Michelle lifted her hand with her fingers up, flagging the attention of the girl at the counter.

"Two more sausage rolls, please." She leaned in to me. "You can't stop now, Maeve. It's not an option."

I fought the muscles in my face at first but the smile spread across anyway. Michelle was exactly what I needed— a reminder of my purpose.

"Girl. Time to bring in the big guns," she said. "I'm in." She folded her arms on the table in resolve. "I might have been a little freaked out at first by your jacked-up sixth sense, but I'm ready now." Her lips pressed to the side and she squirmed in her seat. "At least, I think I am. And you need me." She sat up taller. "Take me on a ghost hunt! I'm your new partner!"

Chapter Six

Ghost Hunt

"Where the hell did you get this?" I threw my body across the hood, in love.

"It's Declan's grandmother's or something. He made me take it." She smirked. "I warned him though. My dyslexia is not gonna make a smooth transition to driving on the other side of the road." Michelle swung the key ring around her finger with a smug expression. "He loves me."

"Oh my god. He's the best!" I gushed.

I always knew I loved Declan. Not only because he was with Michelle, but because he believed in my visions. His sister's similar "awake dreams" gave us endless hours of conversation.

And now, this car!

It was by far the oldest BMW I'd ever seen. A 1972 1500. The true iconic classic. Boxy, with big square windows and straight lines along the body. Huge, thin steering wheel. Solid black exterior. But the best part—the vivid red interior!

"I feel like *Thelma and Louise* meet *007*!" I jumped, clapping my hands.

"Get in." Michelle threw my bags in the back seat. "And fasten your seatbelt!" She snorted a big guffaw. "If it even *has* any."

We flew up the N17 toward Newport in County Mayo. It had only been a week since I was last there with Paul, at Rockfleet Castle. The whispering voices still lingered in my head.

"So did you finally tell Paul you were coming here?" Michelle glanced at me and then swerved back into her lane after scraping the encroaching hedgerows.

"Sort of."

She looked again, so I kept talking to keep her eyes on the road.

"I mean, I told him I was going back. He freaked and made me promise not to. But he's been keeping his distance from the whole thing right now. Thinks it's too dangerous. And I'm still basically pissed about it. Seriously, he can't just pull away like that. I don't care if he's scared. And the whole Patricia thing." I huffed. "Like, that was a little coincidental, no? Her being at the college to see him. Right when he decides to back away from all this. Whatever."

My lips pursed to the side and I looked out my window.

"We're just trying not to talk too much about any of it right now. It's touchy, I guess. He just seems... scared."

I couldn't help feeling angry. His cautious distance made all my insecurities resurface and they choked me. Being alone in the world while fighting a family curse, well, that was enough to raise trust issues in *anyone*. And that made it even worse. If I couldn't trust Paul one hundred percent, then I had nothing.

I tried to keep perspective. He *was* with Patricia for years and their families were friends, so I really shouldn't go crazy about this. But I couldn't help it. She had too much power to win him back and I'd be left with nothing.

I rubbed my eyes, hazy from lack of sleep, and sat up taller. Maybe this was another thing I had to fight for. Maybe it wasn't supposed to come easy.

"Well, diversion is usually an effective way to cope with fear. Basically, avoiding it. Well done." Michelle jabbed at my ribs and flashed a comforting grin. "This will give you a chance to breathe. You know. Like, take some space on your own, to see what this curse thing is all about."

Michelle pulled into an open spot in Westport.

"Come on. Let's get something to eat before we hit the *legendary* Rockfleet Castle." She wiggled her eyebrows at me with exaggerated intrigue.

The big clock tower in the town center stood proudly, welcoming me back since my last visit to Westport—the time when Paul had followed me, trying to be a part of my adventure while keeping a *cautious distance* as my college professor.

My lips pursed to the side to push down the sadness that rose from the sweet memory. I still believed we were connected, beyond this world even, but couldn't stop the worry. He was the only person on this earth with the power to refill my empty soul and make me whole again.

We passed the clock tower, following the smell of seafood chowder and brown bread, scouting for the perfect pub. The main road narrowed and we turned down a lost lonely lane at the far end of town.

"This place is amazing. All of it. It's never like this back home." Michelle spoke to the shops and cobblestone pavers. "Here, there are surprises around every corner. Pubs, shops, ghosts! I love it!"

She reached her hand out as if to feel every experience—the overflowing flower boxes, colorful hand-painted signs, and then, the most intriguing hue of purple filled my every sense.

A vibrant door squished between two storefronts was the gateway to the tiniest shop I'd ever seen. The hand-painted sign hung over the door from a scrolled metal bracket and read, *Palm Reader*.

"Come on." Michelle grabbed my wrist and pulled me to the door. "Let's try it."

She pressed her hand against a plastic sign by the door with a picture of an enlarged palm marking the "Zones of Palmistry."

"No way. That's a waste of money." I rolled my eyes at her, hearing my grandmother's words escape my lips, followed by a perfectly timed clipping from *Dear Abby*.

But I couldn't help notice the cool crystals through the small window—a huge salt rock, lit from within cast an ethereal orange glow, and quartz crystals with magical purple hues seeping along the edges.

A vintage plaque at the back of the crystal display read:

PALMIST and CLAIRVOYANT
Tells Past, Present and Future
Love, Luck, Courtship, and Marriage
Don't Fail to Consult Me

"Let's at least have a look," Michelle said, pushing the door open before finishing her sentence.

My face contorted in horror as our presence was announced by jingling bells on the door.

"No turning back now." She giggled.

The smell of incense overpowered me as we wafted through the patchouli. A young woman, more like a flower child, moved languidly from the back room through a beaded curtain as her long skirt flowed behind in her graceful movement. Her tasseled headpiece reminded me of something I donned for Halloween once, when I was Cleopatra.

I chuckled through my nose and Michelle swatted my hand with a hiss.

"I am Moira of Fire and Water." Her breathy voice added ambiance to her spiritual persona.

Rhythmic chimes filled the air as she swayed her arms to the lulling sound. She reached for Michelle's hand and studied it through half-opened eyes. She pulled Michelle's palm right up to her nose, as if for a closer look, and pulled back in exaggerated surprise. Her arm flew in a large arc, fingers splayed, as if she were about to address the universe.

"Your fate is in your hands." Her mystical tone trailed off into the chimes.

She glanced at me and then back at Michelle. Her finger traced the lines in Michelle's palm as she whispered nonsensical words and phrases that sounded like several people talking at once.

"Your lines are strong. Intuition. Intelligence. Activity." She spoke into Michelle's face, violating her personal space beyond acceptable. Michelle nearly went cross-eyed trying to focus on her. "Your love line is active. You've found your match, no?"

Michelle's eyes widened and stared at me, like, *Oh my god. She's amazing!*

Moira turned to me with a snap of her head, shocking the judgmental expression off my face.

"Would *you* like a sample reading?" She looked me up and down.

"No. Thank you." My curt reply sent clear signals. Or, so I thought.

Michelle hip-bumped me closer to Moira of Wind and Fire, or whatever.

"Go on, Maeve. Don't be a chicken," Michelle pressured.

"No, really. I'm all set." I kept my hands close to my sides in tight balls, like I might catch something or become infected by this nonsense. "Really. Thanks. I'm good." I moved my gaze to the crystals to avoid her penetrating stare. "We actually need to get going."

My pressed lips and stare down nudged Michelle with annoyance.

Moira continued to examine me through squinted eyes and wrinkled nose. Her head tilted.

"Please. One look at your palm. No commitment. Just a peek." She held her hand open and waved her fingers at me, drawing my palm toward her.

My eyes rolled up to the ceiling as I struggled to find the right words of refusal, but I gave her my palm anyway, just to make it stop. She caught it in an instant, without shame and pulled it close to her face, nuzzling it like a dog.

Her eyes darted around every inch of my hand as if studying a treasure map. Then she slowed into intense focus and looked up into my eyes. She held my gaze for an extended amount of time and I didn't know what to do, or where to look. I fidgeted under her intense scrutiny and considered bolting out the door.

"Love. Sympathy. Grace."

She spoke in a rehearsed mystical tone.

"You a time traveler?" Her eyes searched mine for answers.

My eyes widened in surprise and blazed back into hers, unblinking.

She kept hold of my hand as she tipped her head and looked deeper into my soul. Her other hand reached up and slid her Cleopatra headdress off her head and it dropped to the floor with an unceremonious splat.

Without breaking my gaze, she continued.

"You've come a long way. Great distance. By ship. Over the sea."

I pulled my hand back with a gasp and reached for Michelle.

"Obviously." Michelle let her sarcasm fly. "A total Yank." She rolled her eyes at me like I was a fool.

"And over years," Moira continued in a long drawl, attempting a quick recovery.

She leaned in with curious eyes, studying me.

"What are you searching for?" Her head dropped to the side again as she stared.

"The pirate queeeeeen." Michelle flapped her hands in the air for a ghostly effect.

Moira sucked in air as she shot up straight.

"You seek the pirate queen? Grace O'Malley?" Her tone lost all mysticism and flower child cadence as it punched back to reality with sharp focus.

"Yes," I said, pulling back my chin from the whiplash character change. "You know of her?"

My defenses tightened. I wasn't ready to share this journey with anyone else. Particularly if they were just going to get scared off and leave me again. But her sharpshooter response couldn't be ignored. She was right on.

Moira pushed her tarot cards and other craft pieces into a messy pile on the edge of her reading table and rushed to the back room, mumbling lists of items to herself. She returned with a small box of books and clippings.

"Know of her? I've studied Granuaile all m' life." She huffed. "Growing up around here, ya didn't really have a choice. But she's always fascinated me, like to a higher level."

She glanced sideways at me and squinted one eye, for a clearer snapshot.

Moira pulled her relics from the box and displayed her collection of Grace O'Malley history, one piece after another, barely touching them to preserve their delicate condition—news clippings, claims of ghost sightings, treks to find her final resting place, as well as rocks, feathers, and fabric. All tied in to her story of Grace somehow.

I looked up from the collection with a gentle smirk, like, *thanks, that's cool*, but then gazed out the window biting my nails, anxious to get going.

"We're on our way to Rockfleet Castle," Michelle interrupted. "To try to awaken her spirit." Her smile spread for miles.

I eyeballed Michelle in judgment, for divulging our secret mission, but also for sounding as if she were teasing Moira. I mean, Moira was a ruse, I was sure. But my eyes darted to the floor at the same time, in surprise of myself. Was I falling for this crap?

I interjected, "Well, not really *awaken*. Just to try to, ya know, to...."

"Like I said, to awaken her spirit!" Michelle nodded and shot a sinister grin at me like she'd won something.

Moira sent a quick nod to Michelle and skipped to the far side of the shop. She pulled off her fringed shawl and grabbed a North Face from her closet. Her flowing hippie skirt fell from her waist and hit the floor revealing tight black yoga pants underneath.

"Can I come wit'ya? Please. I'll be your conduit. I'm a medium, ya know. A clairvoyant. Sure, I've been dyin' to make contact with her all me life."

Moira's begging eyes jumped from Michelle's to mine, back and forth, waiting for approval.

I kept my eyes averted.

"Seriously," she continued. "I can communicate with the dead. They cross over from the other side and channel their energy through me. It's a family gift. Or, okay, maybe a curse... but it pays the bills. Sure, can I come wit'cha? Please?"

Michelle stared at me with wide, excited eyes, begging for me to say yes.

My jaw clenched as my head shook at her, my lips pleading. "No fucking way."

"No charge. Really," Moira continued to push. "Allowing me to tag along is enough payment. Really."

Arghhhh! My teeth nearly cracked from the pressure.

Fine! She'd better turn out to be a true clairvoyant, even though all signals pointed to hokey palm-reader. But if she had any remote interest in Grace O'Malley, then I guess it made sense to take the risk. She'd better not let me down though. It's not like we needed the extra company.

And, sure, she already had her jacket on and was shutting off lights.

"As long as we can grab some food first, then fine, whatever." I said. "I'm starving."

"I *knew* you were about to say that!" Moira turned to me with bulging eyes.

"Seriously?" Michelle stared at her in shock. Completely won over by her superpowers.

"Just messin'!"

And Moira poked Michelle in the ribs as she grabbed her trendy Orla Keily handbag from under the table and locked up shop.

***

"The original owner of this car's ridin' with us now. Did you know him?" Moira reached her hands out on both sides and rubbed the back seat with fond affection.

"Shut up!" Michelle gawked into the rearview mirror at Moira. "Seriously? Is he mad that I took it?"

"Nah. He's just happy to be cruising again with a buncha lovely ladies." She tossed her head back with a laugh, as if sharing a drive with the owner on a fine Sunday afternoon.

I held my tongue so it wouldn't make enemies. Jury was still out on Moira. But so far, I was pretty sure she was a whack-job.

Michelle took the turns a bit too fast, paying more attention to Moira than the road. My body leaned one way and then the other, struggling to stay upright.

"Slow down, Michelle. I think it's coming up." My senses sharpened as we approached the final bend before Rockfleet.

"Ooh, this is fantastic." Moira bounced in the backseat. "Last time I was here, we held a séance. Sure, we were still in secondary school and had ourselves a stolen bottle of Jameson, but sure, was great craic."

"Are you serious? A séance?" Michelle's eyes locked in the

rearview mirror again. "Did anything strange happen?"

I turned around fully, for the first time, to see Moira's response.

"Ya. Lotsa crazy shite." Her eyes grew wide. "Candles blew out, and, and–" she paused in thought "–and, there were strange winds and yeah, it was crazy. Blame it on the Jamey."

I turned to Michelle with my lips pressed to one side.

Who was this clown? And how did she finagle herself into our trip?

I looked out my window, annoyed by the additional distraction and baggage. It felt a little like betrayal, actually, like I was exploiting Grace. My eyebrows squeezed together and my lips pressed white with regret.

"Did the spirits speak to you, Moira?" Michelle asked, her face hanging in anticipation of more details.

Did she seriously buy this crap? Oh my god. Two clowns.

"Stop here, Michelle. Stop, stop, stop." I pressed my hand into the air to get her to stop.

The castle came into view and a sea of emotions washed over me. It stood exactly as it always was, dark and brooding. Solid and strong. Waiting.

My breath sucked in.

"Park here," I said as my door flew open before the car was fully stopped.

Paul's tire marks scarred the gravelly dirt road from the last time we flew out of here. A shiver ran up my spine and into my fingertips as I remembered the voices… and then Paul's cold response.

A salty breeze blew in from the rising tide, as the sea made its twice-daily trip to the granite steps of the castle.

"So do you feel anything? See anything?" Michelle asked, looking into my eyes for any clues of possession.

Moira stared too.

My face fell, unimpressed. "Seriously?"

"What do you usually see?" Moira moved in closer for inspection of my reactions.

"Castles and stuff," I stated plainly.

I hopped out and walked closer to Grace O'Malley's stronghold, mostly to get away from Moira, but also in response to the steady draw I felt from it.

Michelle leaned in and whispered to Moira, taking her arm like they were besties.

"She's kind of stalked by, you know, the pirate queen. She sees her in these weird visions. And Grace has, like, attacked her." Michelle's voice trailed off as she got lost in her own explanation. "It's crazy."

I guessed it did look pretty weird for a newcomer and even for Michelle. I mean, how *did* you explain this to anyone without sounding like a complete freak?

Moira ran to catch up to me.

"Want me to contact her?" she said with raised eyebrows while reaching for my arm.

"What?" I didn't mean to sound offended, but my tone was sharp.

"I'll conjure her. You know, awaken her?"

I looked at Michelle as she caught up behind Moira.

Michelle blurted, "Yeah! Give it a try. It's about time I met this lady."

My hand went to my forehead as I dropped my eyes in shame. This was already becoming a farce and protecting Grace from this circus was a priority.

"Hey, you're the one with the freaky visions," Moira said, pulling her chin back. "You shouldn't be so judgmental."

Michelle glared at me, like I was a party wrecker.

"Sorry. I just don't know what to believe anymore." I pushed my lip into my teeth with a knuckle and bit.

I was feeling strangely possessive of the pirate queen, like, whatever we had together was personal. Not for Michelle and Moira. But that felt dumb too. I mean, maybe Moira could actually help.

We walked around to the front of the castle and stood at the base of the granite steps, looking up into the black abyss of the large, arched door. The heavy metal ring-pull hung on the wooden panels, waiting to be tugged. My hand reached out to touch it.

"Wait!" Moira's voice pierced my soul, making me jump. "I feel something."

She closed her eyes and waved her hands in front of herself, feeling the air or mystic vibrations of some sort. My cynicism returned and I looked out to sea as she continued.

"There's wind. And screams." She moved her head as if picking up signals from all around us. "A smell of iron. Blood is in the air."

Michelle's jaw hung open as she stared at Moira, absorbing her every word.

Moira moved to the door and placed her hands on the dark, aged wood.

"It's a warning. We shouldn't be here." Moira's voice grew louder as Michelle's eyes grew wider. "We're unwelcome intruders."

The inlet of the sea deepened as the tide moved closer. Clare Island filled the horizon far out in the distance.

"She's coming." Moira opened her eyes and shot a look of alarm at Michelle. "She's coming!" Her voice rose as she attempted to get my attention back from the sea.

The terror in Michelle's bulging eyes made me crack up and I stifled my laugh with my fist. Giggles went straight through me and nearly made me pee.

Moira's hands flew up in the air as she began to wail and flap her arms.

"She's here!" she yelled, gyrating as if she were being electrocuted.

Michelle froze, then began hopping from one foot to the other, not knowing what to do with herself. Her eyes darted around begging for safety, as a shattering crash smashed down on the rocks by our feet.

Michelle and Moira grabbed each other and screamed in unison. They ran screaming and laughing across the road toward the sea. With hands on knees, they leaned panting, looking back at me.

After cringing at the mangled mess of a clam in its broken shell, I turned to the sky and watched a seagull readying itself to swoop down for its smashed-open lunch.

My eyes drooped half-closed in judgment as I glared at Michelle and Moira for their heightened antics. Moira really knocked this one out of the park.

They grabbed each other's arms and burst into nervous laughter.

Michelle's infamous snort shattered the picturesque landscape as she rambled, "Holy shit. You scared the crap out of me."

They walked to the water's edge and Michelle squatted down and rinsed her sweaty hands in the water.

Moira turned back to me and stared through squinted eyes, piercing through me. I pulled my gaze from hers, knowing she was full of crap, but still questioning her accurate account of Grace's presence–the wind, screams, smell of iron in the air. I shook my head, rejecting the notion.

Moira looked away from me then and bent down to collect bits of seashell as she joined Michelle's laughter, shaking away the jitters.

I turned back to the ominous black door, wondering what was inside for me. It was like it knew something and tempted me to enter. I bit my lip, questioning my next move. It would be crazy to go in. Like tempting fate.

A rumble shook under my feet and the heavy door shook on its hinges.

I looked back to Michelle and Moira who appeared unaffected. They were skipping stones into the lapping waves, proving to me that Moira's antics were all a hoax. I huffed, embarrassed that I sort of fell for it.

Another vibration shot my gaze back to the door. It was heaving and expanding in its Gothic stone archway. My feet stepped back, taking me away from what I knew was coming.

A burst of energy from within? An assault of defense against the unknown intruder, me?

The last time that door blasted open, the pirate queen came barreling out, intent on killing me like an enemy caught on private land.

My heart accelerated, causing my breath to pant out of me. She hadn't known it was me then. Once she recognized me, though, she knew not to hurt me. That was when she whispered, "We are one."

I looked back at the girls, then at the door again, considering my next move, though my mind was already made up.

I was going in. And I was scared to death.

If I bumped into the pirate queen, my immediate mission would be to get her to recognize me. That was clear. Then, maybe we would be able to communicate somehow—develop a plan or something. I would show her the ring, for starters.

The door shook and loosened its seal, then opened a crack as if pushed by a steady force. Without looking back, I reached my fingers around the edge and pulled.

Opened just enough for me to squeeze through, I shimmied inside and breathed in the centuries-old air as my eyes adjusted to the darkness.

I pulled the door closed again to conceal my entrance. I didn't want Michelle and Moira following me. This was sacred ground, in my mind, and the violation of their presence would ruin everything. I wish I had realized that before bringing them along. I balled my fists at my amateur move.

Without hesitation, heart pounding, I climbed the ladder to the next floor, and the next, following my footsteps from my first visit last winter until I reached the spiral staircase that led to her chambers. With dizzying speed, I swirled up to the top floor of the stony fortress—Grace's private space.

Light filled the open room through the only large window in the entire towerhouse. I went to it and gazed out to the sea—the same view Grace O'Malley had when she ruled the trade routes and protected the territory of the O'Malley Clan.

My breath hesitated as sharp tingles shot out of my fingers and toes—the kind that alert you when danger is near. I twisted around to survey the open space, expecting to be blasted by the sinister winds—or worse, to see her coming at me with her sword drawn.

My plan was to hold direct eye contact with her until she recognized me. With her sword down, I would reach for my necklace and pull out the ring. I had no idea how she would react to the ring, but my hope was she would have a powerful response to it, as if it were a conduit to reunite her with Hugh, or something.

It was already sounding too easy.

The great room was empty, but my eyes continued to dart from wall to wall, searching for any sign of activity. I stepped forward, listening, smelling, testing all my senses.

My skin picked up on it first.

Starting as a delicate breeze, my arm hairs prickled in response to the movement. Then my ears twitched with sounds almost out of reach. I closed my eyes to focus on my other senses.

My blood flowed through me like electrical impulses and coursed through every vein, concentrating its force in my brain. Then the smell. Musty at first, it grew into something more alive, damp and composting, laced with iron.

My eyes sprung open.

The room came alive with motion and activity, air swirling in every direction. I was knocked and shoved as the gusts grew stronger and I stumbled around the room. The force gained strength as it whirled into itself and pushed me farther. I hit against the wall and then staggered back to the middle of the room, searching the space for whatever or whoever was pushing against me.

It must be her.

My mind raced with the idea of her showing herself to me. I could hardly breathe, thinking about a possible confrontation.

Another hit and I stumbled toward the window.

Again and again it forced me closer to the wide opening. As I fell against the edge, I braced myself on the hard ledge of the sill and dizzying vertigo sent my vision blurry as I imagined plummeting four stories to the ground in a heap of broken mess.

Terror rose in me as a gust pressed me farther and my hair blew out the opening, leading the way for my fall.

This wasn't how I'd planned it. Disposed of before having a chance to reveal my true identity to her.

I dropped to my knees to escape the assault and crawled away from the window, eyes closed from the fury of the blasts.

The gaping shelter of the enormous fireplace called out to me. The O'Malley crest in the top keystone was a clear beacon of safety. I pushed my way into the massive space, batting my flying hair out of my face, and scrunched against the back wall, panting.

I pressed into the stonework, hoping to disappear in soot from centuries past. Peering back out into her chambers, I followed the swirling chaos of browns and blacks swiping at every wall and corner, searching, keeping me tucked deep in my spot.

She was searching for me.

Or worse, eagerly waiting for me to come back out.

My eyes moved up along the jagged stonework of the interior of the chimney. Rough and unfinished, it led up to dull light that penetrated through a small opening at the top where the smoke of a fire would escape. Maybe if I could get a grip on each protruding stone, I could scale the inside of the chimney and escape through the roof.

My hands prodded along the jagged flue, searching for a hold, and I pulled myself up a few inches. I reached for the next piece of stone as my foot searched blindly for a hold. As I pressed my way up another few inches, my sweaty hands slid right off as my feet lost hold and I trailed down the wall landing with a thump back onto the fireplace floor. Shards of broken stone and mortar crumbled and hit down at my feet. Some bounced out of the hearth and into the room.

I froze. Holding my breath with my eyes squeezed shut.

My hands gripped the inner wall for stability, just above the fireplace opening and I willed them to melt right into the stonework with the rest of me.

My fingers wiggled with a curiosity of their own and moved across a small metal door, jutting out from the masonry, like the size of a toaster oven door. My curiosity got the best of me as my focus shifted to the hidden compartment.

My intellect told me it was an alcove for holding cleaning tools or hooks for hanging kettles, but my wild imagination told me it held secrets. Otherwise, it would be in a more obvious place.

A metal ring dangled from the door. I reached for the rusted pull and gave it a yank. It stuck at first, eroded and crusted from time. One more quick pull with the weight of my body and it squeaked open.

I squinted through the darkness into the nook but saw only black in its depth. Against the warnings of my inner voice screaming "mouse" or "spider," I reached in and probed around searching for any trinket.

Whatever could be hidden here would have remained hidden for hundreds of years. Maybe a lost relic of Grace's plundering, or better, hidden treasure beyond compare.

I blinked away the fantasy and continued to grope in the blackness of the hole.

A blast of wind pulled my attention back out of the fireplace and into the room. Black gusts continued to swirl around, hunting. I pressed my shoulders into the back wall of the fireplace as I continue to reach farther into the darkness of the niche.

My hand patted around and then my fingers ran over a round metal object tucked at the very back. I reached my hand around the cold tube and rolled it out. My heartbeat pounded in my ears as guilt washed over me. Like I was touching something that wasn't mine or taking a step into unsafe territory.

The tube was like a paper towel roll, only rusty, and made of a thick, heavy metal. One end of the tube was sealed with a welded metal cap but the other end was packed with a waxy fabric cork.

I pressed the tube into my lap as I looked back out from my hiding place into the great room.

The writhing gusts had died down to mellow swirls of mist and fog.

Now was my chance.

I crept out of the fireplace, clutching the metal tube, and crouched down, scurrying toward the door to the spiral staircase. The stinging tingle in my toes forced me to look back over my shoulder one last time, and there, standing in the middle of the room, commanding all attention through her battle-ready stance and eye-locking glare, was the Pirate Queen, Gráinne Ní Mháille.

My heart dropped into my shoes as my spirit leapt out of my body in panic.

Grace's thick black hair flew in the gusts as her dark cloak flowed all around her, framing a brazen stare of pure intent and defense, like an avenging angel come to protect what was rightfully hers.

At first, she was a hazy apparition a million miles away, but then clear lines formed making her fully present in the room.

Her wild eyes homed in on mine and locked on me like a missile.

My heart jumped into my throat as my hand tightened on the tube.

Her steely gaze moved to my hand and onto the cylinder, then back to my eyes.

It must be hers. Oh my god. I was a robber. In her castle. Shit!

My hair swirled around my face and her haunting voice filled my skull as she commanded me.

"*Troid leo. Ghabháil ar ais a bhfuil linne.* Fight them! Take back what is ours!"

Jesus! My legs buckled under me and I stumbled back toward the steps.

I understood her language. Ancient words that spoke to me from deep in my soul.

"*Is é seo ár n-dtalamh ár farraige ár bhaile.* This is our land! Our home!"

Her commanding voice blasted in my head, generating enough energy to make it explode.

The rage in her eyes sent terror through me and I stumbled to the stairs and flew down them, nearly falling the entire way.

Looking back up the stairs, certain she was following with more commands or assaults, I moved down the ladders and pushed my body through a narrow opening of the black door. I shoved it closed behind me with the force of my entire weight and sucked in my first full breath since the wind began.

I leaned against the wooden door, panting, gathering my wits. Within seconds, I yearned to go back in. To ask questions. To communicate.

My teeth ground on themselves, as I resented my cowardice and fear. My head fell back as I resisted pulling my hair out.

But I had the tube.

My fingers clamped around it like a vice. I wiggled them loose, one at a time, and balanced it in my open palm. My eyes glued themselves to it, staring at the unbelievable relic from the ancient past.

A time capsule.

***

Michelle and Moira studied a rock circle in the sand as Moira used animated gestures to entertain Michelle with her prophecies. Michelle looked up at me and tipped her head. She left Moira, mid-arms-expounding, and walked toward me without breaking eye contact.

"You didn't go in there, did you?" she called over.

I pressed my back harder against the door to be sure it was sealed shut and held the metal tube behind me.

"Nah." I shook my head. "I've already seen inside before. I'm good."

I shoved the tube down the back of my pants and covered the top with my shirt.

The vessel was sacred. For my eyes only.

And what happened in Grace's chamber, that was private too. If Michelle or, god, Moira, found out I went inside, they would probably race in there too. It was my duty to protect Grace from that kind of onslaught.

I blinked in hesitation, noticing my position on protecting Grace, instead of my friends. I blew breath from my lips, realizing where my allegiance lay. My eyebrows scrunched together as a headache throbbed behind my eyes.

"Moira's rocks say there's an angry spirit here. Unsettled."

Michelle pointed back to Moira's rock circle. Moira was still crouched over it, twisting to see new perspectives.

"Come on. I don't want to stay here." I moved back toward the car.

"What do you mean? We just got here," Michelle whined. "And Moira said she would try to contact Grace. She's certain she's already here. It's only a matter of conjuring...."

"No." My tone stopped Michelle in her tracks. "It's not safe. Seriously. We need to leave."

Michelle pouted and walked back over to Moira to share the bad news.

I sat in the car waiting for them as they proved to be in no hurry, still crouching around the stones, waiting for a ghost to appear or a rock to flip on its own.

I reached back for my tube and examined it closely for the first time.

The rough, rusted exterior was covered in worn carvings—Celtic swirls and intricate knots. It was more beautiful than I had anticipated and made me wonder if the possible contents were anywhere near as interesting.

I shook it.

Silence. Nothing rattled. Nothing bounced about.

I turned it around and upside down, examining all features. The waxy seal begged for my attention. Opening it would probably break every archaeological rule in the book but there was no way I was passing up on the opportunity.

I picked at the wax and small crumbled bits fell onto my lap.

I considered waiting for Paul. He'd know how to handle it.

Maybe it should be left in its original condition. Maybe it belonged in a museum.

I chewed my lip and looked back toward the girls. Moira was squatting on her knees and moved around the stones like a troll. Michelle's jaw fell as her eyes glued themselves on her every movement, mesmerized, and I chuckled, shaking my head.

I picked at the wax again. And then some more. A small piece of fabric wiggled free from its waxy hold and I tugged on it. The entire stopper shook loose, so I pulled harder. I pressed my nail along the sealed rim and pulled again. The entire wad moved and then popped out.

My eyes widened as I peered into the dark void and focused on the muted light of yellowed, rolled paper—like a scroll.

I reached in and grabbed an edge of the parchment and gently pulled while tapping the other end of the tube. It came loose and the end revealed itself.

The brown edges of the aged paper were thick and rough, almost like hide. The outer corner of the roll opened up, exposing intricate designs with faded colors of purple and orange.

As I yanked a little more, the doors of the car flew open, making me jump in my seat, nearly bashing my head off the roof.

Michelle and Moira hopped in, giddy with chatter and stories. I stuffed the tube down between my legs and wadded the wax stopper in my fist.

"Maeve, you should've seen it! Moira saw stories in the rocks. Like ancient Druid rituals and tribal stuff." Michelle's eyes bulged.

"That's cool," I lied.

My cynicism hadn't faded in regards to Moira's "gift." Although, I had to admit, she was spot-on with feeling Grace's presence right before I entered the castle. I hesitated and stole a quick glance at Moira's face, wondering what she was truly capable of, if anything.

"Seriously, though," Michelle continued, forcing my undivided attention, as she pulled the car away from the castle. "She picked up vibes on Grace. As if she were around the castle."

I swallowed hard, knowing it to be true, and looked at the tube peeking out from behind my backpack.

"Really?" I turned to Moira in the back and shuffled around to look at her better.

I reeled back in fright when I saw the harrowing look in her eyes. She stared right through me, frozen in terror. Her chin trembled as if she was trying to speak.

"She's... she's in you." Moira's words hardly came out of her mouth, like they were struggling to stay in where it was safe.

Her hands went to her chest and then to her mouth as she stared at me as if I were a ghost.

"What?" I pulled back from her harsh, glaring judgment.

Her voice rose as her tone became shrill.

"She's in you!" she shouted. "She's all around you!" Her lips pulled back and her eyes watered as they darted around the car like her safety was in jeopardy and something cataclysmic was about to happen. "Who *are* you?"

Michelle tightened her grip on the wheel and the car slowed. "Calm down Moira. What's going on? Are you okay?"

"Let me out!" she shrieked. "Stop the car! Let me out!"

"Are you nuts? We're in the middle of nowhere." Michelle's voice shook.

"Jesus Christ. Stop the fucking car! Let me out!" Moira screeched.

Michelle jammed on the brakes in the middle of the road and turned back to see Moira.

She was already getting out of the car and slammed the door. Her body quaked and twitched. Tears rolled down her cheeks.

"Go! Go! Leave me, please!" She stepped back from the car and looked at me one final time. Her arm rose as her finger pointed at me, moving up and down as she spoke. "Sure, my work is mostly bullshit.

But you, I see her in you. All over you. You're cursed! By the Pirate Queen."

She moved back away from the car, as if she might become a victim to the curse. Her head shook as her hands moved through her hair and she spun around. She broke into a sprint in the opposite direction without looking back and we watched her blend into the darkness of the street.

Michelle stared in the direction Moira ran, then turned back to me. Tears laced the corners of her eyes as she looked at me, as if I were a stranger.

My stomach twisted.

"It's *me*, Michelle." My eyebrows scrunched at her. "Moira's nuts."

But the way Michelle looked at me wasn't nuts. It was pure fear.

"I don't know, Maeve."

A tear streamed down from her eye without even a blink. The heavy pull of the tear brought it down her cheek to her chin and then it dropped onto her lap.

My hand pressed onto my chest and my chin tucked in, like I was choking. Short breaths wheezed into me as my world collapsed inward.

Michelle too? It was too much for her too?

"Please, Michelle. It's just me." I begged her to come back to me, but the crushing blow of being left alone held no prisoners. It flattened me.

My jaw clamped in resolve. I could be alone in all of this.

Moira knew exactly what she was talking about. And Michelle bought every word of it.

Funny thing though, I was pretty sure it was the first time Moira realized her "gift" was actually real. But Michelle, she always knew my visions to be real. This was nothing new for her.

So I just needed to win Michelle back. Help her move from "freaked out" to "I got this."

Either way though, it was another sick reminder that I had to be prepared to do this on my own, whether I like it or not.

I looked back at the scroll, hidden from Michelle's sight, and my mind raced with the possibilities. My heart rate jumped to high gear as

I bit my bottom lip.

    This was it. What I'd been waiting for.

Chapter Seven

Ballynahinch

"Jazus!" Paul placed the tube on his desk, like it might disintegrate from over-handling. "It's a flippin' ancient artifact." He recoiled from it, then leaned in for a closer look. "We need to share it with the archaeology department. They'll create a committee to evaluate it, preserve it, send it to a museum, who knows?"

He bent and stretched, examining it from every angle, lost in its timeless hold.

Propped on his wrists, he hovered over the relic, then blinked, turning his attention to me.

"What the hell were you thinking? Going there without me! Maeve!"

His cross glare made me shrink. But then I took a long, slow inhale.

"No. What the hell were *you* thinking? You're the one who walked away from all of this. Leaving me to do it alone. What's your problem?" My eyes bored into his, searching for an explanation.

His lips moved then stopped. Then they moved again. "You shouldn't have gone back there without me. It wasn't safe."

"Well, you left me no choice. And seeing you with Patricia didn't help matters. What the hell? What was I *supposed* to do?" I was sure my eyes were burning red, blazing into his.

He moved closer to me. "It wasn't safe."

He looked to the ground.

"Whatever." I focused back on the tube and exhaled through my nose in exasperation.

"Please." He brought his face close to mine and reached for my cheek. "I'm scared, Maeve. Like I can't move. I'm scared something will happen to you." He rubbed his temples. "And if it was my fault…." He ran his hands over his face and looked to the ceiling. "I couldn't bear it."

A flutter in my stomach told me my butterflies were awakening. I couldn't stay mad at him for long. Not with that scruffy, fresh-air look tucked neatly inside his starched white oxford. But I resisted and kept my eyes on the relic, with a stoic gaze.

"I can't stand that you're holding back from me, Maeve. It's killing me." He stepped closer, exposing the despair deep in his eyes. "Let me back in," he whispered.

His words shattered my guard and it fell to pieces at my feet, but I shook my head in resistance. "I just…."

He closed his eyes at my words and reached for me. He pulled my body close to his and dropped his head onto my shoulder.

"Please," he said as he brushed his lips on my neck and inhaled deeply.

Passion rose in me and burned my cheeks. I imagined popping the buttons off his perfectly pressed shirt.

But I pushed him away.

"Let's look at this thing." I leaned over his desk and put my focus on the tube.

Paul's shoulders slumped and he looked to the ground.

"I'm sorry," he said. "I shouldn't have pulled away from you." He stepped back putting more space between us. "You're right. It was weak of me."

He moved around to the side of the desk and looked at the relic.

"I can't believe you went and got this." He huffed. "Jesus."

"What about Patricia?" I cut the air with her name.

"I told you everything. I'm not sure why she came to the college that day." He frowned. "But, she seemed unstable, like she wasn't as together as she used to be." He looked at the ground. "She had questions about you, so… I figured she was still struggling with it all."

He scratched some glue off the surface of his desk. "I just think she's having a hard time. If there were some way I could help her, I would." He licked his bottom lip and looked at me. "You have nothing to worry about though, Maeve. I can assure ya."

"She had questions about me?" I prodded.

His lips pressed together.

"General stuff, you know. Like how long you were staying. Why you came back." He ran his hand through his hair. "She's just trying to get her head around it all."

My shoulders hitched up as my lips pursed to the side, before I could stop them. My childish response was embarrassing.

"Maeve. You have complete power over me. You have to know that." He reached for my hand. "I would do anything for you."

I smiled a half-smile.

"Well, let's look at this thing then and tell me what you think."

My words were a verbal push away. Difficult to deliver, but necessary. I was still wounded from the distance he had created. And Patricia was, by far, the last person I ever wanted to see him with.

His lips pressed together in resignation. The space between us had closed considerably, but it still had holes.

I needed more proof of his renewed commitment. For now, focusing on my archaeological find was the priority.

Inspecting the tube again, Paul looked up from his desk with wide eyes. The shocking depths of blue caused my breath to suck in. I bit my lip as my chest heaved.

"Show me how you opened it before." His eyebrows rose in anticipation.

I loosened the waxy cloth from the side of the aged metal tube as Paul's eyes widened like a child catching a glimpse of Santa on Christmas Eve. I tapped on the end to get the contents to slide out and Paul winced as if in pain.

"Gently," he spoke through clenched teeth.

"Sorry."

The inner scroll moved toward the opening and stuck out. Paul pulled latex gloves out of his top drawer and grabbed a tweezer-like tool with rubber ends.

He reached in with the tool and gently coaxed the contents out. As the parchment came out of its secure hold, it popped open in its freedom and invited us to unroll it farther.

A tingle tickled my chest and I scratched it. The tingle turned from a slight sensation to a burning one.

The scar on my chest still held faint designs from Grace's ring, burned into my skin when she embraced me last winter. It sizzled back to life. I rubbed at it and stepped back from the scroll.

"What is it?" Paul looked up and noticed my hand at my chest. "Is it burning?"

"Yeah, but it's okay." I rubbed more. "Let's keep going."

I stepped closer to his desk.

"Okay. Stop me if it gets worse."

I nodded, watching *him* more than scroll. His focus and precision were that of a true historian. And his lashes and square jaw framed his concentration perfectly.

Paul held the edge of the parchment and slowly unrolled it. Two or three rolls and it was fully open. Two sheets, stacked on each other with the edges remaining curled. Paul placed a pencil cup, cell phone, and two stones on the four corners to hold them down.

Our eyes widened together as we stared at the lines and shapes of an ancient map. Hand drawn with a faded red stamp on the upper corner—the crest of the O'Malley Clan.

The map was cryptic, lacking modern detail, but a definite representation of the west coast of Ireland. Family names were written in territories and lines delineated sections of rule. The map wasn't marked by cities or villages, but by clans.

"That's Grace's name there. Grany Ni Maille." He pointed to the area of Clare Island and all the surrounding lands. "Her name's there twice to show the expanse of her territory."

He took a step back and focused on the entirety of the map. His eyes jumped to mine.

"This could be the original map Queen Elizabeth created for Grace—proving the land to be O'Malley territory—taking away the rulership of Sir Bingham from the clan lands. And sea."

He stepped back again and looked at me with wide eyes. "Do you know what this could mean?"

I shook my head at him.

"This could be the proof needed to stop the land disputes and return the area to the O'Malleys for good."

"Wait. What do you mean, return it?" My eyebrows scrunched tight.

"Like Padraic said in Warde's, the O'Malleys had scattered. Their land in dispute. Ancient Brehon Law placed land ownership in other hands, but only for a finite amount of time, until the O'Malleys could prove it to be rightfully theirs." His words flew fast.

"Land ownership in other hands? Whose?" My hands ran through my hair as I pictured Grace's despair from my past visions.

Despair for losing her true love to the brutal slaying by her enemy, the MacMahons, but it was also despair for losing the Gaelic Ireland she fought so hard to keep. And it was her land and the sea that was lost.

"Rival clans. I can't be sure." He peeled at the corner of the map to reveal the page beneath it. At first they appeared stuck together, but with gentle motion, they separated. "But the clock is ticking. Without proof, the temporary land ownership becomes permanent after several generations."

The parchment beneath the map was a different quality and material, more fabric-like. The rough edges framed written words that were stained with brown blotchy spots, worn from time. Fancy ink scrawl covered the entire document and was sealed at the bottom with an oval crown in the center.

My eyes jumped to the top where the largest writing decorated the beginning of the document. In large, decorative letters, it read, "Elizabeth." The bottom part of the z carried on and underlined the name, curling back and over two or three more times decorating the underside of the signature.

My hand flew to my mouth to cover my gasp.

"Holy shit." Paul stepped back and looked at me, as if trying to unsee what he had already seen.

I moved closer for a better look.

"Just don't touch it. The oils from your fingers will—"

"I won't." My hand went up to stop him.

The fancy black ink writing filled the page and was nearly impossible to read. I skipped cryptic words and landed on "Queen of England", then "by royal creed" and "in god and on my life."

The swirling letters and dark black blotches pulled my eyes all over the page, searching for something of meaning. As I became familiar with the script, I recognized more words. "Ni Maille" revealed itself in the writing and the word "deed," over and over again. "Grany Ni Maille" again.

I turned to Paul.

"What is this?"

He moved closer to the ancient document. He put his loupe to his eye for magnification and went closer in.

"It appears to be...." His voice trailed off as he inspected it more closely. "Christ!"

He stepped back and ran his hands through his hair.

"It's a deed. From Queen Elizabeth the First. Granting territory to the ownership of Grace O'Malley."

His hands trembled as he took his phone from one corner and took pictures of the two pages from all directions. He carefully rolled them back in the shape they beckoned to return to and slid them inside the metal tube.

He moved his gloved finger over the Celtic designs that ran around the top and bottom circumference of the vessel. The greenish hue of the intricate artwork brought it to life in his hands as he inspected the tarnished carvings. More raised markings covered the body of the container with intricate knotwork that went on without beginning or end.

"Maeve." His blank stare seemed lost. "I'm not sure what to do." His eyebrows edged upward in the middle.

"Can we just do nothing right now? Just for now. I need to figure this out more before it gets into the wrong hands," I begged.

I bit the nails of my right hand, all four fingers at once.

I wasn't ready to let this go yet. It held too much for me and my family. This could be everything I was searching for.

I just had no idea what to do with it.

"I don't know." He looked back at the tube. "It feels like we're doing something wrong. Like it's illegal."

"Just for now. Not long. Please."

I reached for the T-shirt I'd used to wrap the tube and began securing it within. I pushed it into my backpack and snapped it shut.

"This is just the beginning. The start of everything coming together." I reached for his phone. "Let me see the pictures of the map."

Paul found the best one and zoomed in on the area of Clare Island.

"Can we make that bigger? Let's get it onto your computer screen." My impatience made me bounce in my shoes.

This map was incredible. It held ancient secrets and medieval ideas of the land and territories.

Priceless.

Once the map was on his screen, we zoomed in on the details that were faded to the naked eye but easier to see on zoom.

A smudged skull-like symbol sat at the coast of Clare Island, as if looking back toward Rockfleet Castle on the mainland.

Another unusual symbol was farther south toward Galway in the mountainous region of Connemara. I'd been to that area with Rory, climbing the hills of the Twelve Bens, with no idea in the world that the area might have had any significance to Grace O'Malley.

"What is this place?" I pointed to the symbol by the Twelve Bens.

"It must be Ballynahinch Castle. There's nothin' else along that river in the area." He tapped his finger on the screen, right on the location. "The two places must have a connection of some kind."

He leaned in and studied it.

"Okay. Well, if legends are true and Grace's final resting place is somewhere on Clare Island, we need to go there. I mean, skull and crossbones on the map… that doesn't leave much to the imagination."

Paul's lips pursed together. "Unfortunately, for five hundred years, no one has been able to prove where her actual burial site is."

I pointed to the spot where his fingerprint lingered.

"That's why we start here. At Ballynahinch. There must be something there, a clue or a connection. And that will direct us to the right place on Clare Island. It's a lead anyway. A good one, too." My eyes sparkled. "Okay?"

"Okay." His steady tone resonated confidence. "I'm back in. Let's do this."

He reached for my hand and squeezed it, like sealing a deal, though worry lingered at a shallow depth behind his eyes.

***

The horizon filled with peak after peak of the mountain chain known as the Twelve Bens. I gazed out my window at the magnificent view and searched each hill for the one Rory and I climbed last fall.

He had kissed me for the first time on our decent from one of the summits. The thrill of it was etched in my memory, but I also recalled how it awoke the sleeping burn on my chest.

I glanced at Paul to be sure he couldn't read my thoughts, and then went back to Rory.

Soon after, Rory became chieftain of the MacMahon Clan, the ones responsible for the brutal murder of Hugh DeLacy, Grace's love. I rubbed my chest, thinking of how close I got to a clan enemy without realizing it.

Rory and I were connected by a tribal feud that spanned centuries and somehow we landed in each other's arms. I shook my head to clear the thoughts of his lush lashes, flirtatious teasing, and decadent brogue. His allure was surely an evil tactic for gaining leverage in the fight.

My fingers ran through my hair. One mountain blurred into the next, along with my memories of Rory, as Paul and I flew down the narrow pass toward Ballynahinch Castle.

"I'm not too sure about Grace's connection to Ballynahinch, but I think she spent some time there, on retreats maybe." Paul's voice broke through the reels of my secret replay of my time with Rory, and I blinked them away.

I watched Paul's profile as he navigated the narrowing road. Trees and shrubs encroached right out to the street's edge, giving it the feel of a tunnel-like passage. His jaw was tense with focus, almost as tight as his knuckles around the steering wheel.

Unable to stop the persistent reels, I thought of the time he and

Rory met at my blue door for the first time. I was certain they would burst into a fist fight. The tension between them was brittle—ready to shatter at any moment.

It all became clear later when Paul revealed his ancestry to Hugh DeLacy, Grace's murdered lover. Murdered by the MacMahon Clan. It made Rory and Paul undeniable enemies of the ages, right on the spot, MacMahon vs DeLacy.

At the next bend, surrounded by mature landscaping, a regal ivory-colored sign with golden Gaelic letters read *Ballynahinch Castle*, and Paul turned onto the long, meandering drive leading up to the grounds.

We swerved and rounded tight bends as anticipation grew to see the estate open up in front of us.

A shiver ran through me as we approached the unknown and I squeezed my backpack with my knees.

"Do you think it's dangerous that I have these documents? What if someone knew or found out?"

I pulled my pack off the floor, closer to my chest. It held so much—the tube with the scrolls and the tomb key. I wished I could handcuff it to myself.

"Well, right now, it's safe. No one knows about any of it, right?" He turned to me for a sure response.

I nodded my head, hoping that was true.

My eyes fell to my lap and I swallowed. Sickness brewed in my stomach from my nerves. I looked at my pack as if seeing through it with X-ray vision, straight into the contents. The weight of the small items was heavier than anything I'd ever known.

We reached a clearing and the view expanded before us like a wide-screen opening scene of an epic movie.

"There it is," Paul said as he slowed the car.

My eyes lifted to the bright light of the open landscape, leaving the long stretch of dark narrow driveway of overhanging trees behind us.

My hands gripped the sides of my seat like clamps as I braced for impact. I was slammed back in my seat by the view of the landscape.

Topiaries. Sculpted trees on the lawn. Many in the shape of four-sided pyramids, leading up to a stately manor.

"What the hell!" I screamed and hid my face in my hands. "Oh my god." I mumbled into my palms.

Tears of panic filled my eyes and spilled. I peeked out through my splayed fingers and saw the familiar lawn ornaments and the path that led to the terrace and enormous front doors. My fingers tightened to block the image, willing it away.

The car stopped short, jolting me in my seat.

"You know this place?" Paul's voice held a heavy tone of ominous premonition.

"Mmhmm." My breathing tightened to short, rapid puffs. "I had a vision of this place. Right after our trip to Rockfleet, when we heard the voices. It's exactly the same. This…." My hand gestured out across the view.

Paul's eyebrows shot up as his muscles tensed.

"What happened in the vision?"

I pictured the brown-cloaked figure who chased me. And then the portrait inside. The one that looked exactly like me.

Chills ran through my body straight to my toes and finger tips. I bit the inside of my cheek, wondering how much to tell Paul. In the past, I'd just gushed everything, but now, I had to be more guarded. In case he'd shut down again. I exhaled in resignation to the new complicated layers.

"Come on." I hopped out, surveying my surroundings. "What is this place?" My voice trailed after me.

"It's a hotel of sorts now and a restaurant at the back, I think," Paul said as he checked out the signs for parking at the far side. "Slow down now. Tell me about the vision, Maeve. I need to know what we might be heading into."

I surveyed him through half-open eyes, choosing which filters to put in place. He was right, though. He needed to know.

"I was chased and stuff, just like at the cemetery. The brown cloak. You know." I hesitated, watching his response.

His lips pressed into a white line.

"Brown cloak?" He perused the landscape with a suspicious eye.

"Yeah. In the vision, it was Fergal." I lowered my eyes and looked down at my nails. "I don't know."

"It's okay, Maeve. I'm here. And I'm not going anywhere. I promise." He reached for my hand and took it in his. "Come on."

His intimate touch shot tingles and warmth through me. I held his hand and for a moment, felt like everything was going to be okay.

We left the car and walked along a manicured garden path of white stones through the topiary gardens.

I focused on a direct line of vision toward the huge double doors—my destination.

"I need to see inside. Do you think it's open to visitors?" I held my gaze on the doors.

"Not sure." Paul's voice trailed into the landscape as his heightened attention scanned the perimeter.

We followed the stone gravel path through the topiary garden along the front of the estate. The setting was peaceful and less intimidating in bright daylight, with rays of sunshine breaking through the gray skies. Though I kept my wits about me, looking around every bush and statue for any possible danger.

My pack hung loosely from one shoulder, so I swung the other shoulder strap onto my free arm and pulled the adjustment cords, securing it tightly to my back.

I climbed the granite steps of the terrace and approached the enormous double doors. One side was permanently bolted shut, but the other pulled open with relative ease for such immense size and weight.

We entered the grand space and sailed back in time in the blink of an eye—swept away by faded antique tapestries, heirloom portraits, and fragile ceramics. Fine dark oak woodwork and brass fixtures decorated the museum quality estate, accentuating its time travel quality. The classic musty smell of aged furniture and fabrics wafted through my senses, carrying me deeper into the past.

Clanging dishes and quiet conversation drifted from the back rooms, reminding us of other guests and fine dining.

"May I help you?" The cordial, gracious voice of an older woman came out of nowhere and made my heart leap out of my chest and into my mouth.

I spun around, wide-eyed, as my muscles tensed around my bones. I hadn't expected contact with anyone so soon and startled from the unnatural velvet sound of her voice.

Her formal black dress was buttoned to the top with a regal white lace collar, and her polished black single-strap shoes set a tone of high class and fine dining.

I adjusted my jacket, stood up straight, and ran my fingers through my hair to settle it down.

"We were hoping to have a look around, if that's okay," Paul asked, adding his swoon-worthy smile.

"Ah, sure. Feel free to have a look-see. These rooms and the grounds are open to visitors." She motioned to the space we were in as well as the adjoining room.

With minimal movement, she turned and walked back toward the sound of the other guests.

She slowed and turned her shoulders to me, then added, "Stop over for a cup of tea and scones, if you like. We'd love to have you."

Her head tipped as she held my gaze. She hesitated, as if studying me. And then she left us.

My eyes followed her as she moved out of sight and my muscles relaxed once she was gone. I took Paul's arm and pulled myself close to him.

"That's the room with the family portraits, I think." I pointed to the adjoining space.

We moved in silence toward the archway that framed the entrance to the great room. The glow of the coal fire drew us farther in.

With light steps, I crept to the center of the space for a full view of the surrounding walls. My eyes darted around the room, fearing what I might see, but refusing to miss any of it.

As my eyes met hers, I snapped my gaze away in terror and turned into Paul's body. He held my shoulders and then pushed me back enough to look into my face.

"What is it?" He glanced around the room.

Then his grip on my shoulders fell. He dropped his hold of me and moved to the far wall. I kept my eyes on the ground.

"What the hell?" His voice trailed off into the years.

I lifted my gaze to find him, afraid of what his face might reveal.

He stood in front of her portrait, hands by his sides, without a single flinch. He just stared at it.

The trembling in my body made it difficult to move. I closed my eyes and breathed, then took one step, and another, over to Paul.

"Jesus, Maeve." He glanced at me in disbelief.

He looked at me and then back to the portrait and back to me again. His wide eyes exposed his shock and confirmed my deepest fear.

"She's the spittin' image of ya." He shook his head to clear it. "Even that freckle on your cheek."

The plaque beneath the painting revealed what I already knew to be true.

Maeve Grace O'Malley
"The Lost Daughter"
1555 —

I slapped my hand over my mouth and stepped backward for the door—space, open air, anything but that room. As I pulled the door open, I turned back for Paul but he was motionless, staring at the portrait, as if he were in a trance.

I left him there and threw my body down the terrace stairs and onto the green lawn. Hands on my knees, I breathed through the dizzying overload.

My head shook back and forth in denial the more I thought about it.

The lost daughter? What was this all about?

Brigid had said the same thing, and now, here it was. My exact reflection, every detail and imperfection, painted in the 1500s.

My mind scrambled from history's proof in the portrait. I'd gazed into my own eyes from five hundred years ago. I rubbed my temples and closed my eyes through a long inhale.

After my slow, deliberate exhale, my eyes narrowed and I swatted at the air in anger. Every time I thought I was finding answers, I was only uncovering new questions. Frustration ground my teeth.

But this… this scared me the most. My whole identity was crashing in on me and I struggled to keep hold of who I was.

I knew I was a descendant of Grace O'Malley, my sixteenth great-grandmother, but this was bigger. Like a more immediate connection.

A familiar feeling of home washed over me and my breathing steadied. "We are one," she had said to me once, and now, it repeated in my soul and I believed it to my core. If I had been lost to her at some point in time, I was now found.

And I was ready to go to Clare Island with this new understanding of my identity.

An inner light gleamed out from my eyes, brightening my way, without any doubt of who I was anymore and what I needed to do.

Chapter Eight
The Lost Daughter

The fresh air cleansed my senses as I watched dark gray clouds roll in. The portrait, and everything it implied, just didn't seem real... as if it weren't possible.

My fingers pulled through my hair as I stared up into the sky. Thoughts of my family raced in my mind. My mother, my grandparents. And Brigid. I didn't just need to fight for Grace. I needed to fight for Brigid, too. She deserved some peace. And all the women of my family, past and future.

I looked out across the yard at the fancy gardens of topiary shrubs, absorbing my new reality, and my breath sucked in as my eyes darted toward the far end, following quick movement.

A deer maybe? Or a badger?

My gut told me worse.

I raced up to a tall pyramid bush, as least ten feet high, just like the one in my vision, and hid. I peered back toward the large doors to the estate, praying Paul would walk out any second. I peeked around the four-sided shrub and let out a shriek of terror as a brown-cloaked figure darted straight for me.

I turned and bolted back toward the castle entrance.

"Paul! Paul!"

The shriek of my own voice sent higher levels of fear through my soul and accelerated my legs faster than they'd ever moved.

I lost speed as I was pulled backward by my pack. I yanked to break free from the grip and spun to the side, losing my balance. My vision filled with the brown flapping cloak everywhere I turned.

He held strong to my pack and I struggled again. This time, pushing back on him with my entire force.

"Get away!" I shouted.

His grip remained strong and a shudder of terror bolted through me, convincing me I was outmatched.

With a crash, the huge wooden door smashed open and Paul flew out of it with a snarl of aggression etched across his face. I recoiled as he came bounding down the stairs like a steamroller.

Without a word, he lunged at the man and knocked him away from me. The cloaked stranger turned to run, but Paul caught the point of his hood that trailed behind him. He pulled it off the man's head and held tight, stopping him in his tracks as he was choked by it.

The stench of his filth permeated the air and hit me square between the eyes, causing me to gag. The foul decay repelled Paul's face as he turned away with a grimace, but he held on and restrained him.

The man turned on Paul, swinging, ready for a fight.

I stepped back in horror as his face came into view.

Fergal!

Horrible, creeping Fergal.

I knew it!

He'd been stalking me from the start. Trying to stop me for reasons I didn't understand. But now, here he was again.

Following us.

Me.

He pointed into my face, baring his vile teeth.

"She must be stopped!" He spat from the rot of his mouth.

He pulled from Paul's grip and leapt for me again with venom shooting from his eyes.

Paul clamped onto his back and forced him to the ground.

"Run, Maeve. Get out of here. Lock yourself in the car or get inside the castle. Go!"

He threw himself back on Fergal and they struggled in the grass, throwing chunks of sod into the air.

Paul's strength outmatched Fergal's by far, but I still worried about what Fergal might be capable of.

I flew through the topiary gardens toward the safety of the car, my mind racing on how I would help Paul.

A crowbar maybe? Or blast the horn?

I panicked about where the keys might be or a phone. Too many unknowns. I redirected my escape toward the back of the castle to get help.

From my peripheral vision, my head jerked toward sudden movement from behind another bush, close by. I jolted in terror from the sight of a second brown cloak.

With my imagination running frantic, I wasn't sure if it was real, but I hid around a large topiary anyway.

Panting to catch my breath, I peeked around the far side of the shrub, to check that the coast was clear. Terror blinded me as I caught sight of the cloaked figure barreling toward me. I turned with a yelp and ran for my life.

His speed was double mine and he reached me in an instant. His overpowering strength halted me as he grabbed my pack and pulled. My entire body fell backward from his swift tug and I bounced off him.

I rounded in my shoulders to keep the pack on my back and yanked around as hard as I could to release his grip. In the same motion, I clenched my fist and swung at his head. The hood of his cloak buffered my contact point but the unexpected strike surprised him and he stepped back.

Shaking my fist loose, assuming at least two knuckles had just been shattered on his thick skull, I stepped back for balance and lunged at him with a kick to his crotch. He went down like a ton of bricks, reeling in a fetal position from the pain.

I kicked again, aiming for the same spot, but only hit his wrists, strategically protecting his injury from further assault. I kicked at his ribs and heard a sickening groan escape from his lips.

I turned to see what was happening with Paul and Fergal. They had moved out of sight, so I hoisted my pack securely and turned to tear across to the rear of the estate for help.

As I took my first step, the cloaked man grabbed my ankle and yanked me to the ground. I hit down on my elbows with a thud and kicked to get away. He rolled on top of me and pinned me with little effort as I squirmed under his weight.

Fear pounded my heart. But it was a new fear. Not for my personal safety anymore, but for losing ground in my mission. Protecting my backpack was my focus and I was ready to defend it with all I had.

I swung my arms at him, trying to scratch his face and took hold of his hood and yanked it. As it came away from his face, he turned from me to hide his identity.

His dark hair fell across his cheek, framing his sharp jawline, as my eyes flew wide open. He flicked his head, shifting the hair off his face and moved his gaze to mine. My heart stopped and I gasped as I looked into his familiar deep blue eyes.

Rory.

"Christ! Ya tryin' ta kill me, Maeve?" He keeled over, holding his side and his crotch, wincing.

I wiggled to try to get out from under his weight as terror widened my eyes.

Nothing made sense. If Rory was trying to harm me, then I truly had no idea what was going on. I was in *way* over my head.

"Stop. I'm not going to hurt you." He reached for my hair to move it from my face. "Please."

I shrank from his touch.

"What the hell are you doing, Rory?" I yelled in his face. The pressure in my scream nearly burst my head. "Get off me!"

"I'm not going to hurt you. I promise. I never would." He moved his weight off me and sat to my side, hunched over, wincing.

I pushed myself up to sitting and dusted off any leaves or debris.

"What the hell, Rory?" I stared at him with loathing. "Fergal attacked me. Paul is over there. Stop him!"

"Fergal ran. Paul kicked the shit out of him." Rory chuckled. "I just saw your *boyfriend* run into the castle looking for you."

I jumped up.

"I need to find him."

"Wait! Maeve." Rory stood and grabbed my hand. "We need to talk. You have something we want."

I yanked my hand from his.

"Get away from me, Rory."

"Please, Maeve." He reached for me again and I pulled with every ounce of energy in my body to get away from him.

As I jerked away, my leg twisted under me and I lost balance and began to fall. I reached for the fabric of Rory's cloak and knocked his balance off as well. As I grabbed for him, he stumbled and we both fell into a beautifully sculpted shrub with a cracking, snapping crash.

I landed on top of him with a splat, forcing him to take the prickly part of the fall. I shimmied clumsily across his body to move myself off and caught the sinister twinkle in his eye.

A wide smile spread across his face. Then laughter. I couldn't help but laugh too and I punched him in the chest.

"Jerk!"

He reached up and grabbed me, pulling me close to him.

"I miss you, Maeve."

I pushed against his chest and wriggled away.

"Funny way of showing it. What the hell are you doing in that creepy robe, stalking me? Rory!" I searched him for answers. "You're with Fergal?"

The accusation flew with ease from my lips.

I scrambled to my feet, brushing off bits of the bush, as Rory pushed himself out of the deeper part of the hole.

We'd left a huge indentation in the once-perfectly-manicured shrub.

"Sure, they'll hardly notice," Rory said as he tried to replace some broken branches to their original location.

"Stop avoiding my question. What are you doing here? You attacked me!" I stared him down and hitched my backpack onto the center of my back.

I took a few steps toward the estate, looking in every direction for Paul. Just at the far corner, I caught a glimpse of him and waved my arms above my head.

The relief that washed over him was visible for miles as he ran toward me.

"There he is!" I said to Rory as I started running to Paul.

I looked back to see what Rory would do, but he was gone. Without a trace.

If the gaping hole in the topiary hadn't still been there, I'd have thought he was a dream. The big black scar in the bush was wide open, but Rory had vanished.

I ran to Paul, clutching the straps of my pack like they were my lifeline.

***

"Can we just go inside for a minute?" I begged Paul as he beeped his clicker to unlock the car.

"We need to get the hell out of here, Maeve." He scoffed at my request.

"Seriously. I need to pee. Badly."

A strange sense that there was unfinished business here stopped me from leaving with him that instant. It was clear Paul wanted to vacate the premises immediately, but I needed some resolution to this nagging feeling first.

He darted his eyes around the grounds, searching for clues of our attackers. The landscape was silent. He pursed his lips together as his nostrils flared.

"Fine. Let's be quick." He beeped his clicker again to relock the doors.

"It was Rory."

"What?" Paul's tone was curt, placing extra emphasis on the T.

"Rory. He was here too."

"I knew it. Did he touch you? I'll fookin' kill 'im. Can't be trusted." He kicked the gravel drive.

"He didn't hurt me. But he wanted my pack." I chewed my lip.

"He's an enemy now, Maeve. You know that, right?"

I nodded my head in agreement, though my heart felt different.

When my head and my heart disagreed, I was lost.

He took my hand and pulled me along to the rear of the building where the restaurant entrance was.

An odd sense of normality washed over me as the sight and sound of happy patrons filled the air. Cups of tea, scones, and salmon platters mixed with lively conversation and gentle laughter invited us in.

Paul sat tall in the foyer, in full-blown lookout mode, as I staggered into the ladies room. His shoulders hadn't fallen from his ears yet and he brushed dirt from his knees while surveying every corner of the establishment. The muscle in his jaw twitched from its vice-grip clench.

I leaned on the sink in the bathroom and gazed into the mirror.

I was safe. Unharmed.

After a few deep breaths, my tense thoughts of Fergal dissipated and the memory of falling into the bush with Rory took over. I relaxed and chuckled to myself at the thought of it.

I stared up at the ceiling, wondering how I could still have butterflies when I thought of Rory. Even now.

Warm soap on my hands cleansed the trauma of the attack down the drain and I ran my wet fingers through my blown hair. My cheeks flushed crimson and my eyes sparkled with bright light. I felt more alive in the moment than ever before. My senses were sharp and alert.

As I stepped out of the door marked "Powder Room," Paul jumped to his feet and fixed his eyes on me. He closed the space between us in a millisecond and I reached for him, feeling his angst cut through the air.

I wanted to hold him close and never let go. As I opened my mouth to speak, the words were lost in the voices approaching us from behind.

"There she is. The one I told you about." The polished black strapped shoes darted toward me, clomping on the wood floor, followed by two sets of formal gentleman loafers.

Paul stepped in front of me and reached his arm back around me, holding me close behind him.

The hostess who had greeted us earlier, at the front great room, slowed with the two older gentlemen as they reached us.

"Ah, I see you've come for that fine cup of tea." She ran her velvet voice over us.

Paul stood taller as I peeked around him at the curious hostess and her posse.

One of the graying men, wearing a dated but stately brown suit, leaned his head around and studied me like I was a picture.

"It's uncanny." He spoke to no one in particular. "The resemblance." He rubbed his chin. "Come out, dear. Let's have a look at ya. Seems to me we have a special visitor to Ballynahinch today."

I reached for Paul's hand and squeezed it tight.

"We were just leaving. We appreciate your hospitality, but must be on our way." Paul's words left no room for negotiation.

The other man pushed his glasses up his nose for a better look.

"Would you stay a bit longer?" He nodded and straightened his waistcoat. "Tell us who ya are. It's clear to us you've come a long way, for a reason, no?"

Chills ran up the backs of my legs.

"What's your name, miss?" The man in the brown suit stared into my face.

My protective nature for Grace put up a strong wall to these people. Disclosing my true identity to strangers, and unusual strangers to say the least, could put everything in jeopardy. There was no way to know if they'd try to stop me. It was best I remained anonymous for now.

I searched for my voice which was hiding deep in my throat. I cleared it.

"I'm Maggie. Maggie McPhee. From the States." My eyes pulled to the floor, attempting to conceal my lame lie.

"Mm." The gentleman in the waistcoat pushed his specs higher up his nose again. "Are you of O'Malley descent by chance? Your resemblance to our, ah, relation, shall we say, is quite shockin'."

"Um, no. No connection to O'Malleys that I'm aware of. Sorry." My head shook more than necessary.

Relation? Could they be O'Malleys?

My heart leapt into my throat as I considered the possibility of finding some of my distant relatives.

All in good time. I would come back to them. Hopefully with good news of laying to rest land disputes and feuds over historical O'Malley territories. But before then, I had work to do.

I pulled on Paul's hand, shimmied the straps of my pack up my shoulders, and took a step back toward the door. Paul stepped back with me. As we put space between ourselves and the Inquisition, the three moved closer to us again.

Paul put his hand up to establish a barrier and said, "Sorry for any trouble or disappointment. We must be going now."

He turned and wrapped his arm firmly around my shoulders and we moved out the door in a blur that left the three frozen and speechless.

One final look back as the door closed behind us and I met three sets of eyes boring into my soul with questions of centuries gone by.

Guilt washed over me as we raced for the car. They knew something in there. And believed I held the answers they were seeking.

Paul's silence emphasized his full attention to our surroundings as he ushered me into the car without blinking or missing a beat. The secure sound of locking doors around me confirmed we were safe.

In a hasty three-point turn, Paul had the car sailing toward the long driveway that brought us here. My head turned to a dark spot in a large topiary, the gaping hole left by Rory and me. Motion from the corner of my eye spun my head further back to where we'd come from.

The three hosts had come out and walked, side by side, toward us. They covered ground faster than their feet moved, giving an eerie sense of something supernatural. Their eyes were fixed on me and I spun around to Paul.

"Shit!" I spat through clenched teeth.

"What is it!" His tone rose to alarm in an instant.

"They're coming after us!" I yelped.

I threw my hands on the backs of our seats and peered through the rear window as Paul struggled for a look in the side and rearview mirrors.

They were gone. Vanished into thin air.

Paul reached for my waist and coaxed me back into my seat.

"Buckle up."

He swerved through the bends of the winding, heavily wooded drive like a professional race car driver. The hum of the engine whirred through each gear, adding to the intensity of the escape. As light emerged at the end of the drive, leading out onto the main road, we burst out from the thick of ancient tree cover and flew along the open road toward home.

As the miles grew between us and Ballynahinch, the tension in the car dissipated and Paul's foot lightened on the gas. The lush green countryside stole my breath away as we drove past the hills and through the open expanse. Fresh breeze blew across my face from my open window and I breathed the clean, damp air.

The car slowed further and then swerved to a rest area on the side of the road.

I turned to Paul with raised eyebrows.

"The *Quiet Man* bridge," he stated.

"What?" The corner of my lip lifted.

"Come on." He opened his door and climbed out, coming around to my side.

Still shaken from Ballynahinch, I resisted leaving the sanctuary of his car. I looked back down the long stretch of open road, to be sure... well, just to be sure.

He opened my door and reached for my hand.

"Come on. It's beautiful out here." He pulled and helped my reluctance give in to his coaxing. "We can clear our heads."

He walked me over to a low stone wall and we sat, overlooking a river with a majestic mountain backdrop of greens, blues, and purples. Like a painting in a museum, we gazed at the picturesque wooden footbridge in the distance, leading across the river.

"It's the bridge from a famous scene in *The Quiet Man*. Quite a tourist attraction, actually." He smiled.

"That's cool. My grandfather loved that movie."

I'd seen parts of *The Quiet Man* throughout my entire life. Never from start to finish, but definitely the entire thing. My grandfather loved John Wayne and watched the movie any time it was on.

We stared out across the panoramic view.

"Well, you never fail to keep me entertained, Maeve O'Malley." Paul huffed and pulled me closer.

"I know. I'm sorry." I pressed my lips to the side.

He reached for my chin.

"I'm afraid, Maeve." He brushed his thumb across my lower lip and pulled it down a little, sending heated butterflies through me. "I need to keep you safe. But I keep walking you straight into trouble. You're killin' me."

He stared at my mouth.

"I'll do anything fer ya. To make this right." He gazed into my eyes with wide pupils, allowing me into his soul.

I inched closer to him and reached my hands into his unzipped coat and wrapped my arms around his warm waist, pulling myself into him. I craved to be close to him, like I was starved.

His hands ran through my hair and around the back of my neck, lifting my face toward his. He brushed his lips across mine and breathed me in.

"I love you, Maeve. Always have."

His words washed over me like warm honey and filled every empty crevice.

He kissed me as if it were our first kiss. Our last kiss. And every kiss in between. My strong armor melted and in that instant, I trusted him.

My mind spiraled with thoughts of being close to him. His hands on me, his warm body on mine. Holding me forever. It was everything I wanted and needed.

"Take me home," I whispered into his ear.

Chapter Nine

Red King

Time lost all measurement as minutes, hours, and days blurred together. Entwined in each other and wrapped in my fluffy duvet, we emerged for food and water only. The guilty pleasure was a welcome break from the craziness.

I blinked into the air at the memory of my bliss with Paul. Greedy for more, I sulked about his having to get back to work.

"Okay, wow." Michelle's voice shattered my daydream and scattered the images around the pub. "Are you thinking about him again? That's just gross." She pushed on my arm. "Pay attention to *meeee*," she whined.

I turned beet red, wondering if she could see my uncensored thoughts.

She'd begged me to come out with her and Declan, and my stomach twisted in guilt wishing to be with Paul again instead. But the fact that Michelle was back in the game with me, in any way, was critical. Her support meant the world to me.

Staying home alone wasn't really an option anyway. I was in a mindset of "avoid awake dreams and aggressive run-ins at all costs." So, being in this pub with my friends was a no-brainer.

"Sorry! I'm so distracted. I need to focus." I shook my head. "You guys are my normal. You're like the most important part of my existence right now. Keeping me sane."

Michelle's lips pressed to the side. "Yeah. About that...."

"What?" My eyebrows shot up as my stomach took a dive.

"I know you were hoping to talk about your trip to Clare Island and such, and we have your back on that, really...." Michelle swallowed. "But you just need to hear Declan first. Okay? I don't mean to be a spoiler. But just listen. 'Kay?" Michelle hesitated, then nodded for my agreement.

"Um. Okay."

My knees clasped together as I reached for the ring on my necklace. I had the feeling now that they had dragged me out for more than pints.

My eyes moved across the bar, watching the barman pull pints amidst the plethora of Irish antiques hanging above and on every wall. I stared at Oley, the life-size statue of a Gaelic-speaking resident of Inishmore who stood at the bar, just as he was about to leave for America to escape the famine. His head hung in heavy sadness that made my throat constrict.

Declan's melodic voice pulled my attention back to him.

"So, my sister. Her dreams are worse now. Like, more vivid and frightening." Declan leaned in over the drinks as he began to describe his sister's recent visions.

I pushed back in my seat. "Wait. I thought her visions were just, like, symbolic. Like the Great Famine and stuff."

Michelle leaned in, with her hand on his knee.

"Yeah, but they're changin' now. Izzy's dreams are gettin' more violent. She screams through them." Declan's face grimaced and his voice cracked.

The blood drained from my head as my hand covered my mouth.

"What is she seeing?" I asked through my fingers.

Declan hesitated. He looked at Michelle.

"What?" I pressed.

"We don't want to freak you out or anything. But you just need to know." He kept his eyes on Michelle instead of me. "Everything you've been seeing. She sees it too."

"What do you mean? Declan! Stop trying to sugarcoat this. What does she see?"

My heart rate accelerated as I thought about Izzy's visions

becoming more violent like mine. It wasn't fair. She was only eleven.

I rubbed my temples. Izzy's dreams were more prophetic than assaults. She saw things that had happened and felt lost in the visions. She was more of an observer than the hunted. So at least that was good. I hoped.

"Tell me, Declan. What does she see?" I was starved for details. Maybe something would be helpful.

Declan pursed his lips and stared into his pint.

His eyes rose to meet mine as he said, "A pirate queen."

My eyes widened and I sat back at full attention. "Seriously?"

His face pinched as he swallowed. "She's killing everyone."

My muscled tightened around my bones as my breath shook.

"What? How would she even know about the pirate queen?" I asked.

"That's the thing," Declan said. "She doesn't."

I crossed my arms and then reached my knuckles to my mouth in thought.

Izzy might be seeing the events on Grace's galley, after Hugh was murdered. Or when Grace went after MacMahon castle and decimated it in revenge.

But I couldn't help but wonder if she was seeing future events to come. I had to be open to anything.

"So, there's more," Declan added in a low tone, almost as if he were hoping to go unheard.

I dropped my hand from my face and waited.

"When she screams, she shrieks, 'She's coming!' or 'She's almost here!'" Declan looked down again, and then at Michelle. Anywhere but at me.

I swallowed hard.

"Okay. That's scary, not gonna lie." I exhaled, thinking of poor little Izzy. "I want your sister to be okay, Declan. I'm going to stop this. I promise."

One of my eyelids twitched. I rubbed it while contemplating her visions.

A storm was coming. And I was at the center of it.

The musicians at the rear of the pub warmed up their instruments.

O'Connor's was known for the impromptu trad sessions, but once the fiddle started along with the thumping of the bodhran drum, my head began pounding.

"I think I'm ready to head home," I whispered, holding my stomach as a grimace covered my face. "Are you guys gonna stay a while?"

"Yeah." Michelle eyed their full pints. "For a bit, I think. Do you mind?"

Her eyebrows inched up and she looked to Declan.

"No. I'm just gonna go to bed." My head swirled with thoughts of the pirate queen. Izzy's visions. Ballynahinch and the unusual three innkeepers.

"Paul said you shouldn't be alone...." Michelle's eyebrows scrunched together as she tried to figure out what to do.

"It's fine. I'm just gonna sleep. I'll see Paul tomorrow."

Declan grabbed his phone.

"I'll get you a lift. It's too far to walk. And, well, you know, just not safe." He messed with his phone app for two seconds. "On their way."

The driver arrived in a matter of minutes and left me at my door on Bohermore. The sound of his engine faded into the night air as I fumbled for my key and dropped my phone. *Shit.* I picked it up and checked the screen.

Intact. Shocking.

I needed to text Paul to let him know I was home safe.

As I wiggled the key through the lock and pressed on the door to open it, a sudden heavy weight smashed me from behind, forcing me through the door with a violent crash.

With the wind knocked out of me, I fell inside with the force of a large person shoving me from behind. The angry assault kept me off balance as I was hurled through the alley space.

A blur of dark color and rough motion clouded my sight as I gasped in panic to fill my lungs again. Thrown against the wall, I scrunched my eyes closed as a foul smell curled my hair and sharpened my focus, sending terror through my veins.

Fergal!

The shock of him all over me filled my lungs with a heave, just enough to allow for an ear-piercing scream as his grimy hand smacked over my mouth and squeezed with an intensity that shot fear through me, stifling any sound.

He forced his full weight, pressing me against the wall as the speckled plaster cut into my cheek. His hot breath wet my ear as he slurred slow terror into my mind. Each vile word making me fear for my life to the point of believing it.

"You've fooked with us long enough, ya bitch. It's my duty to stop ye."

He pressed me harder against the gritty wall, keeping a strong hold over my mouth.

Tears spilled from my eyes and whimpers escaped my throat. The taste of dirty salt and sweat from his palm, seeped through my lips, branding the trauma onto my soul.

"My apologies for havin' to do this to ya, miss, but you've the power to ruin us. And we can't have that now, can we?"

I wiggled and begged with my muffled voice, but his only response was his knee digging into my ribs to hold me still.

My inner voice pleaded with him

I would stop. I'd go back to Boston and never come back. Just please let go of me. Leave me alone.

"Ya thought you'd show up in the final hour, yeah? To foil our plans of claimin' the land permanently." He pressed harder. "Well, not so fast, lassie. Sure, you don't have the formal power, anyway. And I'll make sure it stays that way."

He pushed his shoulders into me, grinding my face deeper on the jagged plaster wall, allowing freedom of his other hand. He dug around in his back pocket. Maybe for a knife. It was my last chance.

If I could just get my legs free. Or an arm. I'd tear my face open on the rough points of the wall that poked deeply in my cheek, but maybe I could break away. I'd probably be killed anyway… but at least on my terms

"It'll be quick, now, O'Malley, I assure ya. Just close your eyes and…."

Smash!

My door burst open, having never fully latched after Fergal pushed me in.

In an instant, Fergal's foul hand was off my face and he flew against the opposite wall with a crash as his head smacked off it. He crumpled to the ground in a moaning heap.

Peeling my face off the rough wall, I sucked in the first full breath since the attack, and my senses jumped to a new level of awareness.

I beaded in on Fergal's crouched form and moved to him with stealth, only noticing the pacing black boots next to him as an added detail. The familiar black boots kicked Fergal and spat angry words at him. I followed the black boots and kicked at Fergal too. Adrenaline shot through my veins and turned me into a raging bull.

My fingers clamped onto a clump of his matted hair and held on like a vice grip. The power in my muscles was ten times my strength as I yanked him around like a rag doll, kicking at his scrambling body as he tried to escape my wrath.

He was going to kill me.

I kicked at him more.

He planned to end my life tonight.

I dragged him down the alley by his hair, snarling at him through clenched teeth.

The black boots followed and stood with me.

Their steady stance soothed me, assuring me we were in control once again. They encouraged me to release my grip, and move myself away from Fergal's squirming heap.

The black boots took on larger form as their lyrical voice filled the alleyway.

"Yer blackballed now, Fergal. An outcast!" A boot connected with Fergal's ribs one more time, causing him to wince. "The clan will punish you for this. *Yer* the defector. Scum. Always have been."

The brogue was almost too thick to decipher.

One last kick and Fergal was out the door, staggering, crouched over on his right side.

I crumpled down the wall onto the cold cement and hid my face in my knees.

The black boots came to me, pacing around my crouched form. Then he stopped and spoke.

"Maeve." He knelt down to me.

Rory's voice filled me with sweet intoxication. The sound of my savior.

"Maeve, are you okay? Did he hurt you?" His voice cracked in fear.

My face remained buried in my knees. I was frozen, unable to respond.

Rory's voice faded in and out as he ranted, not knowing what to do next.

"I'll kill the fooker for putting his hands on you." He paced again. "Jesus!"

He kicked the wall, over and over, sending paint and plaster shards flying.

"Maeve. Come on! Don't do this to me." He knelt down to me again and wrapped his arms around my shoulders. "Come on. Up," he pleaded.

I lifted my gaze to meet his and could only see Fergal's face and could only taste and smell the rancid stench of Fergal. My stomach heaved and I dropped my face back down into my knees and whimpered.

Rory's arms wrapped me in warm safety as he lifted me to my feet.

"Maeve, I gotcha. Let's get you inside."

He nudged me to start walking. My knees betrayed me and buckled under my weight.

Rory's hold surrounded me again as he lifted me in one swift enveloping scoop. Curled in a ball, I buried my face in his chest.

Jumping two steps at a time, he brought me up to my flat without a single bump and nestled me in the soft chair by my fireplace.

Unable to look him in the eye, I hid my face in my knees again, but not before noticing his scrunched, pained expression. His face contorted with bared teeth and trembling lips. His eyes were wet and lingered on me as if viewing my dead body.

The sight of him threw my body into a fit of quaking twitches as my muscles released the tension of the attack.

"I'll get a blanket. Hang there." Rory pressed his hand on me to be sure I sat tight as he scanned the room for something to comfort me.

He poked into the hall and glanced toward my bedroom.

"Rory!" The scream flew out of my mouth like fire. "Don't leave me!"

Panic surged through me as I clamped the arms of the chair, bracing for a crash.

He raced back in, eyes wide, and fell to his knees at my chair. He reached for my face.

"I won't leave ya. Ever. I promise."

He pulled me off the chair and into his arms, cradling me on the floor. My body melted into his as the shuddering quakes dissipated into his warmth.

"I need to call the gards. I'll deal with their questions." His voice was solid with authority. "The clan will be dealin' with Fergal, I assure ya. But a bit o' modern day police work can't hurt either. Pressure from all sides." He huffed. "I'll need ta be callin' McGratt, too," he mumbled as his lips pressed together into a tight line.

Rory stroked my hair and ran his fingers along the sides of my face. He played with my hand and drew lines in my palm. My breathing slowed and grew deep as I drifted off in the security of his hold.

***

Light twinkled on my lids as I made the slow decent from floating sleep to heavy wakefulness. My eyes fluttered open and watched a beam of morning sunshine stream through my bedroom window. In less than a millisecond, the memory of Fergal's stinking hand pressed on my mouth and the weight of his body overpowering me filled my mind with terror and I sat straight up with a gasp.

My rapid breathing sent me into a panic and I grabbed my sheets and pulled them up around my neck. My eyes darted around my room, certain Fergal would be lurking, waiting to press his knife into my throat.

In a heap in the corner, black boots stuck out of worn jeans and the black fabric of a big dark coat moved in slow motion. Rory picked his head up off the wall and blinked a few exaggerated blinks.

"Mornin'." He smacked his lips like he'd had a good rest.

I looked around the room again, not remembering how I got there or why Rory was on my floor.

"Um. Hi."

I gave a half-smile and checked under my sheets to be sure I was dressed. Realizing that my outfit from the previous evening was still on me brought back more heinous memories of Fergal's assault and my face grimaced.

"You're okay, Maeve. Ya just have ta keep tellin' yerself that." Rory's voice caressed me, smooth as butter.

"He was going to…." My trembling voice stuck in my throat.

"No. That fooker doesn't have it in him. Don't give him so much credit." Rory picked himself up and stretched his back, sticking out his chest. "Come on, now."

He came over to my bed to get me moving.

"Let's get you cleaned up."

"Rory…." The next words got stuck behind the first, causing my lip to tremble.

I looked at him as heavy pools filled my lower lids.

"Ah, sure. You're welcome." He looked away and at the floor. "I'll make some coffee."

I gathered fresh clothes and a towel and headed for the bathroom. The stairs leading down to the door of my flat, out into the alleyway, were right next to the bathroom door. I stared down the steps, seeing Fergal lingering in every shadow.

"Rory…" My voice shook and rose to a high pitch.

He bolted from the kitchen in an instant.

"Ya, what?" His eyes moved up and down me, checking for signs of distress.

"Do you mind staying here, at the door, while I shower?" I looked at the floor, feeling stupid.

"Ya, sure, o' course. Go on." He waved his head at me to git.

The warm water cascaded down my body, cleansing every piece of grime and spit left by Fergal. Soap made sure to destroy any residual bits of his assault. My senses cleared and my inner self peeked out from behind the wall of terror. My audible sigh welcomed her back.

I needed to call Paul.

My eyes pressed shut in a hard squint.

He was going to be pissed. He told me not to be alone. Ever.

My head fell back.

I wondered if Rory spoke to him already. Probably not, or he'd be here by now.

I wrapped my towel around my hair and flipped it back. The warm mist of the shower hung in the air and kept my body warm, as I looked at my reflection in the mirror.

A shuffle outside the door reminded me of Rory's presence, making my skin prickle in mini-goosebumps. I imagined opening the door and inviting him in, allowing him to hold me again and make it all better.

My eyes widened and I shook my head to clear it.

I must be truly traumatized.

I grabbed my clothes and threw them on in a hurry. To clear any of my prior devious thoughts, I exercised my jaw, stretching my mouth open and then closed, and cracked my neck both ways.

Then opened the door.

Chapter Ten

Tribal Feud

With my hair still wrapped in a twist of towel, I peeked out the bathroom door and looked at Rory, leaning against the wall scrolling through his phone.

He glanced up at me.

"Ah. Now that's better." His bright smile flashed in my eyes.

I couldn't help but smile back and reached for the towel on my head, wondering if it looked dumb or if maybe I looked pretty to him.

Oh god. What was wrong with me?

"Thanks, Rory. For everything." My eyes dropped to the floor. More words formed but I couldn't get them out.

He followed me into the kitchen as I moved toward the undeniable pull of morning coffee. Two mugs sat by the pot and he filled the big one and gave it to me. He reached for the pint of cream and poured it in while I held the mug with two hands. I pulled it to my face and inhaled as my eyes flickered shut.

"I make a mean cup o' joe." He snickered.

The mess of grounds, spilled cream, and dirty spoons gave the appearance of a coffee-making battle scene, but he was right. It was a beautiful thing.

I inhaled more of the swirling steam and took a long, deep sip. It filled me with the comfort of home, friendship, and normalcy.

"It's the best coffee I've ever had." I looked up and met his eyes as I continued to slurp.

He smiled with a boyish grin.

"Did you call Paul, Rory? And the gards?" I searched his face for details, wondering if he'd called Paul and then pictured cruisers pulling up to my flat with the blinding reflective letters GARDA written across the sides.

Rory rubbed the back of his neck.

"The gards want you to go to the station to make a statement. When you're ready."

"What about Paul?" I pressed.

Rory moved closer to me without breaking his gaze into my eyes. He took the cup from my hands and put it on the counter.

I pressed back against the sink as he stood in front of me, his feet on either side of mine. He reached for the towel on my head and unraveled it in slow loops, dropping it to the ground as my wet hair fell around my shoulders, never breaking eye contact.

He took my face in his strong hands. "*I* can take care of you, Maeve. Can't you see that?"

My lips parted to speak but I found no words. Shock ran through me as my mind went blank.

"Maeve." His voice turned my name into a melody. "I want you to be with *me*. Always have." He whispered along my cheek and held his head next to mine, inhaling the scent of me. "Not being with you has been... impossible for me."

If Rory hadn't come, I'd be dead. I owed him my life.

He moved his warm, full lips along my jawline and onto my neck. The thrill of his touch ignited a torch inside me that sent me spiraling.

But Paul had come back to me, fully. I hoped. Would he betray me again?

My head dropped back by instinct, inviting him further. The scratch of his stubble along my face heightened my senses, churning desire in every nerve. Being with him was as easy as breathing.

My inner voice sent an awakening shout of resistance trying to break me from his spell.

I pushed Rory away with a hard shove.

"Stop!" I caught my breath and my wits. "Rory! What are you doing?"

Guilt washed over me for falling so easily for his charm.

He backed away as if he were wounded.

"I'm with Paul, Rory. You know that."

The chime of my phone tweaked my brain.

"I know it." He rubbed his bottom lip. "I'm sorry."

Another chime.

I pressed my hand into my forehead. My exhaustion was making me lightheaded. I shook my head.

"I shouldn't have done that. It wasn't fair." He stared at the ground. "I just couldn't help m'self. You're just... you're all I think about."

I dropped my face into my hands.

I was a wreck. I had no clue how I got here. In this moment. I needed Paul. He had the power to stabilize this situation. Pull me together again.

"No. It's my fault too. I should have stopped you quicker. I'm sorry." My hand covered my mouth, then pulled away. "I'm not myself right now."

My eyes fell to the ground in shame.

My phone chimed a third time and I stared at it across the room, knowing it was Paul.

"I'll take you to him. You shouldn't be alone." He looked at his shoes and shrugged.

I pushed away from the counter to get to my phone. In my haste, my elbow bumped into Rory's side.

"Ack!"

He keeled over in pain, holding his ribs. At first, I thought he was kidding, but he looked up with a grimace, baring his teeth.

I grabbed his shoulder for a better look.

"Rory, you're hurt!"

I reached for his hands and pulled them away, to see what he was hiding. Small spots of blood seeped through his T-shirt.

"Oh my god. You're bleeding!"

I tugged on his shirt for a better look and he pulled away.

"Did Fergal hurt you?" My eyes bulged in fear.

"I'm fine. It's old. Sure, bloody thing won't heal right."

He stepped to the sink and pulled his shirt up for a better look.

Elaborate artwork covered his ribs. Tribal symbols and Celtic designs. The tattoo covered much more skin than his original "Ruaraidh" script, which I'd noticed last winter, right before I left to go back to Boston.

That was back when I first realized Rory had accepted his role as chieftain of the MacMahon Clan. The ink marked him as Red King for his tribe. But *now* it took on a more aggressive look, almost threatening.

My hand reached out to examine it and I moved in for a closer look.

"Rory. What is this?"

My eyes followed a thick black swirl, along his ribs and over his sculpted abs. Closer to the center, it looked raw and unhealed. He flinched from my breath on it.

"You need to have someone look at that. It might be infected."

"That's the thing, see. I can't. It's not public yet."

He wet a paper towel and dabbed the sore.

"What's not public?" I pulled back and looked into his face.

"The whole chieftain thing. It's done, though. The initiation." He looked at his ribs. "This is the mark of the tribe chieftain."

I stepped back and sucked in a quick breath.

"What does that mean?"

"Well, that's the problem, really. It's kind of a big deal. Ancient rituals, treaties, duties to the clan. It's all on me."

"So, Fergal?"

The connection within his clan was obvious. I just didn't understand the details. *Or* the big picture.

"He's dangerous, Maeve. You know that now. He's a rogue clansman, looking to change the course of history. Centuries-old pacts. He'll stop at nothin'."

My shoulders slumped as my hands began wringing.

"What does he want?"

Rory stopped dabbing his wound.

"He wants the MacMahons to hold permanent claim to the territory. The land and sea of the west. It's rich land. Legend says it's riddled with treasure." He smirked, hearing his own words. "You're a major threat to us, Maeve. Connected to the pirate queen. *I* know. *Fergal* knows. He thinks you're *her*, come back to reclaim the land." He put his shirt down and looked into my eyes. "Dumb, right?"

I stared back into his dark pupils as they seemed to try to pull information out of me that I didn't know I held.

"I didn't know you knew that much about the pirate queen." I stared at Rory.

"The clan told me. And sure, you'd rambled on about it back in the day, so it made sense." He rubbed his jaw. "Sure, when I saw ya first at Lynch's, when you'd just come back here, I saw ya in a new light—as a true enemy. Surprised me. My glare scared ya, I think."

He smirked but then his face fell.

"You're a threat to us now, Maeve."

His words shocked me and sent a chill into my core.

It explained why he stared at me with such a caustic gaze that night at Lynch's, though. But I couldn't get my head around being enemies with Rory. *Eternal* enemies. It didn't seem to fit.

"And Fergal? He's with you?"

"No! He's an outlier, Maeve. Headin' up his own revolt."

I pressed the bridge of my nose, between my eyes. Fergal's revolt nearly killed me.

"We knew he'd be comin' fer ya, at some point. So we had a bit of a lookout set. Good thing, too." He sniffled in triumph. "Or we mighta missed him last night."

The doorbell rang and I jumped back like I'd been shot.

I ran to my room to look out the window.

Paul's car reflected bright light into my eyes as if to mock: *We're here*….

My heart leapt into my throat.

"Shit, Rory! It's Paul."

I grabbed my phone and looked at his text messages.

"Oh my god. This looks so bad," I said out loud.

I paced for a second then ran down the stairs, panting.

Rory hadn't contacted Paul last night. I knew that now. And I still hadn't had a chance.

Crap. Oh god.

I pulled the door open.

The relief that washed over Paul's face made me sick with guilt.

He reached for me and took me by the waist, pulling me in to him.

"Hi." He smiled into my eyes. "I was worried about you."

His cheek brushed mine and he kissed my face.

"I haven't heard from you and I... I just don't want you to be alone," he whispered into my ear.

He hugged me and lifted me off my feet in his strong embrace.

My body went limp as I remembered the attack and then Rory in my kitchen. Panic surged through me like poison.

Paul lowered me down and pressed some of my hair away from my face.

"Are you okay?"

He studied my expression but his lost eyes showed he couldn't get a good read.

"Actually, no." I tore my eyes from his before I got physically sick. "A lot has happened. I need to tell you."

I pinched between my eyebrows to think, then pressed my lips with my fingers, not knowing where to begin.

"What's going on, Maeve? Tell me."

He moved farther into my alleyway, but then glanced down the corridor to the door of my flat as we heard the heavy footsteps coming down.

I swallowed hard and closed my eyes, hoping to evaporate into thin air.

Rory stepped out of the door and into the alleyway, pulling his arm through the sleeve of his black jacket. He turned toward us and gave a sideways glance through his hair.

"Hey, man." He nodded at Paul. "I was just leavin'."

Paul released his grip on me and stepped back, like he'd taken a bullet. He moved his wide eyes back and forth, from Rory to me. He swallowed hard.

Rory turned his body and pressed past us in the narrow space. He pulled on the blue door and looked back over his shoulder.

"See ya, Maeve."

His arrogance wasn't lost in the tone of his voice and he was gone with a slam.

Paul's silence made me shrink to the size of a mouse. His blank eyes stared like he'd been hollowed out. He fell back against the wall and looked to the ground.

I reached for his hands, hanging lifeless by his sides.

I never wanted to hurt him. Ever. I had to fix this, fast.

Seeing him crumble before my eyes made me love him even more. I wanted him to come back to me. Strong as ever so the two of us could move forward, together.

"It's okay, Paul. He helped me." I lifted his hands to my heart and stepped closer to him. "My heart is with you. I promise." I brought my face close to his and looked him in the eye. "Come on. I have a lot to tell you."

I pulled him toward my door that led up to my flat, but he didn't budge.

"Maeve. Did you sleep with him?" His eyes stayed fixed to the ground.

My heart rate plummeted through the floor.

"No. It wasn't like that. He was here to protect me. That's all." My voice took a commanding tone to reassure him.

His knees buckled and he bent over as if he were going to vomit.

"Are ya tryin' ta kill me, Maeve? Ya might as well be pullin' me guts out." He choked on his words. "*He's* protecting ya now? Why? How is *he* here and not me?"

His shoulders slumped as his lost eyes searched mine.

I stared back at him. His vulnerability was raw and he made no effort to hide it.

I just wanted to hold him. To love him. To pour myself into him forever. How could he not know that?

I reached for him, as if he were a wounded soldier, and held his face in my hands. I kissed his soft lips as he remained motionless, defeated. I kissed him again, this time with a smile on my lips. I spoke through the kiss in a whisper that blew gently on his mouth.

"I love you, Paul McGratt."

He struggled to hide his smile, but it pulled up one side of his mouth enough to show he liked it.

I pulled on him more, to get him to bring his strength back.

"Fergal was here," I said.

Paul's eyes widened and he straightened in an instant.

"How the hell was Fergal here?" he blasted through clenched teeth as molten lava erupted in his pupils. His strength returned full force.

"Last night. Rory followed him. If Rory hadn't come, I don't know what would have happened." My voice cracked along with the scattered fragments of my story.

"Are you hurt? Did he touch you?" His face fell as his eyes searched me again for damage. He reached for the redness on my cheek, subtle scratches from the wall, and stroked it with his thumb.

"Come on." I tugged on him to follow me upstairs. "I'll make coffee."

He was right on my heels, but then stopped. I turned back.

"What?" I asked.

"You said last night." His blank stare faded as his eyebrows scrunched down.

"Hm?"

Oh shit.

"Last night," he repeated. "Rory's been here since last night?"

***

Paul fidgeted in the hard, straight-backed dining chair. With an elbow on the table, he clamped his chin in his fist and watched me as I made a new pot of coffee.

I wiped the counters of loose grounds and spilled cream, whisking away any evidence of Rory's presence.

I grabbed the mug he had taken from my hands earlier and rinsed it warm water. Then hot water. I left it under the tap and let scalding water course in and splash out.

Paul's gaze moved out the window across the stretch of green fields and into oblivion. I pulled the other chair close to his and sat with my knees pressing into his leg.

Leaning in, I whispered, "Look at me."

He turned his head and blinked into my eyes as his chest imploded with his slow exhale. Sitting up taller, pushing himself back into his chair, he pressed his jaw to the side and looked at me through half-closed eyes.

"So, are you going to tell me what happened?"

My stomach clenched like a vice sending vile sickness through me, turning my gentle smile into a twisted scowl.

"Fergal tried to kill me." My voice remained flat to avoid reliving the emotions of the event.

Paul jolted up to his feet, sending the table forward, and his chair tipped and smashed off the tile floor.

The thunderous bang sent me flying, like a cat stuck to the ceiling, shooting electrified sparks through my body.

The shock brought tears and then convulsions that shook my body into terror and then darkness. The world closed in and spun around me in a whir as I became weightless and released myself to the slow-motion haze.

In the same instant, I was awakened with a jolt as Paul collided into me, catching me before I hit the floor. My body quaked in his arms as I smelled Fergal's hand over my mouth and tasted his foul stench with the clarity of the moment it happened.

Paul held me with such an intensity of strength I was sure it would hurt, but instead, he held me together. He lifted me and stared into my face, as if I'd been mortally wounded and these were our final moments.

His tortured face turned up to the ceiling as if looking for strength, or answers, or a death wish on his enemy.

I sank into a cloud of soft covers that cradled and soothed me. The safety of his strong arms and my warm bed allowed for the tears to unleash without shame. With quakes that could easily have been mistaken for the first heaves of vomit, the tears flowed out of me.

I cried every detail of the story to Paul, slobbering and rambling, shouting and struggling, until I was exhausted.

Staring at the fresh drizzle on the window, I swallowed and sat up, picking pieces of stuck hair off my wet cheeks.

Paul's nostrils flared as he ground his teeth.

"I'm gonna kill that fucker."

"He said he had to stop me." I rubbed my temples and laid back down on the bed, curled up with my blankets.

"I need to contact the garda. They'll need to make an arrest."

"Rory spoke with them last night. They want me to come to the station today to file a formal report," I muttered.

Paul balled his fists at the sound of Rory's name. He paced the room like a trapped animal.

I thought about what Rory told me, of the land in dispute. Fergal's intentions.

"It's all about the land disputes. The territory up for grabs." I picked my head up off the pillow and peeked at him.

He pursed his lips and looked up in thought.

"The deadline for resolution must be closer than we know. That would explain Fergal's attacks." His teeth clenched as he mumbled to himself, shaking his head in anger. "Legends say there's treasure in the territory. Fergal's greed has taken priority over his clan." He cocked his head to the side.

I spun around in the bed and propped myself up.

"He must know I have the map. And the deed to the land." My hands flew to my mouth to muffle the words.

My eyes darted to my backpack, filled with Grace's truths. The truths of the O'Malley Clan.

"What do we do? He nearly killed me for it." My voice sounded more steady.

Paul huffed. "Yeah. 'Tis ironic."

He shook his head in disbelief and went to the window.

"What is?" My eyebrows squeezed together.

He stared out at the rain and then turned to me.

"The fact that I need to go to Rory." His lips pressed together until they were white. "For help."

Chapter Eleven

Chieftains

We hurried down Shop Street through the middle of Galway City, dodging the rain, and the levity brought a smile to my face that I hadn't felt in days—since before the Fergal thing, anyway. The misty rain had turned to streaks of wetness as Paul pulled me along by my hand over the bumpy cobblestones. Late-afternoon shoppers dispersed and the streets opened up.

The bright red door of Lynch's pub caught my eye and I slowed our pace.

"Thanks for doing this," I said to Paul, as he turned to see why I'd stopped.

"Yeah. Certainly not my first choice of person to share space with." He pressed his lips together. "But Rory has information we need. I get that." He paused and checked his phone.

I bent forward to get a clear view down the street and felt anxiety tighten in my core. It was going to be awkward to share space with Paul and Rory again.

And the moment Rory and I shared, right before Paul arrived that morning after the Fergal attack, haunted me. My gut twisted whenever I tried to rationalize it. I lumped it in with the moment Paul shared with Patricia at Smokey Joe's, as if the two events were similar in some way. Though I prayed they weren't, and hated that they happened at all.

"And Maeve." Paul's voice snapped me back. "I've found some

more information in my research this morning. Might explain why Fergal's so hell-bent on stopping you."

I looked into Paul's intense face and loved him for caring so much. For making all of this a priority.

"What is it?" I swallowed the lump in my throat.

"A momentous clan council meeting. Next week. It's makin' headlines as an historical event, with magnitude that could effect the future of the clans involved."

I watched droplets of water collect on the ends of his hair and fall. I knew nothing of council meetings.

He added, "Sounds like it could be related to the land disputes possibly. It would explain the rising angst in the MacMahons anyway."

He watched my eyes glaze over.

"What kind of power do the clans have anymore, anyway? It seems like an ancient thing. More like tradition stuff." I shook my head, trying to understand the enormity of what was at stake.

I looked out along the cobblestone toward Lynch's Castle, imagining the same road set in its original medieval time.

Paul smirked.

"Right. The clans hold on to their ancient customs, quietly. They hold more power than common folk know. The rituals and treaties, they're all honored to this day, protected under Brehon Law." He blinked rain from his eyes. "People tread on the land like it's theirs. But sure, it's sacred."

"Well, at home, in the States, if you buy land, it's yours. Doesn't matter if a clan had it before you." My head tipped, suddenly questioning the rules back home.

"There's vast quantities of land in Ireland, not owned by individuals, but held, as territory, in clan names. It's the true power of Ireland. Its soul." He pressed his lips together and nodded his head.

He squeezed my hand and shook the rain from his hair. The wetness splashed my face and went in my eyes. I squealed as I brushed the drops from my cheeks and pushed him.

"Jerk!" I jeered.

I took the ends of my hair and whipped them at him, sending drops back at him. He stepped back, under the shelter of a shopfront awning. He pulled me into him and held me, looking into my face with a steady gaze.

"Tread easy in there. You know… on me." He gave a half-smile of worry and the furrowed lines on his forehead stressed his concern. "I don't like that guy."

I reached up on my toes and kissed him. He lingered with his eyes closed to prolong the moment.

"No worries," I said.

But in my heart I was nervous—unsure how this meeting with go, with the three of us.

Rory was arrogant and cocky. I prayed he wouldn't piss off Paul. Especially with Paul still feeling insecure about the other night.

But I was also uncertain of Paul's ability to get Rory to talk. If anything, Paul would shut him down with his first word and Rory would walk away with whatever it was we needed.

"Come on." I pulled Paul away from the wall and tugged him to Lynch's.

I had to face this head on.

Now.

***

Rory was slouched at the back of the pub in the shadows by the ancient stone arch. His legs splayed out, taking up more space than he needed. His pint half gone. Paul lingered at the bar to order drinks and I went to sit with Rory.

He pulled himself up to standing as I approached the table and his eyes moved over me like silk. He leaned forward for a hug but hesitated, noticing Paul's watchful glare, and instead, gestured for me to sit.

"You look better, Maeve. Are ya feelin' okay?"

He sat back in his seat across from me, taking up more space with the span of his outstretched arms—one propped with confidence on the back of his chair.

I peeled off my wet jacket and shook my hair away from my face.

"Actually, yes. Much better. I slept straight through last night, for the first time since… you know. So that's good." I half-smiled.

"Well, I've reported everything to the clan elders and they've contacted Fergal's outlier clan. He shouldn't be botherin' ya again. Ya can be sure o' that." He took a slug of his pint and wiped his mouth with the back of his hand.

"Who are the clan elders?" I watched his mouth more than I should have.

"The wise ones, basically. More in tune with the rhythms of the earth. Druid priests mostly. They're the ones saw ya comin'." He nudged his chin at me and then looked into his dwindling pint.

I pulled my head back and scrunched my eyebrows.

"How'd they see me coming?"

"Ah, come on, Maeve. We all know you're connected to 'er. To the great O'Malley chieftain." His eyes grew wide with mocking exaggeration. "Sure, the elders know things. They're connected to the past, ya see."

Paul came to the table with two pints and a coffee.

"Hey, Rory." He nodded with little expression. "What's this about an O'Malley chieftain?"

He set a pint for Rory and placed my coffee into my eager hands.

"Thanks, man." Rory finished the end of his pint and placed the fresh one on its coaster.

Silence. Awkward.

I looked at Rory and then at Paul. Neither flinched.

"So the police still have no information," I stated. "No leads."

Rory nodded and closed his eyes.

"No surprise," he said.

The silence returned and stretched for miles.

"Um, so," I stuttered, "we need your help, Rory."

"Ya, I figured." He lifted his eyebrows and tilted his head, waiting for details. "It's about time, I s'pose."

Paul cleared his throat.

"Can you tell us why Fergal attacked Maeve? What did he want?"

Rory glanced around the pub to be sure it was still close to empty and said, "Yeah. Fergal wants something from 'er, all right." He sat back farther in his seat and took a deep breath. "There's a feud between the clans, ya know—the MacMahons an' the O'Malleys. Goes back over five hundred years."

"I'm aware." Paul's voice fell flat.

Rory squinted at him with an annoyed nod.

"Well, there's land involved." He paused. "Lots of it. And riches, supposedly. The MacMahons have control over the land but still, no treasure's been found." Rory looked down his nose at me. "But you've upset all that now. Did ya know that, Maeve?"

I squirmed in my seat, like an accused criminal.

"They say yer here to finish her business." He watched my shaking hands.

"*Who* says that?" Paul interrupted.

"The Druids. Elders of me clan." Rory spoke to Paul, then turned back to me with narrow examining eyes. "Are they right, Maeve?"

Paul reached his hand over to me to stop me from responding, protecting me from Rory's interrogation. I took his hand and moved it back.

I thought about his question.

To finish her business.

Rory's clan was right. That was exactly what I intended to do. To restore the land that was rightfully hers. To get it back from the clutches of the MacMahons before it was too late. I couldn't let their resistance stop me, or kill me even, and had to move fast.

Maybe it *was* time to approach the O'Malley clan council with the scrolls. I had a week before the big hearing Paul was talking about.

But who was I? Just an immigrant's granddaughter from Boston. They wouldn't take me seriously.

Plus, it was all connected to Grace and I had to keep her at the forefront. I had to make the right decisions for her. She reached out to *me*. She wants *me* to do this. Not only reclaiming her territory to that of her original Gaelic Ireland, but reuniting her with Hugh. Returning peace and prosperity to the O'Malley Clan.

I deflated at the enormity of the task. I was lacking the actual power to make it all happen… although the MacMahons seemed to think otherwise.

"Well? Are they right? You here to finish her business?" he asked again with raised eyebrows.

"Yes. They are right," I stated with a clear, firm tone.

Rory's chin pulled back at my gumption and then he nodded. "I see. Then we *do* have a problem here."

Rory and I stared into each other's eyes—neither of us blinking.

I pulled power from his gaze and didn't back down. All peripheral vision blurred out and I only saw into his deep pupils and all the secrets they held. The baby hairs all over my body bristled.

A slow breeze blew my hair forward, tickling my face, and then with a heavy burst, the red door flew open, allowing a forceful surge of wind into the pub. The space lost pressurization and my ears popped as all sound mixed together into a loud hum. Then all went silent in the blast.

My eyes darted around searching for an explanation. Just as my hair settled around me, a huge whoosh of energy picked up again, causing my eyes to squint.

Swirling chaos of wind and salty mist filled the space with screeching sound and alarm.

I turned to find shelter or a place to hide as my flight instinct took over. The squalls avoided the back of the pub, like the edge of a tornado, and the ancient stone arch remained clear.

I reached for Paul and yanked him with me into the shelter of the arch. He grabbed my arms and pulled me close, wiping my hair out of my face.

Rory jumped up from his seat and stepped farther into the wind with his arm shielding his wide, bewildered eyes.

"Rory! Get in here!" I screamed through the torrents.

He turned and peered through the gusts with squinted eyes, trying to hear me.

"Rory!" I reached for him. "It's not safe!"

My voice turned to a scream as I saw her taking form in the wind. I reached for him again.

"It's her!" My voice was lost in the wind. "She's coming!"

I grabbed his jacket sleeve and tugged him in with us.

The wind tore past the archway and continued to churn through every other space of the pub.

The burn on my chest awakened and sizzled under the weight of her ring hanging from my necklace. I reached into my shirt, grasping the chain, and pulled it out. My head fell back as I cried out in pain. The ring swung on the chain in my hand and twisted in its agitated freedom.

A dark blur flew across the pub toward us and yanked the ring from my neck. The chain broke and fell to the floor as I scrambled for the relic that was gone in an instant.

"Paul! The ring!" I cried out, rubbing the back of my neck where the chain broke.

Paul froze, gazing into the swirling mist as if entranced in the eyes of a cobra. I spun to Rory for help but he had the same lost look, staring in the exact direction as Paul.

I followed their line of vision, breathing through the blistering burn on my chest, and squinted into the swirling black mist as it took the form of Gráinne Ní Mháille, pirate queen.

Grace stood tall in the gusts with her blue cloak flowing all around her, exposing a white ruffled blouse held tight to her waist with a laced leather vest. Her broad stance held steady as the lines in her face and intent in her eyes became clear through the squall. She locked her piercing gaze on me and moved closer as her jet-black hair flew all around, framing her in striking beauty.

She glanced to my left at Paul, then right at Rory, and they dropped to their knees in an instant and bent their heads down in respect.

My legs quaked under me as she reached out to touch my hand. My eyes looked away in terror as I froze, waiting.

She took my hand and lifted it in front of my face. Her weightless touch felt like air moving through me. My timid gaze remained planted on the floor, scared to death to look up into her magnificent face.

"*Méabh*." Her smooth poetic voice filled my head with the sound of an ancient language as she spoke my name like prose. "*Taoiseach*."

She held my hand up and waited. I lifted my gaze from the floor and looked at her through half-shut eyes, like looking into the sun.

"*Taoiseach Ni Maille*." Her eyes smiled into mine.

She pushed the ring onto my middle finger.

The scorching heat from the band, like liquid metal, bonded onto my skin without pain as it became a part of me.

Like a strange mix of venom and morphine, a surge of energy burst from the ring and ran through me like hot streaking light. In an instant, I looked straight into the eyes of Gráinne Ní Mháille with a confidence that grounded me, as if I were home.

She allowed me to gaze into her soul and joined it to mine.

My eyes brimmed with tears as her mystical knowledge filled my mind. I gasped for air as my eyes rolled back. Visions of my life ran backward on rewind, flipping through the years to my infancy, but then continued on.

I traveled through generations and centuries of O'Malley women and their life experiences. All focusing in on a single point of enlightenment. The true essence of the O'Malley Clan.

My heart connected with hers as I filled my lungs with new life. New understanding. She was my soul now. My beating heart. And I wanted to stay with her.

I opened my eyes and reached for her blue cloak, desperate to touch her.

She nodded in satisfaction with my transformation but faded as I moved closer.

I stepped toward her and watched the power in her eyes and strength in her stance blur into the mist.

Panic shot through me with a shudder as the wind died down and her streaks of color settled into the haze.

"Grace!" My voice cracked in anguish as the dark edges of the pub came back into clarity. "Don't leave me!"

And she was gone.

I stared, panting, into the space under the arch where she once stood.

My heartache tightened, reminding me of the cruel pain of grief. But then, in my next breath, it turned to something new, where there was no pain. Something that gave me new strength and courage. I had a battle to fight for *her*. For my *clan*. And what I was feeling was determination.

Determination to fight and win.

If I could restore my ancestral lands, I would live out my life here. My true home.

And if I could put Grace's soul to rest, at peace, then I would have hope for a peaceful future. For me and for coming generations of O'Malley women.

I lifted my hand and stared at Grace's ring.

The Celtic designs danced in my eyes, encouraging me to take on my new role with courage and grace. She'd given me the power I needed to lead the fight. To face the MacMahon chieftain with equality. To face the clan council elders with the validation of an ancestral title passed down directly from the our most honored leader.

"Jazus Christ! What the fook wuz'at?" Rory's brogue thickened with fright. "Feckin' Grace O'Malley, it was." His eyes bugged out of his head as he rubbed his hands through his hair. "Bloody hell."

He made no effort at hiding his trembling limbs.

Paul pushed up from his knees and stumbled to me. His energy had been sapped from his body and he nearly fell. I grabbed onto him with solid strength and moved him back to our table. He collapsed into his chair and coughed.

"Come on, Rory."

I pulled him up and moved him to *his* chair. He followed along like a rag doll.

I stood at the table with a wide stance, shoulders squared, waiting as they gathered themselves together.

Rory rubbed his eyes and tried to sit up straight as Paul propped himself on his elbows, squinting to clear any remaining disturbing images.

I smacked my knuckles on the table, presenting to them the ring on my hand.

Their jaws fell as they stared at it with wide, unbelieving eyes.

Paul stated, "She made you chieftain."

"Yes." I smiled.

***

"Can I getcha somethin', miss?" the barman called over to me, unfazed by any of the windblown, anointing events.

"Pint a' Guinness, please," I called back.

Paul and Rory sat taller, regaining their energy through each new breath. They took long pulls from their pints as if it were life-giving elixir—like it might have been their last.

"What now?" Paul asked.

"The skull marking on the map, on Clare Island. It's our final clue." My eyes widened in hope.

Rory leaned in. "Whatcha mean? What map?"

I darted a look at Paul first. He raised his eyebrows and nudged his chin at me, leaving the decision to tell Rory up to me.

I wanted to become allies with Rory. Now that we were each in charge of our clans, it provided us an opportunity to unite and work out an agreement. Without violence.

I had to take a chance and trust Rory. He could be the link to making this work out right.

"Grace led me to a hidden map in Rockfleet Castle," I started.

Rory readjusted his position at full attention.

"It has two markings. One is Ballynahinch Castle, as you're well aware." I glared at him with a smirk, holding him accountable for his amateur attack. "The other is Clare Island. And I'm pretty sure whatever might be on Clare Island will give us the final answers to all this."

"How can you be so sure?" Rory asked as he went to the bar and brought back my well-settled pint.

He placed it in front of me, waiting for my reply.

"Because the map came with another document." I picked up my pint. "Signed by Queen Elizabeth I."

Rory eyes widened. "What kind of document?"

I pressed my lips together in silence and held the tight seal.

He picked up his pint.

"Well, to Queen Elizabeth I."

Paul reluctantly lifted his pint to ours and we cheered to the Virgin Queen.

"*Sláinte*," we said in unison as our glasses clinked.

I took a long drink from my pint and wiped my foamy mustache ceremoniously with the back of my hand.

"So, two chieftains, sharin' a pint?" Rory flashed an arrogant smile Paul's way.

He chugged the rest of his pint and clonked the glass down. He pressed on the table and lifted himself to delicate standing, still weakened from Grace's visit.

"This does present a problem, however." He pressed his lips together and straightened up as best he could. "We're at odds now, I'd say. More than ever."

He stepped back from the table.

I watched his every move, uncertain of what he might do or say. Paul sat tall with his shoulders broad, probably using every ounce of energy he had, and his eyes followed Rory like a hawk.

Rory nodded formally to both of us and said, "I'm sure we'll meet again."

And he left without another word or glance back.

***

With my celebratory pint in hand, I looked across to Paul, as the growing weight of the pint dropped it back to the table.

We sat in silence, finishing our Guinness, absorbing our new reality and stealing glimpses of the ring, over and over, to be sure it was still there on my hand.

I was chieftain of the O'Malley Clan now. Clan leader. Lost kin of Grace O'Malley.

I was the chosen one to carry forward whatever Gráinne Ní Mháille had begun. To return her land and her fortune to the O'Malleys and to reconnect her to her lost love, Hugh.

I thought of her sword, lost in the ivy. It was another piece that needed to be restored. I resolved to get my hands on it.

"We gotta get to Clare Island," I told Paul without wasting a moment. "To find the skull on the map." My eyes widened. "You always said her final resting place was most likely on that island. What if that's what it marks? It could be the solution to this puzzle." I leaned forward, rambling, ready to pack my bags.

"Maeve. Slow down." Paul ran his hands through his hair. "We have no idea what any of this is. I mean, chieftain! Christ!" He glanced to the side, avoiding my face. "Think about it. If Fergal was willing to kill you, who else is out there ready to pounce?"

He turned to me with a tension on his face I'd never seen before. The look of loss deep in his eyes twisted my gut.

I stopped my racing brain from planning my trip to Clare Island and considered his words. I hadn't thought about other creeps that might exist. Other brown cloaks. My spine straightened with the reality it presented.

Paul exhaled and pursed his lips. "I don't think you should be alone *at all* anymore. Not until we really know what's going on."

"Seriously? You too?" I rolled my eyes. "Michelle and Declan said the same thing."

I'd been staying at Michelle's since the attack but never expected to make it a longer-term thing.

"I want you to stay with me," Paul said. "I won't feel safe any other way."

My eyes nearly fell out of my head.

"No way. I won't put your reputation on the line like that, not ever again."

I thought back to how our relationship began, when I was a student in his class. No matter how cautious we'd been, it had still gotten away from us.

"It's too risky, " I added.

I closed my eyes, trying to erase the memory of the time we were once seen in public together by a former student and then the whole Patricia confrontation.

I rubbed my temples. Somehow, his ex-girlfriend Patricia got wind of it and then came to him, trying to pressure him back to her. What a mess.

"I can't take that chance." I shook my head.

"It doesn't matter. I need to keep you safe." His eyes held mine as he clenched his teeth. "I want this." He hesitated. "I need this."

"It's too risky, Paul. I'll be okay. I'll move my things to Michelle's for a while. Declan's there most of the time, too. It'll be okay." I reached for his hands on the table and squeezed. "Really."

He pressed his lips together, knowing he'd lost the debate and moved his gaze out the door of the pub.

"I've got a bad feeling." He shook his head in resolve and closed his eyes.

Chapter Twelve

Soul Mates

"So, do you want to come to the O'Malley cemetery with me?" My nodding head and high eyebrows left Michelle little wiggle room.

With Paul stuck on an unexpected assignment at the college, I was antsy to get moving. My impatience gnawed at me as I considered my next steps—as chieftain.

The title nearly blew my mind as I considered the responsibility that came with it. The clan system went back in Irish history to medieval times and held families together like tribes. My entire clan, wherever they were, was counting on me and they didn't even know it yet. Truth was, I didn't even know yet if I could live up to it. But the idea of bringing my clan together again was like rebuilding my lost family.

It was what my heart beat for, what I was meant to do.

Now that I was chieftain, though, getting my hands on Grace's sword seemed imperative, before moving on to any other task. It called to me from its hidden ivy bed every time I closed my eyes.

I placed my wineglass on the red stain that bled through my brainstorming paper—covered with flow charts of what to do next, what could happen, where to go, et cetera. The paper was covered in scribbles, cross-outs, and arrows.

"Hell no!" Michelle blasted. "I refuse to go to that freaky cemetery. I'm staying away from all that crazy shit. Far away!" Michelle swung her arm for emphasis on the "far" and sloshed her wine on the couch.

I shook my head and huffed.

"Seriously, Michelle. You have to come! There's no way I can go alone," I begged. "Paul is trapped with his college stuff and can't get out of it. If I can't leave for Clare Island yet, then I have to do *something*."

The whine in my voice annoyed even me, but I had to take some form of action, and getting back to the cemetery seemed to make perfect sense.

If Fergal was "taken care of," as Rory alluded, then he wouldn't be guarding the cemetery anymore. Assuming that *was* Fergal, I guessed, but I was pretty confident it was.

The thought of the sword at the cemetery, in the ivy, haunted me. It was calling to me—popping into my mind, morning and night. I had to get it.

"You guys shouldn't go there," Declan chimed in from the kitchen, sounding more like a dad.

He dropped a bag of Tayto's on the coffee table and we launched at it.

"You're just lookin' fer trouble that way."

"Her mind's kinda made up," Michelle said to Declan as she shot him a look I couldn't interpret.

He paused with his lips pursed to the side.

"You're going, either way, right?"

I sucked air through my clenched teeth, apologetically. "Yeah, kinda. Sorry."

I had to go.

If I could get my hands on Grace's sword... it was her power. It might give me the power to ward off enemies. Not that I would slash them or anything, or even be capable of wielding it in any fashion. But I believed it held more than that. Like an unspoken, unwritten law. And it would be proof of my chieftainship, along with the ring.

I couldn't stand the thought of it just lying there in the wet ivy. When she dropped it last winter, the look on her face twisted my guts. Her stately features contorted with shock and stricken grief as she stared at Paul after nearly killing him—as if she were gazing on Hugh himself.

My drive to reconnect Grace with Hugh was stronger than ever.

I felt so close.

I needed that sword. It was a symbol of her power and leadership but also a conduit through time of centuries of struggles, fights, and victories. And I definitely had to keep it out of enemy hands.

Declan moved to the couch and plopped next to me.

"Well, it's safe here. You should stay. And wait for Paul. I mean, anything could happen, and go wrong."

He glanced at me from the corner of his eye like he knew something.

He scratched his head, as if he were re-evaluating me, and I squirmed under his scrutiny.

"Declan. Cut it out. It's still me!" I punched his arm and threw a look at Michelle like, *What the hell? What's his deal?*

She laughed at Declan.

"Yeah, he's a worrier. Can't blame him, though." She rubbed his knee as Declan looked at his phone.

Her hand shook slightly as she forced a fake smile.

"Ah, jazus." His fingers tapped across his phone, texting someone. "Mum needs my help with Izzy."

He rolled his eyes at Michelle.

"Tell her to drop her here," Michelle said. "That way, you won't have to leave."

She shot him a wicked smile that left no options.

His fingers flew across his phone again. His eyes lifted from the screen and looked into mine with a filter of caution.

"Sure, I guess you'll be meetin' Izzy." His lips pressed together. "They're on their way."

Michelle's eyes went wide without reason.

Insecurity washed through me.

I wasn't ready to meet her. I needed to work up to it. Take time to figure out how I'd talk with her. What I would say? I fidgeted in my seat.

"Hey, I don't want anything bad to go down either," Declan said. "Don't go sayin' stuff to scare her, now."

"I won't, Declan. Shit, I'm more scared of her than she will be of me."

I laughed at myself. Frightened of an eleven-year-old.

But she knew stuff. She saw things.

I shook my head, realizing how my friends must see *me*. Kind of a freak too, I supposed.

"Her vision are still getting worse." Michelle broke the tension but added a new level at the same time.

"Wait. Seriously?"

I turned to Declan and readjusted myself on the couch so I could look directly at him.

"What's going on *now*?" I asked, holding my breath.

Declan glared at Michelle in a micro-beat, not meant for me to see.

A car door slammed out front and Declan jumped from his seat.

"Well," he said as he looked out the window, "you're about to find out, I guess."

***

Izzy bounced in with fresh air and sunshine beaming from her eyes. Her smile lit up the room as her feathery blond hair flowed around her as she looked around.

"Hi, Michelle!" she squeaked in a high-pitched sweetness that melted me.

She ran to Michelle and hugged her. She grabbed hold of Michelle's wrist and examined her bracelet.

"Oh, I love this! You have the best accessories."

Declan interjected, "Izzy, this is our friend, Maeve."

Izzy barely pulled her eyes from the bracelet.

"Oh, hi." She flashed a bright smile of little Chiclet teeth and I smiled back in insta-love.

She was so sweet and full of life.

She looked up at Michelle.

"Wanna bake? We can make a sponge cake or Black Forest gateau...." Her huge eyes could win any debate.

Michelle's face fell and she looked to Declan. She could hardly make boxed mac and cheese, so I was sure she had no idea how to make *those* things, let alone have any of the ingredients.

"Gotta pee." Izzy hopped on one foot and Declan pointed the way.

She scampered off to the bathroom.

"Now don't freak her out, Maeve. Promise?" He begged with his puppy eyes.

"Jeez. What did *I* do?" I mocked him with my palms turned up in innocence.

When she got back, Declan sat her down and handed her his phone. She dove right into his apps looking for her favorite.

"You're not gonna be here long enough to bake, Izzy. Mum'll be back soon for you," Declan said.

"Awwww." Her eyes stayed glued to the phone screen as she tapped away on it.

"Maeve," Michelle yelled for me from the kitchen. "Get in here. I need to make a snack for Izzy."

I jumped up, thinking of good kid snacks. Grilled cheese, chopped fruit, cereal. I browsed Michelle's cabinets and we agreed on pasta. Plain, buttered pasta.

I plopped back down on the couch across from Izzy as Declan went to the kitchen.

I watched her playing on his phone and a small smile crossed my lips. Then, she looked up at me and caught my gaze.

Her eyes popped open and she stared at me.

"You're the girl," she said. "Right? With the visions."

She looked straight into my eyes.

My chin pulled back, like I'd been caught or exposed.

"I can see it in you." She looked at Declan's phone then looked up again. "Can you see it in me?"

I stared into her eyes and suddenly understood the term "old soul."

"Yes, Izzy. I see it in you too."

She dropped Declan's phone onto her chair and scrambled over to me on her knees. She knelt in front of me and took a closer look with a drawn face and slackened jaw.

"I think you're in trouble." Her voice fell flat. "My dreams are gettin' worse. And they're to do with you." She leaned in closer. "Do you want to hear 'em?"

I nodded my head.

"Yeah."

The sunshine in her eyes dulled and she took on a darker appearance, as if she were sinking into herself to an unpleasant place.

"There's death all around." She looked to the side.

My fingers gripped the upholstery as she continued.

"The pirate queen is near. She fights. She's brave. But there's an enemy." Her eyes squinted as she leaned even closer.

My breath sucked in as I hovered on the edge of my seat.

"He's strong. Smart."

I stared into Izzy's eyes, hanging on her every word as my skin prickled in reaction to her story.

"He wants to stop you. He has the power to lead others, to stop you." Her eyes grew wide and she leaned even closer. "He's coming for you."

I swallowed through my tight throat.

Who could this enemy be?

"So you've made friends," Declan's booming voice made me jump out of my seat.

Izzy's intense gaze bounced to him and lightened.

"Jeez, Declan! You gave me a heart attack." Panting, my hand flew to my heart.

"Tellin' her stories already, I see," Declan jabbed at Izzy.

"She's got the visions, too, Declan. I need to tell her *all* of it," she whined and brushed her hand at him to stop interrupting.

"Tell me what?" I looked from Declan to Izzy and back again.

Declan nodded.

"I know, Izzy. 'Tis as good a time as any. Go on. Don't let me stop ya." He nudged at her with his chin.

I stared at her, wide-eyed.

How could Izzy's dreams have become worse, to visions more like mine? She always had similar awake dreams like me, but not as violent, and she was so much younger.

I dropped my face into my hands in thought. Her visions were what brought Declan and me together as friends in the first place, but now, they were more serious.

Izzy looked at me and chewed on her bottom lip.

"You tell her, Declan." She turned to her big brother with hopeful eyes.

Declan nodded. "Well…I was gonna tell ya this anyway, Maeve. I just didn't get to it yet."

He cleared his throat with his fist at his mouth.

"She sees a sword. Like the one you talk about. Ancient and regal, with the Celtic swirls and all." He took a breath.

"Yeah…?" I leaned in.

"She says some bad guy has it…." He bared his teeth.

"A real baddy," Izzy interjected.

"Like a crazed maniac, actually," Declan continued. "And he, ah, he kills a man with it." He huffed in an attempt to dismiss the heft of what he just said. "So, yeah. That's it."

He looked to Izzy and she nodded in agreement while looking down at her hands.

A chill ran through me and I shook it off.

Then I thought of the murder scene in my nightmare and my eyebrows scrunched together.

"Well, that sounds just like what happened on the ship, in my nightmare last winter—when I saw Hugh murdered by the MacMahons during their attack on Gráinne's galley. They were like pirates who boarded her ship. It's the same vision, right?"

I looked to Izzy for confirmation.

She kept her eyes on the floor.

"I know. I thought that too." Declan hesitated and bit the inside of his cheek. "At first."

"Tell her," Michelle prodded, as she came out of the kitchen. "She needs to know. Especially now that she's thinking of going back to that cemetery."

I fixed my wide-eyed gaze on Michelle, trying to freeze time, and held it there as Declan's words continued.

"It wasn't from the past, Maeve." His words ate through my armor. "Izzy said *you* were there. The man who was killed… was with *you.*"

My hand flew to my mouth with a smack, stinging my lips.

"Paul?"

My eyes widened in fear at the thought of Paul being harmed in any way. It would be my fault. I couldn't let it happen.

Declan nodded and Michelle closed her eyes in resignation.

"It's just one of my episodes," Izzy burst out. "It doesn't mean it's going to happen!"

Her voice cracked in panic as if she were going to cry.

I sat up tall and felt my face grow rigid as my teeth clenched.

It was a prophecy. One I knew was coming. I'd known it from the beginning.

Paul and I were destined to be together, but doomed to be apart. Like Grace and Hugh.

My heart tightened and shortened my breath.

"So, I'm going then." My commanding tone filled the room. "I'm getting the sword before anyone else does… and I really don't want to go alone."

My words left no room for negotiation as my eyes pleaded with them.

There was no way I could go alone now. Not with the idea of some creeper out there, probably Fergal, hell-bent not only on killing me, but on replaying history.

The danger was palpable.

Paul *needed* to stay away. I had to do this without him.

If I could get the sword, I could prevent him from being hurt.

The tingling warmth of the wine had left my veins, replaced by frozen shots of adrenaline and terror.

"You'll be okay, though," Izzy added. "The original three will help you." She smiled with innocence.

My eyebrows scrunched as I leaned in to her.

"The who?"

"The original three. They follow you. Everywhere. Waiting. They know you've come to free them." She picked at her nails and bit the corner of her thumb.

I looked at Michelle and Declan, who were both watching Izzy for more details. I turned back to Izzy.

"I'm not sure who you mean, Izzy. Who are the 'Original Three?'"

"I dunno. Some old people. The lady wears a black dress with a white collar and the old guys wear bad suits. They seem kinda lost or something."

She reached for Declan's phone again.

My eyes rounded as my breath sucked in.

The innkeepers from Ballynahinch! Who were they?

My heart rate accelerated to bursting as I pictured them following me.

I shot a death stare at Declan and said, "And you thought *I* was going to scare *her*?"

He huffed and moved his eyes away in feigned innocence.

With a huge inhale, I turned back to Izzy.

"I'm sorry you're seeing such strange and scary visions, Izzy." My heart broke for her. "I'm going to make it stop. I know what to do to make it stop, and I will."

My resolve strengthened even further now that I felt responsible for restoring Izzy's sunshine as well.

My teeth ground together, thinking of the trouble Fergal and his generations of minions had caused for the O'Malleys and anyone else connected in any way to the rhythms of the Druids or the earth or whatever it was that enchanted Izzy.

"I'm sorry, Declan. I feel responsible for all of this." I shifted in discomfort. "I'm going to help Izzy. I promise. I'll find a way to stop all of this. Will you help me?" My eyes pleaded. "I could use a getaway driver."

My guilty smile spread across my face.

Izzy bounced up and down.

"Help her, Declan! Help her. Pleeeease…," she pleaded.

Declan fidgeted and looked at Michelle.

"Yep." He sniffed into his curt reply. "For Izzy."

He lifted his sixteen-ounce can of Heineken into the air. "But also for Granuaile. To bringing balance back to ancient Gaelic Ireland and her pirate queen."

He reached his can higher.

"*Sláinte.*"

Michelle and I raised our wineglasses, eyes wide in surprise at his sudden shift.

Izzy raised Declan's phone and we all chinked.

"*Sláinte.*"

***

The cotton wool in my head cleared after the second cup of coffee.

I'd tossed and turned all night replaying Izzy's story. It scared the crap out of me. But Michelle and Declan were on board to help, so that was good.

We'd made a plan; I'd do some last-ditch research today and then we'd go to retrieve the sword tonight, without Paul.

Our aim was to keep him out of it. To keep him safe.

Paul was busy and distracted at the college anyway, so I figured I'd find him while I was there and fill him in on the Izzy stuff and my cemetery plans.

He'd probably try to stop me, but at least I wasn't going alone. Michelle and Declan were my perfect excuse for making it work, leaving little room for argument. I hoped.

My array of strategies for convincing him it would be okay consumed my every thought.

***

I snuck out of Michelle's into the blinding morning sun. My sluggish stride to NUIG dragged the journey into what felt like an epic Tour de Galway.

As I entered the campus library half-asleep, my senses awakened to the familiar smell of old books, the rows and stacks of well-worn reference guides, and the awesome historical architecture of the high ceilings and arched windows.

My shoulders relaxed as a feeling of security surrounded me, a sense of support basically, whether it was the wealth of information, shelf upon shelf of answers, or the quiet solitude. The library never disappointed me insofar as ancient Celtic history or any form of archaeological digging.

I navigated my way through tables and reference desks to my

favorite spot at the far corner.

My computer buzzed to life as I splayed my favorite books across the table, surrounding myself with the mysteries of ancient Ireland. The pictures on the book covers danced in my eyes, showing me history through their titles, fonts, and medieval designs.

My phone sat next to my foam coffee cup from Smokey Joe's and lit up with a cheerful chime. I flicked it onto silent, looking around like a guilty library criminal, and checked my text message.

Paul: Mornin U up yet
Me: Ya Lots o coffee
Paul: Doing what
Me: Lookin for grace stuff. How bout u

Pause. Waiting.

Paul: Not now. Working. Talk later maybe?
Me: ???

Pause. Waiting.

Me: Hello
Paul: Sorry. Meant for someone else

Okay...?
My throat constricted.
Was he seeing Patricia again?
My insecurity washed over me.
That's all that could mean, though. Right?
It was meant for Patricia. Holy crap.
A sickness rose up my neck and coated my tongue green. Oh my god.

Was he pulling away again now that I was chieftain? Or because Rory was there to save me from Fergal and he wasn't?

My eyes climbed the pile of books in front of me but I could only think of Paul with *her.*

My face scrunched in a grimace.

The time she confronted Paul outside his classroom flashed in my mind… and her stare-down when she saw me with him. She knew then that we were together, just by the energy between us.

A twang of guilt washed through me again, but Paul had assured me they were over. But I'd always felt awkward about it. Like I was the "other" woman.

I knew this might happen again. Like karma, I guess. She had a hold over him that I couldn't compete with. Years together. And family ties. And she was gorgeous. And. And. Ugh!

I was losing my mind. But I saw them together in Smokey Joe's a couple weeks ago. When Paul had pulled away.

Ahhhh! I grabbed my hair. I didn't know what to think.

I shook my head. There was no way it could be true.

Paul and I were meant to be. It was real. Like truth.

He was Hugh DeLacy's descendant. Grace and Hugh were soul mates. I stared at my foam cup in complete distraction. *We* were meant to be together *too*.

Grace and Hugh had been ripped apart by violent, evil ways. But somehow their love continued through centuries of separation.

I pieced it together. Paul and I were their hope. We were the chance for Grace and Hugh's love to stay alive. And I felt like I was home with him. He made me whole again.

I texted.

Me: Paul. What are you doing?
Silence.

I laid my head on my crossed arms on the table, allowing fear and insecurity to reawaken in me. The familiar feeling wasted no time reacquainting itself with me. It had been waiting, just a layer or two under my skin, to gnaw away again at my weakened inner structure.

The thick history books surrounded me like a fortress. They mocked me now, though. Each one holding answers just out of my reach. They reminded me I was a stranger, with little knowledge of the magic of their world. New to their land.

"Sorry, no sleepin' on school grounds."

The lyrical brogue brought me back to the present. I blinked and lifted my hazy head.

My half-open misty eyes looked into the bright, smiling eyes of Rory.

The heavy gray fog around me cleared away in a blink.

"What are *you* doing here?"

My surprise at seeing him at the college was too obvious. He'd dropped out a long time ago.

His hands went up in defense as his eyes narrowed.

"Easy. Can't a guy seek a bit o' knowledge now and again without bein' judged so harshly? Sheesh."

"I'm sorry. I'm just surprised to see you." I shook my head with a grin, to clear the air between us. "Seriously though. Why are you here?"

I stared at the stack of books in his arms and smirked. "Research?"

"You could say that." He glanced at my impressive spread of texts. "And you? Investigatin' something?"

"You could say that," I retorted with a smug grin.

"Can I join ya? Got room for me?"

He pushed his stack of books onto my table, causing mine to shift and nearly spill off.

"Hey!" I grabbed the edge of a stack before it went crashing down. "Seriously? Not so pushy!"

I sat up straighter with a wide grin, wondering if I looked as bad as I felt. Blush rose to my cheeks for even caring.

"So, what are ya lookin' fer?" He pulled one of my books over and flipped through it.

His thick black hair flowed up at the front, possibly with a bit of hair clay rubbed through it.

"Gimme that!" I grabbed for it as he yanked it out of my reach, teasing.

"Hmmm." He leafed through it again. "Celtic history. The Druids…." He scratched his chin stubble. "One might think you were looking into ancient ways. Tryin' to solve age-ol' mysteries perhaps."

He threw a suspicious side-glance my way.

I swiped the book from him.

"Well, what are *you* looking for?" I pressed.

I reached for the book on top of his stack. He stopped me by a mile before I got to it and held my wrist.

"Not so quick, lassie. These are *my* secrets." He winked at me.

The old Celtic lettering on the top book read *Ireland's Clans and Chieftains*.

"Hmm. That looks like a good one." I reached for it again.

This time he let me take it.

I flipped through it and nodded.

Maps and family names jumped out at me, and writing, lots of writing. This was definitely a book I needed to study.

He pulled another book off my table and read the title aloud.

"*Great Tribal Chieftains of Ireland*. Hmm. One might think we're here for the same thing, ay?"

His innocent expression and lost puppy eyes lifted any apprehension I had about his possible bad intentions. He was just as confused as I was in this whole chieftain thing.

"What have you learned so far? Anything helpful?" I asked, keeping my head tipped down but lifting my eyes just enough to meet his.

"Well–" his eyebrows rose in arrogance "–it appears all the land along the west of Mayo, you know, the castles, the bay, and all surrounding territories, treasures too, it all belongs to the MacMahons. Says so right here, in one of these books." He nodded his head, waving his hand at the big pile. "And the O'Malleys, well, I'm sorry to tell ya, but they're to do as we say. Yield to our wishes, that sort of thing. It's here, somewhere." He flipped through hundreds of pages of the book in his hand. "And you? Find anything of interest?"

I huffed, ready to dump his pile onto the floor.

"Well, *my* books show clear maps of the west of Mayo." My voice held exaggerated confidence. "All marked as O'Malley land. Control over the land and sea, and all relics and treasures too. And it says here, explicitly, that the MacMahons are a bunch of shitheads."

Rory pushed my books to the edge of the table and one fell off with a loud thump.

"That's a load a' shite! My books are the real ones. Sure, yers are ancient tabloids." He pressed his lips to the side and shot a judgmental glare at my piles.

My smile exposed all my teeth as I cracked up and pushed myself up out of my seat. I reached for the book in his hands and slapped it down. He lost grip of it and fumbled to catch it, flipping it in midair. It splatted on the floor with a heavy *whap* and he gawked up at me like I'd broken his favorite Christmas toy.

He lunged at me and wrapped his arm around my shoulders in a loose headlock.

"Take it back." He laughed. "Say the MacMahons rule! We control it all!"

He pressed into me farther, trying to get me to say uncle, causing me to bend over in resistance. His jeans filled my vision and smelled of wood and wet air.

I reached for his thigh and trailed down to find the back of his knee. I grabbed hold of the two tendons, running up the back of it, with my fingers and squeezed—hard. A monkey bite, as my grandfather once taught me. I pinched and pulled on the tendons until he fell over.

"Never!" I shrieked.

He dropped his hold on me instantly and leaped back, hopping on one leg to shake the willies out of the other.

"Not fair! You know I hate that!" He hobbled around to get rid of the queasy feeling that shot through his knee.

I dropped my face into my hands and laughed.

"You're a total goofball," I snickered.

"Shhhhhh," commanded an annoyed librarian who appeared out of nowhere. She eyeballed the books on the floor and glared at us like we were heretics.

"It was her!" He pointed an accusing finger at me as I withered in the librarian's glare. My jaw dropped as I stared back at Rory while pointing a weak finger at him to prove he was the true library criminal.

He gathered his book up while rubbing the back of his squeamish knee and whispered, "No, O'Malley. I got you beat on this chieftain thing."

"We'll see about that, MacMahon." I scowled.

"Shhhhh." His finger at his pursed lips hushed me.

Chapter Thirteen

Ancient Cemetery

We settled into our books after calling a truce, finishing our coffees, and thoroughly checking our phones. Rory flipped through his chieftain book, mostly looking at pictures, and I focused on maps of ancient Ireland, making careful note of family names for each territory.

Grace O'Malley's name was last seen on maps in the 1600s, written as Grany NiMaille. After that her first name went away, but the O'Maille surname remained, though it moved around and shared space with other prominent clans, particularly the MacMahons.

I shielded the maps from Rory's view.

"What'cha got there? Somethin' good, no doubt. Your squintin' eyes betray you." He leaned in to steal a peek.

I pulled the book close.

"Nothing. How about you?"

His smirk mellowed and he said, "There's actually some interesting stuff here."

He moved closer with his chair and opened the book for me to see.

"Says here, about the O'Malley Clan… Grace O'Malley was a businesswoman. Held contracts and deeds. Was likely buried with them."

My eyes darted up and met his.

He watched my every flinch.

"I know."

I pulled my eyes away from his. They were too distracting.

"I plan to find her final resting place. I just can't seem to confirm its location anywhere." I scanned the book piles.

"Seriously? You're unstoppable." His eyebrows shot up. "Good luck with that though. People have been searchin' for her grave for five hundred years."

"What about the MacMahons? What do you guys have, to prove your side of the dispute?"

I cocked my head and smirked, like he had nothing.

"We got Brehon Law." He flashed a smug smile. "We got ancient tribal law on our side."

He lifted his eyebrows at me.

I shook my head at him.

"But what are you going to *do* about that? Come on. I told *you* something. You have to tell *me* something now," I prodded.

His twinkling, lighthearted gaze took a more serious shade of dark night blue.

"You're beautiful," he said with a mellow tone, like poetry.

My blush blazed under his stare and I fell into the deep blue abyss of his gentle eyes.

"Shut up." I looked back at my books. "You know what I meant."

"It's true." He held his gaze on me.

"Rory! Stop messing with me. We have work to do."

I stood up and threw my empty cup into the trash.

"It's *true*." His tone remained constant, his gaze unblinking.

Speechless, I glanced at him sideways.

He sat watching me, as if he were hoping for something. Waiting.

I bit my bottom lip and looked anywhere but at him. I grabbed my computer and my bag and moved away from the table.

"I'm gonna grab another coffee. Want one?" I asked.

He nodded without breaking his lock on me.

"Hopefully, you'll regain your sanity by the time I get back," I added.

I forced my legs to carry me out of the library toward Smokey Joe's.

My brain was a scrambled mess.

Rory was super-cute and fun but how could he play me so easily? How did he have that power? I should hate him. He was my enemy. Right? So why did I still have feelings for him?

My breath filled my lungs for an eternity and I exhaled as I entered the campus coffee house.

Smoky Joe's was quiet, silently anticipating the return of the fall semester and all its coffee lovers. I perused the counter of limited goodies and grabbed two scones and ordered two coffees.

As I waited, I looked around at the mostly vacant seats, half expecting to see Harry again—NUIG's permanent fixture.

Instead, in the corner, overlooking the Corrib River, I saw Paul's unruly windblown hair and my heart skipped twenty beats. He radiated his famous "outdoorsman" look and my pining smile ran away with itself. His head was down in full concentration, studying papers and jotting notes.

I balanced my items, scones in my elbow and coffees in my hands, and headed over to him. It felt like years since I'd seen him, though it was no more than a full day. His work had him under a deadline and he was buried in it, but that wouldn't stop me from stealing a moment of bliss with him.

Just one kiss.

My desire to feel his warm lips on mine made me dizzy. Desperate, even.

Rory had confused me again, raising my emotions, and my teeth clenched at his ability to do that to me. I'd have to fight harder to keep him within proper boundaries.

My focus was clear though.

And it was Paul.

As I shimmied through the tables, envisioning his face as he would look up at me, I was cut off by another person making her way over to him with equal fervor. Her pace showed guided determination that stopped me short. My coffees sloshed as I jerked to a halt and some spilled out onto my boot.

When I looked back up, I caught a glimpse of her intense, focused profile. Her pointed expression didn't distract from her beauty and I crumpled under her superiority.

It was Patricia.

I slowed and redirected as if going somewhere else and then watched her. She touched his shoulder and sat with him.

I knew it. How could I have been so naive?

My head fell back and I stared at the ceiling. My legs began to buckle, threatening the wobbling coffees, as I dropped myself into a chair and watched them from afar. My shoulders slumped as my head retracted into the collar of my jacket.

Her flawless smile and gracious animated features made me want to puke. She leaned in as she spoke to him and placed her hand on her chest every time she laughed at something he said. Probably not even funny. She was literally in full-blown flirt mode.

My throat squeezed and I pushed a swallow down through it, to keep from being sick all over Smokey Joe's.

I pulled myself up with extreme effort as if glued to the chair. My limbs wobbled under me like an under-stuffed scarecrow, barely following my commands. I abandoned the coffees and scones on the table, hightailed it out of there, and flew off campus into the bustle of the city center where the air was finally breathable.

***

"You at least have to tell him you're going." Declan's tone was like a parent's.

"No, she doesn't," Michelle interjected. "He's a dick and that's all there is to it."

I cringed at her words, hoping for a magical explanation to it all, but my gut twisted and heaved, and I had to listen to it.

"I need to go *now*, even without him knowing. So much for being busy with his work. He's busy messing with her, so his loss." I pouted.

My rationalization was child-like, I was well aware, but going without even telling him was my best revenge.

It was all I had.

"Will you at least text him? Just so he knows what's up," Declan pressed. "It's a safety issue."

I sighed for miles.

"Fine. If that means we can get going."

I waited for Declan's nod of approval.

He grabbed the keys to his grandmother's BMW.

"Thanks. Let's go," he said.

Michelle jumped up as if she were heading on vacation.

I settled into the back seat as Michelle and Declan chatted and bickered about which playlist to select on Michelle's phone.

I typed.

Me: Saw you with Patricia. Again.
Send.
Me: On my way to cemetery. Looking for sword.
Send.

There. I hoped Declan was happy.

Nausea rose in my throat. The acid bile burned it.

I waited for his dialogue dots to appear.

Nothing.

The sour taste in my mouth thickened and a foul shudder ran through me as I pictured Patricia manipulating him or worse, seducing him.

The silence of my phone drove me crazy. I shut it off and chucked it onto the floor by my feet. I stared out the window at nothing.

"Is this the turn? It's the fork by the church." Michelle twisted back to see why I wasn't responding. "Maeve. We're here. Is this it?"

I blinked to clear my vision and my menacing thoughts. They'd gone into some seriously dismal places, hollowing out my insides.

We were in Claremorris, near the O'Malley boneyard.

Already.

"Yes, turn left. Then the next left."

My body stiffened with the thought of approaching the cemetery without Paul.

What was I thinking? It wasn't safe. But after hearing about Izzy's visions, it wouldn't be safe for Paul either.

Hmm. Probably should have brought him, now that I thought about it. I huffed to myself.

I reached for my phone at my feet and pressed it. No new text messages. I threw it down again, harder.

"Slow down. The right-hand turn is coming up by those trees," I said.

My mind flashed with memories of my previous visits. All terrifying. Brown cloaks filled my mind and then the stench of Fergal crushed down on me.

I watched my phone, waiting for it to light up. Praying for it to.

The darkness at my feet confirmed its silence.

Michelle turned back to me. "Is this it?"

Declan slowed to a crawl as we approached the glen of spruce that hid the O'Malley cemetery from view—from time and all existence.

"Yup. Stop here," I said. "Over that low wall. The boneyard is in there."

"Don't call it *that*," Michelle whined. "That makes it creepy."

She hid her face in her elbow.

"That's what the locals call it," I whispered as an afterthought.

Michelle and Declan dug in their packs and checked their phones as I stepped toward the shrouded grounds of the graveyard.

The stillness all around caused me to pause and check my surroundings. Mist and fog hovered around the perimeter and I pushed through it, stepping over the ancient stone wall, into the sanctuary of the hallowed ground.

Each gravestone peeked out from the overgrown moss under the darkness of the overhanging spruce boughs and welcomed me. Their presence gave the sense of a family gathering as they seemed to awaken and respond to my arrival.

My eyes came into focus in the low light and letters appeared on the stones and markers. The O'Malley name spoke out in unison from every gravestone, in every form of the historical name—O'Malley, O'Maille, NiMaille, Mailey.

I surveyed the boundaries by the ancient trees, half-expecting a brown cloak to jump out at any moment. The silent stillness of the sacred space was reassuring.

Toward the back was the burial mound where I'd once seen the image of Hugh DeLacy chained and struggling. It led my gaze to the area where Grace had dropped her sword last winter. It had fallen into the ivy as I stopped her from striking Paul with it. When she halted her attack and recognized him, the sword fell from her grasp and she crumpled to her knees. Paul was Hugh's blood. And she realized it in that moment.

But when Paul and I returned here a few weeks ago, Fergal was here. I prayed he hadn't found it. And double-prayed he wouldn't return.

"This is so cool," Michelle whispered. "It's just like a horror movie. But no chainsaws or creepy wells. Thank god."

The unexpected sound of her voice sent my heart into my mouth.

"You just scared the crap out of me," I chuckled. "Don't sneak up like that."

But her running commentary lightened my heavy mood.

"Sorry. Declan, get over here." She waved for him to hurry up.

His sharp focus was intent on keeping watch. He kept his eyes on the area around us, half-expecting an attack from all sides. His army-green jacket and black Doc Martens added to his combat-ready stature.

I let my breath out, for the first time since getting out of the car, and felt my shoulders drop by at least five inches.

"It's over here. In that ivy." I pointed. "That's where she dropped it. And where I tripped. All in that ivy." I swirled my finger at the area where the confrontation went down.

It must be somewhere near the low stone where I'd dropped the crucifix when I was trying to ward off her ghost, old-fashioned-movie-style. I chuckled at how ineffective my amateur move was and was happy to be able to laugh about it now.

I dropped to my hands and knees and rooted in the ivy.

"I saw the glint of light from right around here," I said to Michelle and Declan.

When Paul flew out of the cemetery with me last winter after the attack, I looked back and saw the glint of light. It had to still be there. It had to be.

"I'll get my flashlight. It might help reflect the light off the sword and back at us." Declan turned and jogged to the car.

Michelle watched him and brought her hands to her mouth,

looking around from the corners of her eyes.

"Um, I'll wait right here. For him." She stepped back toward the outer edge of the cemetery, taking long, exaggerated strides. "I feel like we're doing exactly what people make fun of when watching horror movies. We're the idiots!"

I scrunched my eyebrows at her but then looked down, ashamed. She was right.

I looked over my shoulder and then continued moving my fingers through the tangled ivy. Maybe the passing months and wet weather created more overgrowth, burying the sword. My hands wove into the depths of the vines. I crept and searched until my knees were black from dirt and wet from the damp.

"It's not here." I looked up and realized I'd spoken to myself. "It's gone."

Michelle was at the outer stone wall of the boneyard now, looking toward Declan and the car, waiting for the signal that it was time to leave.

As I looked across the cemetery in slumped disappointment, my eyes were drawn to a bright flash of light at the top of the burial mound. My spine stiffened and my eyes widened in horror as I stared at a brown-cloaked figure in a wide stance holding the sword high above his head.

I pushed myself to standing and stole several steps back, blinking away the possible hallucination.

As I retreated, I caught the movement of another cloaked person at the tree line. My eyes traveled along the perimeter and saw cloak after cloak lining the edges of the cemetery.

I scrambled backward, stumbling, and yelled to Michelle, "Run! They're here!"

I looked back to the one with the sword and he was in mid-air pounce as the others ran in response to his attack. They were all coming straight for me.

The grotesque battle cry, gargled with phlegm, from the man with the sword couldn't be mistaken. It was Fergal in all his heinous disgust. And he held Grace's sword in his rancid hands. Anger seethed in me at the sight of the sword in his grip, but rising terror for my life beat it down and took over.

I turned to run and saw Michelle and Declan's wide-eyed horror take over their bodies. They bolted for the car like their lives depended on it.

Instant regret poisoned my veins as I realized the danger I'd placed them in.

"Run, Maeve! Don't look back!" Michelle's words blasted my thoughts to bits and shot fear through my soul as I flew after them.

The war cry and aggressive snarls of the band of cloaked ones filled my ears and raised my terror to levels I couldn't contain. My mind exploded into fragments as I took flight into mid-air. The ivy vines entwined my ankles and pulled me down in a slow-motion crash of hair, limbs, and swears, flying in all directions.

The spongy ground welcomed me in its cradle and time slowed to molasses as I rolled through the wipeout. The wind picked up and blew fresh salty mist into my senses, returning balance to my mind and time to normal speed.

The swirling gusts shot streams of black through the chaos, like dark bolts of lightening. I ran my hands through my hair in shock. The flashes of black light screeched toward the cloaked ones, knocking them off balance.

It was *her*.

She'd come to defend her sacred ground. Her sword.

My finger buzzed as her ring sent electrified energy up my arm and into my heart. I looked back on my attackers and watched them battling the wind.

At first, they lashed out at the swirls and black mist. As they punched at nothing, they spiraled in confusion and searched the squall for their unseen enemy.

Fergal swung the sword into the bursts, striking at whatever he might connect with. The gusts struck him from all sides, knocking him about like a plaything. Squinting his eyes against the blasting assault, he snarled and sliced the sword into the thick mist in a clumsy figure-eight.

I scrambled back toward the edge of the cemetery, listening to the uniform battle cry turn from aggressive attack to frantic pleas for help.

Then blood-curdling screams.

My hands flew to my ears to stop the horrifying sounds of terror and pain. The brown cloaks flapped and sailed on the wind along with their wails. Like tortured souls, they begged for it to stop, dropping to their knees, covering their heads. Some fell and writhed in the pain of the attack while others retreated, seeking shelter and escape.

I searched for Fergal through the chaos, hoping the surge would make him drop the sword and writhe against her wrath. Gone from my sight—he'd abandoned his fellow outliers, maybe to suffer her vengeance on his own.

I raced to the car and jumped in.

Before my door was even closed, Declan gunned the engine and peeled out. I slammed the door and bounced around in my seat to look back behind us.

Staring back at the sheltered O'Malley boneyard, once again silent and still, I was blinded by the bright flash of reflected light.

Light from the sword of Gráinne Ní Mháille.

My hand flew up to block the glare and I stared through the powerful beam.

Fergal stood on the highest stone of the cemetery wall, his power stance wide as he held Grace's sword high above his head, shaking it in victory.

Victory over Gráinne.

Victory over me.

Chapter Fourteen
Clare Island

Michelle and Declan's energized voices filled the car with fast-paced questions, angry accusations, and giddy retellings of what they saw. Their words ricocheted through the car and around my head like a flock of trapped swallows, but none of them reached me.

My phone shook in my unsteady hands as I willed my fingers to hit the right letters.

Me: Fergal has her sword
Send.
Me: Why aren't you answering
Send.
Me: Please don't leave me
Send.
Me: Don't leave me

My face fell into my hands and down to my lap as the tears flowed. Quakes of nervous tension jolted out of my body with each sob.

Sniffling, I peered at my silent phone.
Send.

Michelle pulled herself over the front seat and shimmied her way into the back. Her awkward wiggling plopped her into the backseat onto her shoulder and she twisted and kicked her way to upright.

A smile pushed its way across my soggy face and I shoved her knee.

"Hi," she said. "You okay?"

"Yeah. You?" I raised my eyebrows, assessing her condition.

She darted a look over her shoulder and out the windows, nervous as a skittish mouse.

"Like I said before, not a fan of your freaky visions." Her lips pressed to the side and head tilted in judgment. "But it's Declan I'm worried about. I think he nearly crapped himself." She laughed, poking at Declan.

"I'm fine." His curt tone spat his words out onto the road ahead. "Let's just get ta hell outta Mayo."

He hit the gas harder.

Michelle squeezed my knee, trying to suppress her laugh, but the vibrating snort that escaped her nostrils shook the entire car.

Declan's foot went heavier on the gas.

I shook my head at Michelle, grateful for the comic relief, and silently wished I could be in her skin instead. It was safer. And more fun.

Time stretched into a blur of instant-replays and emotional tidal waves in the protected bubble of the BMW, broken only by the growing traffic and lights of Galway City.

"You guys wanna get some food? Decompress a tad?" Declan glanced over his shoulder to gauge our response.

Michelle was slumped, half-asleep and half-drooling, and straightened up after hearing his voice.

I lifted my gaze from my lap.

"Can we drive by Paul's first?"

Michelle shot her wide eyes at me, wiping wetness from her chin.

"Are you sure? What if she's there?" she warned.

Her words were like taking a bullet and my face winced in pain.

"Sorry." She bared her teeth. "But what if she *is?*"

"I have to. I need to know what's going on. Please, Declan. Can you take me there?"

"Sure."

He took the turn for Taylor's Hill.

The homes grew larger and more estate-like as we entered the prominent neighborhood. It seemed a bit high-end for a college professor, but Paul lived in one of his family's regal properties. Apparently they had several.

His red car sat in the driveway, confirming the right house, and I sucked in a gulp of air.

Declan pulled up in front of the house and parked.

"Wow. Not bad." Michelle pressed her face on the car window. "Friggin' hot, actually."

The large windows and master stonework were pristine Irish architecture at its finest.

"You don't have to...." Declan's voice faded as I left the car without haste.

Paul's overstuffed mail poked out of the slot in the door, needing one extra push to gain full entry. I stared at the high-shine, massive front window, framed in glossy teak, expecting to see a curtain move, maybe by a sneaking, guilt-ridden woman.

My shaking hand reached for the doorbell and pressed.

The chime filled the inside of the house and echoed emptiness back to me.

I imagined the sound of his feet thumping toward the door and then his strong arms pulling it open.

I waited.

I pressed the bell again and leaned into the narrow, frosted window at the side of the door. I cupped my hands around my face to block any glare in hopes of being able to see through the translucent glass. Maybe see movement or light.

Silence.

I balled my fist and pounded. Each effort got harder and louder. I reeled my arm back for an earth-shattering thump as Declan grabbed hold of my wrist.

"Come on." He led me back to the car where Michelle stood with her face hanging in despair, mouth agape.

Her face said it all.

He was gone.

The pain started in my stomach and forced its way through my heart. I bent over to soften its assault on my insides, but nothing helped. It tore at me, shredding my fragile core like a vicious, hunting beast.

I dropped my beaten body into the back seat.

Michelle and Declan stood motionless in silence. Michelle climbed in the back with me and held me in her arms as Declan drove.

Patricia was always a danger. I was never safe from her power to pull Paul back into her arms. They had a history together and were meant for each other.

My thoughts sickened me further. Who did I think I was anyway? Maeve Grace O'Malley, from Boston, the small and meek.

My toxic thoughts poisoned me and I crumbled like a house of cards.

We pulled into Tirrelan Heights and Michelle dragged me out of the car.

The sick taste in my mouth soured my entire being and I spat into the grass. I spat out Paul's promise but it remained on my tongue. I spat again but it wouldn't leave me. It lingered, with full intent of torturing me.

***

Of all the insane events of the past few days, the one detail that nagged me most was Fergal at the cemetery.

How did he know I'd be at the cemetery that day? It was as if he were waiting for me, with his henchmen. He knew I'd be there, but how?

The only person who knew I was going, besides Declan and Michelle, was Paul. Declan made me send him that damn text.

I shook the thought from my head. It wasn't possible. There was no way Paul would betray me like that. But the seething toxin was already planted and it permeated my every cell, sickening me.

"Don't tell anyone where I'm going," I said to Michelle and Declan. "Please. I don't want to run into any more trouble. Unless Fergal's psychic or something, I should be fine."

"You still shouldn't go alone. It's just a bad idea. You should know that by now." Declan paced in the kitchen while Michelle stood in the middle of the room and stared at me, as her half-eaten apple hung from her hand. "Izzy screamed through the night again last night. That means something." His eyes widened, as if he were waiting for me to drop everything.

But I had another little secret that fueled my decision to go to Clare Island. Now.

A letter.

I found it stuck in the seam of my blue door, wedged in tight so it wouldn't blow away. The return address read only: BALLYNAHINCH, in golden Old World cursive.

Without question, I knew the Original Three had found me and left me a message.

In the envelope was a hand-written letter. The script was blotched as if scrawled with a quill and black liquid ink. The letter wrapped its way around a smaller envelope, sealed with a red wax stamp of the O'Malley crest.

It was addressed to The Lost Daughter of Gráinne Ní Mháille and directed me to not open the wax seal until the right time.

Signed by "The O'Malley Clan Tribal Council," it also held the three names, scrawled in their own hand, beneath. They were the three last remaining council members.

I breathed in, holding the significance in my lungs and allowing it to spread through my body. The letter was snug in my backpack with the other relics.

"I love you guys. Just keep in touch with my text messages. Don't fall out of communication. Not even for a minute. Promise?" I begged.

Declan nodded once.

"Yep."

***

I waved as my bus pulled out and watched Michelle's head drop onto Declan's shoulder as I drove out of view. Her despair haunted me for the first leg of the journey, as if she were resigning herself to the fact that I wasn't coming back... in one piece, anyway.

My hand rooted around inside my backpack to confirm I had everything I needed. My fingers wrapped around the ancient tube holding the map and the signed document from Queen Elizabeth. I rifled around more and grabbed the leather satchel holding the ancient tomb key that was hidden for years in my grandfather's garden. And the letter from the Original Three of Ballynahinch. My treasured relics—they had to come on the trip with me in case they might come in handy.

I missed having the sword. Though it wouldn't have traveled well in my pack, getting it back from Fergal was a mission that smoldered in my soul. Whatever I gained from Clare Island—knowledge, power, or more relics—would help me when I went back to confront Fergal for the sword, preferably in his sleep.

My arm hugged my pack close to my body, under full protection, like a small child. The more I thought about the contents, the more I realized I should probably have hired a security guard or two.

If Michelle and Declan knew that I was traveling with these things—or worse, if Paul knew—they would all kill me.

I lifted my hand and it hovered in front of my face as I gazed at Gráinne's ring and drew courage from it. A tingle in my stomach grew into full, winged butterflies. The fluttering tickled a smile onto my face as I recognized my adventurous self emerging, blinking into the sun.

***

The Clare Island ferryman held out his hand for my ticket. His weathered, bony fingers unfurled, one at a time, in a slow fan-like gesture. My air sucked in as my eyes darted to his face, half-expecting to see a skeleton in a black shroud. His twinkling eyes and friendly grin smacked me back and I shook my head, handing him my ticket.

I shimmied past the few other passengers and ran straight to the front of the boat and, cautious to not appear too much like Rose from *The Titanic*, I lifted my face into the wind and kept a bead on my destination, Clare Island.

Thoughts and images of Paul jumped to mind every other second and made my heart hurt. He was determined to come on the trip one way or another.

It was true, though; he should be here. This was the biggest part of our journey—finding Grace's final resting place and connecting everything together.

Anything could happen.

My eyes fell closed under heavy lids and I dove into the deep blue depths of Paul's warm, passionate eyes as tears streamed back into my hair from the wind and mixed into the gusts of salty sea mist.

A bone-jarring horn sounded, unhinging my joints, as clear details of the pier and rocky headland came into view. The quiet docks cowered beneath the shadow of a tall, square castle that kept watch over the harbor.

Grace O'Malley's tower house was one of the pinnacle sights of the island. She'd spent her final years in the castle and many say she was buried nearby or maybe even inside.

My eyes traced every feature of the fortress. It was nearly identical to Rockfleet, though this one had a parapet, right over the front door. My lips pursed as I thought of Paul telling me stories of clans attacking intruders—dropping rocks or hot oil on their heads, "from the parapets."

My knuckles turned white on the rail and I released it as if it had turned red-hot, and ran my fingers through my hair to dispel any unsavory feelings or regrets.

I could do this.

I shot my gaze back to the castle that stood five hundred years strong without any sign of age or weakening. Though I'd heard legend that Grace's head was buried somewhere around it, my intrigue was drawn elsewhere—to the abbey I'd researched.

Somewhere on the island was the ruin of a 12th century abbey and it supposedly held an O'Malley crest and other ancient relics. Most of my recent research of Clare Island, and okay, my gut, pointed to the abbey as her final resting place, not the castle, so I kept that idea close in mind.

I clung to the rails of the ferry again, bouncing in my shoes anticipating our mooring, and was then first in line to disembark.

"Tourist, are ya?" The deckhand wrapped huge ropes around a post and tied massive knots. His traditional cap covered his gray and the deep weathered lines in his face proved he'd been working the docks his entire life.

I slung my pack over my shoulder.

"You could say that," I replied with a smile.

"Best B and B in Ireland right over that way." He pointed to a white house with red trim and the words Granuaile House painted in Celtic lettering on the side. "And, sure, don't miss the ghost village at the far side of the island. Tell us if you figure out the mystery of where they all went."

Ghost village? I hadn't heard about that. My intrigue rose ten notches.

"Thank you." I waved to him as I hopped onto dry land and looked up the road ahead.

"*Cead mil falte, Inish Clare.*" His voice trailed off behind me as I barreled toward the castle.

My adrenaline spiked the minute I felt the island under my feet and an urgency rose in me, like the feeling of coming home after years of being away. Getting to the castle was suddenly the only mission on Earth and I charged for it.

Its ominous brooding stature grew in size as I got closer. The dark gray walls, three stories high, threw shadows all around it and added a bone-reaching chill to the air. It stood strong and proud in its solid foundation, daring me to come closer.

As I approached the stony fortress, my pace slowed as my breathing became louder. With each small step, more detail of the structure came into clarity. My hand flew to my mouth as I noticed its state of disrepair. The crumbling walls and moss-colored exterior stopped me in my tracks.

Crumbling from the pressure of time, the castle was a broken ruin. My hand hit my forehead and pulled back into my hair. The castle's state of disrepair shattered me with disappointment, and I shook my head for my naiveté in assuming it would be in its original steadfast condition.

I dropped my pack off my back and searched for water for my suddenly-parched throat. I turned toward the doorway of the castle, swallowing a painful gulp of air along with my water. It squeaked and squirmed all the way down my tight throat.

Unlike Rockfleet, there was no heavy black door to this castle concealing centuries of secrets. The entry was wide open allowing the elements, and anything else, in.

My hand rested on the door jamb and hit a rusty nub that was likely a hinge at one point. Stepping over the slab-stone threshold, my eyes flew around the interior, searching for structure and purpose but it was only a bare skeleton of its former self—exterior walls only.

The upper floors were gone—anything made of timber, gone. No stairs. Just moss-covered stone walls, three stories high. Birds flew around the inside as I looked up into the grayish-blue sky above.

My heart sank with disappointment.

I had expected more—more like Rockfleet, with levels and chambers and spiral staircases.

Looking out through a narrow slit of a window, I gazed at the hills and the sea that surrounded the location and envisioned Grace's daily view. I wondered what it was like for her. living in this remote and isolated location.

Granted, it was perfect for protecting Clew Bay and Rockfleet, as well as keeping an eye on the Atlantic for intruders, but it was lonely in the same breath.

I stepped out of the ruin and followed the single road farther into the island, away from the docks. The late morning sun shone on the Granuaile House, confirming it would be my base.

My *Clare Island Guide* brochure was already worn and torn at the edges from overuse. I reread every word, hoping for secret messages or hidden clues.

The contents described the mountainous terrain, home to about 145 people, walking trails, and a brief history of Granuaile, Ireland's Pirate Queen. The first line explained the variation of Grace O'Malley's name, Granuaile being a medieval combination of Gráinne and Ní Mháille.

Looking back, the docks hid from my view, and rolling hills of green filled my vision. I stopped and pulled the tube from my pack and tugged out the ancient map. I unrolled it just enough to see the skull and the approximate area of the island it marked.

My feet turned left, then right, and with a few more adjustments, I lined up the map with the spot where I stood. The accuracy was surprising, but with each step taking me farther from the docks, a new level of insecurity ramped up.

Being alone reared its ugly head.

After scrambling over a steep ridge in the road and panting to catch my breath, I stopped short as a field of gravestones took over the view. My shoulders relaxed as my breathing settled into a smooth rhythm.

My rising angst was soothed by the appearance of the tranquil graveyard and its numerous inhabitants. The stone monuments rolled in waves across the lawn that surrounded the ruins of an old church.

My shaking fingers pulled at the edges of the map to double-check the location. It confirmed my suspicion.

It was the abbey.

The stonework of the abandoned structure was bone-white and the two small windows, high up at the second floor, were water-marked with dark stains running down the front of the building, like tears. The top of the abbey rose to a sharp point. The lower level had two vertical ornate windows with thick glass, still intact but worn to a fogged opaque.

Excitement shot through me as hope rose.

Maybe I would find answers inside. Answers on how to settle Grace O'Malley's soul. To get the final puzzle pieces so I could end this curse, once and for all.

Behind the abbey was a smaller roofless ruin, possibly the original structure from the 12th century. Grave sites marked the yard all around the abbey. Some were ancient, weathered chunks of stone with hand etching, some shiny and new with modern machine carvings.

No matter where I looked, though, my eyes were drawn back to an ancient monolith grave marker. A course-cut tower of limestone with a single hand-carved marking on it. It stood away from the others and overlooked the abbey and the rest of the island.

I walked up to the monolith and touched it. The rough surface pressed back and sent a warm current through me.

Was it my imagination? Maybe I was trying too hard.

I looked back toward the abbey as if it called out to me.

From the front, there was no way in, only the big double windows. I stumbled over the uneven terrain and moved around the back, noticing the church went much deeper than it appeared, almost like two buildings attached, front to back.

The immense size of it started my heart pounding. The gray stones of the back building were stacked one on top of the other, forming solid walls with no windows. I wondered how light could enter the structure.

What could be inside? So much… or maybe so little.

At the rear, I found a gothic, gray, wooden door, arched to a point at the top. I snuck a guilty look around to confirm I was alone and gave a half-smile to the garden of gravestones watching my every move.

I took hold of the rusted handle in the center of the door and pulled for a second before noticing the inner hinges, then pushed.

The wood squeaked against its solid stone casement. I threw my body weight into it and the door shoved open, throwing a reverberating echo of life through the vast interior.

My footsteps bounced off the walls as light flooded the entry from the open door. I tiptoed into the hollow deep space, leaving the door open for whatever light it provided. Subtle rays shone through from the front of the abbey, showing me the way.

Staying close to the side wall, in hopes of not being detected by whoever—or whatever—I noticed frescos of horses and mythical beasts dancing on the walls and the ceiling in the dusty beams of light. It was as if they were celebrating this rare opportunity of life and light in their usually dark and silent world.

A chill shuddered through me from the cool, damp air inside and I rubbed my hands together. I followed the dusty yellow beams of light coming from the front section of the abbey, walking on the outer edges of my feet to remain silent.

I held my breath as I stepped into the doorway leading into the front, brighter section of the church.

As my eyes adjusted to the new level of light, they darted in all directions, straining to take in all the rich architectural detail and historic ornamentation. My wide eyes flew around the room, detecting hidden alcoves and mysterious corners shrouding secrets or protecting ghosts.

It was like entering an ancient pyramid tomb, where you could tell it was beautiful at one time but now, after the ravages of time, it withered while its secrets became more powerful.

A clang to my right startled me as I jumped back into the doorway, grabbing onto the edge with a vice-grip, and piqued my senses to full operation. My breath froze along with every muscle. I listened with my entire body and my skin awakened to feel the subtlest vibrations in the air as my eyes darted around the space.

My head snapped to the right, following another sound before I'd even registered that I heard it. Movement, subtle motion, came from the far side, like someone, or something, was trying to hide.

The sound of moving fabric and quiet steps filled my ears as I pictured a cloaked beast in my mind, guarding its abbey. My heartbeat rose up my neck and throbbed in my head as my breathing accelerated to near panting.

My frantic thoughts made it impossible to plan my next move with any confidence. The back door to the outside might be reachable, if I ran fast enough. That was one option. Or I could investigate.

Determining which option was smarter was proving more challenging than necessary as I remained in my frozen position without even a flinch. I pursed my lips and balled my fists in frustration with my terrified paralysis.

My feet inched forward before my mind was made up and they carried me deeper into the ornate space. My hearing was muffled by the deafening pounding of my heart. I crept with each footstep barely touching the floor and moved to the edge of the concealed space where the sound had come from.

I stopped and listened, breathing through pursed lips.

A bird, I guessed, or hoped.

Probably a bird trapped in these cold walls, unable to find its way back out a small open window at the top.

Or a badger. Maybe a badger family called this place home.

I leaned on the room-dividing wall and rolled my shoulders and head around the corner and peeked around it.

No sound. Nothing startled.

So I stepped into the hidden space for a better look and stopped short as a tall, dark form spun around to face me. I jumped back in shock and terror as it stood strong, shoulders squared.

"Shit!"

My hand flew to my mouth to stop the curse word from filling the abbey's holy tranquility.

I stumbled back to escape from the dark stranger and scrambled to run.

Who the hell was that? And why was he here, hiding?

Whatever it was or whoever it was, I would figure that out in the safety of the open air and daylight.

I flew toward the door leading to the back building, keeping my eyes set on the light that poured in from the safe outdoors.

The figure followed with heavy steps that ground on the dirt and gravel as he tried to keep up with me. I peered over my shoulder for the stranger, expecting him to be on top of me any second.

"Maeve!"

The voice filled the abbey with a command that halted me in my tracks.

I willed myself to continue my escape from the abbey but I froze, waiting for another word before turning around.

"Maeve. It's me."

Rory's voice echoed off the walls and colored them with his lyrical cadence.

My shoulders remained fixed to my ears.

What the hell was he doing here?

It could only be bad.

My head shook to dispel my negative thoughts.

But this could only mean he was conspiring against me, trying to derail me.

My legs crept closer to the Gothic arched door leading outside, seeking safety as if by instinct. Getting outside and away from him was the priority.

I shouldn't have trusted Rory. I should have been more suspicious of him all along. He'd given me enough reason to be already, but somehow I'd always forgiven him.

My teeth ground together as if I were chewing gravel.

I'd trusted Paul too. And look where that got me. My instincts had misled me too many times, leaving me helpless in my decisions.

I reached for the edge of the open door and pulled myself toward the lifesaving opening. As I threw myself into the doorway to my freedom, my first step to the outside was halted, mid-air, by a strong hold on my arm.

I yanked with panic as I tried to break free from Rory's grip.

"Maeve. Stop. It's me." He loosened his hold. "Jazus. Ya'd think I was a monster or something."

I stumbled back in the doorway, feeling the fresh air at my back.

"Why are you here?" Tears betrayed me and rolled from the outer corners of my eyes.

My terror at his sudden appearance tore at my core. I'd been so cautious to tell no one I was coming.

How did he know? He must be here to stop me or worse. There was no other explanation of his presence.

He stepped back, giving me space to catch my breath.

"I'm sorry. I didn't mean to frighten ya." His eyes studied me with worry lines in his forehead. "Do ya think I'm here to harm you?" He tipped his head in disbelief.

"I… I don't know anymore." I wiped at the annoying tears that continued to roll from my eyes.

"Ah, fer Chrissake, Maeve. Haven't ya figured out we're lookin' for the same damn things?"

His tone held a slap of anger in it, as if he were insulted.

He took my chin and made me look at him.

"Lookin' for answers, right?" He dropped his head to catch my eyes in his and gazed at me from the hypnotizing depths of his dark blue eyes.

I exhaled and let my shoulders fall.

Then embarrassment washed over me and pulled my eyes to the floor in shame.

"You scared the crap out of me." I brushed my foot along the stone floor. "I just wasn't expecting to see anyone. And, well, shit, it's creepy in here!"

"No kidding. I wasn't exactly expecting company either." He pushed my shoulder. "Your reaction was a little insulting though, I must say. I never had anyone run from the sight of me like that before. I'm really not *that* bad-lookin'." He smirked and got me to smile. "Come on. I want to show you some of the stuff in there. It's fascinatin'."

He held the door open like a well-seasoned host, inviting me to re-enter.

I looked at the open sky and the safety of my freedom and then looked back into the darkness of the abbey.

Rory's inviting expression with raised eyebrows and schoolboy innocence pulled me back in.

Chapter Fifteen
Ghost Village

I trailed behind him at first, through the dark backside of the abbey but once we entered the brighter front end, I broke away from him to inspect the carved features in the walls. Rory stood back, watching me, and leaned near a big front window with one foot lifted behind him.

A rectangular plaque of carved stone stood out from its mounting in the wall. My fingers reached for it and ran down the face. The relief played every detail in my memory of the O'Maille plaque in Rockfleet Castle, over the grand fireplace in Grace's chambers, though this one was much larger.

The crest of the O'Maille Clan.

I leaned in to inspect the details more closely in the diffused light and then saw it come together clearly. The boar, the galley, and three sets of bows with arrows. My fingers traced the letters of unknown words above the O'Maille name.

"It's the O'Malley crest." My voice ricocheted around the abbey. "Did you see it?"

I turned to Rory with my hand still on the plaque.

"Strong by land and sea," he said back to me, pushing himself from the wall.

"What?" I cocked my head.

"The O'Malley clan motto?" His condescending tone suggested this was something everyone knew. "*Terra Marique Potens.* Strong by land and sea."

I looked back at the letters and rubbed them with my fingers. "Oh. I didn't know that."

"Bit o' learnin' ta be done, I'd say. Bein' chieftain and all." He smirked.

I stepped back from the crest for a better look at its overall form.

"So how's it been for you, so far? Being chieftain." I turned to him as he gazed at the O'Malley crest.

His head tipped.

"I don't know. It's a lot, you could say. Ya kinda feel responsible. Not just for the clan now. But for all the clan that came before ya." He ran his hand through his purposefully messy black hair, brushing it off his forehead. "There's somethin' mystical to it, too. I'm still just learnin' about that part." He turned to me and his eyes focused in. "But, sure, you know all about that, don't cha."

He eyeballed me with suspicion.

"A bit." I pulled my eyes away.

"A bit? Jazus! You've tapped into something the elders only speculate about. Sure, Grace O'Malley herself visits ya. Nearly made me crap myself in Lynch's, that did." He laughed at his words but grew silent again as he looked around the ornate space. "And don't think I've forgotten how she tried to kill me at the cliffs of Dun Aengus that time. Seems I'm not one of her favorites."

My jaw dropped. I had no idea he'd made the connection that his near-death experience at the cliffs had anything to do with Grace.

"Ya know," he continued, "your contact with her sure gives ya a leg up in all this. I mean, I got my clan to keep, and traitors like Fergal adding to my stress there… I could use a little visit from a past chieftain too, ya know. Ya shouldn't take it so much for granted." He chuffed.

My eyebrows scrunched. I'd never considered it like that. He was jealous of my mystical connection to my clan.

I bit my thumbnail and watched him step away from me.

My eyes moved along his broad shoulders and down to his narrow waist. His jeans hung at his hip and, as my eyes moved lower, he turned to me. Blush burned my cheeks like I'd been caught in the middle of an illicit daydream.

"Come see this." He waved me over to a narrow alcove.

I looked to the ground and moved toward him, annoyed at how easily he distracted me.

A high archway with detailed carving all along its edge led into a small room with a thin double window. Old, broken iron railings attempted to close off the area, but they were rusted open.

We stepped into the recess and our feet crunched on gravel from the crumbling walls.

Rory broke the thick, still silence.

"It's an O'Malley crypt. They say it could be the final resting place of Grace herself."

My eyes widened and I wondered if we should even be standing in the sacred space.

"I don't know." I looked around the small inlet of the abbey and lifted my face to the stillness. "It doesn't feel like it."

I walked out of the crypt and back toward a decorative fixture on the wall near the O'Malley crest. Stone carvings framed an indentation in the wall. It was almost like a recessed bench space, maybe six feet wide, where one could sit but with no headroom.

A dark shadow covered the would-be-seat area and ran up the sides and back by about two feet, as if something large, like a box, was stored there for a very long time and then moved, leaving the mark of its memory behind it.

"What do you think this is?" I asked Rory as I inspected the fine detail framing the edge of the opening.

The detailed stonework started at the outer edges of the space and curved into an ornate peak at the top. Circles were cut into the stone designs and repeating patterns of similar shapes ran along the bottom of the space.

"It looks like something was kept in here." My hand ran along the length of the depression on the wall.

"Yeah. Like a coffin." He blurted out exactly what I was thinking.

I glared at him as if he were being disrespectful and said, "Come on. Let's look around outside, in the graveyard."

We left the sanctuary of the abbey and I pulled the door tight behind us, knowing in my heart it wouldn't be my last time exploring it.

I was tempted to actually crawl into the coffin space and lie there, as creepy as that sounds, but not in front of Rory. Maybe if I had been with Michelle. She'd probably try to jump in first. I chuckled at the thought.

I walked straight to the monolith.

Something about it drew me in. It was powerful and knowing, yet held its secrets close—offering no information but the single unknown symbol.

Was it a guidepost? Or maybe a grave marker.

"Hey!" Rory's voice went through me like lightening and I jumped. "There's supposed to be a ghost village on the other side of the island. Want to find it?"

His playful tone made me forget why I'd even come.

I pulled my eyes from the monolith and looked back at Rory.

His boyish grin was eager for an adventure.

My eyes widened in response to the temptation and I returned his mischievous smile.

***

We rambled along the lonely road that swung around the outer part of the island. A lone farmer off in the hills or a small pack of sheep added to the postcard-worthy view of rolling green hills that poured into the sparkling navy blue sea.

"Water?" Rory handed his water bottle to me after taking a big gulp.

I took it and looked at the opening, knowing his mouth had been on it, and felt like it might be wrong or something. I brought it up to my lips and took a sip as Rory watched me.

"Thanks." I wiped the wetness from my bottom lip and looked away.

As we made our climb over the final rise, the barren, skeletal stone structures came into view. Where the hills met the sea, a line of stony foundations marked the coast. The roofs were gone, along with any furnishings or possessions, leaving only stone walls with open windows and door frames.

A true ghost town.

The loneliness was palpable. Where had everyone gone?

The ancient mystery likely enticed archaeologists to browse the site regularly, searching for clues, always hoping to be the one to make the big discovery.

We approached the ghost village in silence and passed one lonely house at a time, eighty to a hundred of them. Remains of an earlier time, another realm, closed off from the 21st century and all the centuries before that.

"It's like its own world. These people knew this place only," I whispered as we walked through the ruins.

"Farmers and fishermen, I'd say. A tough life." Rory's voice was low and solemn.

His serious tone brought me back to my original mission. It was time for me to focus again.

"What are *you* hoping to find here, Rory?" I stood in my spot. "... exactly?" My head tilted as I watched him develop his response.

He stepped closer to me, causing my heart rate to increase. Heat filled my cheeks as he entered my personal space.

"Now, I thought that was quite obvious." He tipped his head and looked into my eyes.

His hand reached up and stroked my cheek. He leaned closer and his breath warmed my face and sent shivers through me.

I froze in the thrill of his closeness. Paul flashed in my mind and I pushed him out. He'd allowed this to happen, forced it even, and now look.

I imagined Rory's warm, soft lips moving across my jaw and brushing over my mouth. The wetness on his lips awakening something in me that raged to be set free. My mind swam with the excitement of being so close to him. Being with him would be so easy.

Then, I jolted back to reality, as if being slapped across the face. I pushed Rory away from me with a hard shove.

Paul.

My clan.

They were my focus and everything I had to fight for.

Rory's clever cunning nearly derailed me, and rage coursed through my veins in response. He knew my weakness and went for it, ruthlessly.

"Keep away from me, Rory. I'm warning you." I held my hand out to stop him.

He flashed his sad puppy-dog eyes at me.

"I'm sorry, Maeve. I can't help m'self. You make me nuts."

He stared at my mouth as he bit his lower lip. He stepped away, running his fingers through his hair in exasperation.

"It's just your way of getting to me. To win. For your clan." I shot dagger eyes at him.

His face grimaced like a dagger hit him in the chest.

His gaze met mine again as he stood taller and narrowed his eyes. His shoulders seemed to broaden farther.

"It's no secret, Maeve. You and me. We want the same thing. And we're ultimately gonna have to fight fer it." He stared into my eyes. "Everything I do is fer the benefit of me clan. You know that. I'm sorry, but clan first."

The deep blue in his eyes seemed to turn darker.

His words hit my heart like a sword. But he was right. Everything *I* did was for *my* clan as well. I couldn't expect him to be any different.

I looked around at the village ruins, the desolate rolling hills, and the lost sea lapping at the bones of the decaying homes, and a chill shot through me.

I'd wandered off into distant isolation with Rory. My enemy against everything I was trying to accomplish.

My eyes shot to his like a skittish animal.

His hands moved up and pressed the air between us.

"Now don't do that. We'll handle this like two mature, consenting chieftains." His smile calmed my tense muscles. "But, Maeve, ya need ta know. I do want'cha to give me *that* map. It's just too damaging to the MacMahon's territory holds. Right?"

He nodded at me with pressed lips.

I hitched my pack higher onto my back.

"We can discuss that back in Galway." I swallowed hard.

He looked at my pack. "Or now."

He took a step toward me.

"Can I just have a look-see?" He reached his hand out and waved his fingers as if I'd put the map in his hand.

I stepped back.

"Stop. I don't have it with me. That would be stupid, right?" My voice shook, betraying me.

"Ya. T'would be." He stepped closer.

Blood drained from my head, making me dizzy. I gulped for fresh air.

A breeze off the sea washed across my face, carrying time in its mist and the memory of what was once here.

I looked at Rory to see if he felt it too. He stood rigid, staring at me through narrowed, distant eyes.

"What?" I looked down to be sure I was still me.

He turned toward the sea and shook his head. "Something's not right."

Dark clouds stretched across the sky, painting a layer of somber gray across everything.

"*What?*" My shoulders tightened and I swallowed, hating the words he just spoke.

"Somethin's coming. A storm." He looked to the sky and out to the sea—beads of sweat forming on his brow.

I exhaled half my body weight.

"Thank god. You scared me. I thought you meant...."

Blast!

A burst of frenzied energy knocked me back, sending my hair flying in every direction.

I dug my feet into the ground for stability and searched for Rory in the chaos. He was leaning into the blast with his arms outstretched, squinting for a better view.

It was the wind.

"She's coming!" I yelled and lunged for him.

"Hell no!" He grabbed my hand and turned on his heels. "I've walked right into her trap!"

He shot a look of suspicion at me, as if I had something to do with it.

We ran with matched pace and timing and flew past the broken structures, only to be blasted back from another direction, as if we were being corralled.

I searched the squall for Gráinne's form and only saw forceful wind and debris-filled mist.

My head spun toward the sound of a mind-shattering war cry. It quaked through my body disjointing all my bones.

A powerful man's voice, full of venomous condemnation and hate, filled the wind and every space with its bone shaking roar.

Standing on a boulder, overlooking the ghost village and sea, was a tall, dark warrior in full battle regalia. His helmet, with a high spike on top and cheek plates down the sides, cut through the wind and sent chills to my core. He held his sword overhead as blood dripped from the blade, scattering into the wind.

Rory stared, mouth open, at the terrifying warrior and turned to me wide-eyed for instruction.

My gaze froze on the warrior's face as his features conjured an old memory. One I knew well.

I recognized him.

A bolt of terror shot through me as I pieced it together.

The helmet. The blood. The hate.

He was Hugh's murderer. The leader of the MacMahon clan. He overtook Grace's ship and brutally slain her lover.

"Rory! He's a MacMahon. The chieftain!" Tears choked me as fear rose. "He's a killer!"

My feet wouldn't move no matter how I tried. I was welded to the earth.

Rory locked eyes with the savage clansman and then walked to him in a confident, steady gait.

"Rory! No!" I screamed.

He nodded to the aggressive captain as if taking instruction and turned to me with a hollow stare. His eyes empty, like he was gone.

Before I could speak, he lunged at me.

He knocked me from my frozen spot and sent me staggering. He came at me again and grabbed my arms, holding them at my back. I yanked my shoulders to free myself but his grip only tightened. He pushed at my back with his chest and marched me toward the frothing warrior.

I struggled and squirmed to break loose.

"Rory, what are you doing. Stop!" I strained to free my arms, pulling the muscles in my shoulders.

He continued to move me closer to the eager captain.

I turned my head to avoid his heinous death stare and the thick blood oozing off his sword. Hugh's blood.

I envisioned the sword burying into my body—the tearing, the breaking and the pain. The thought sent my adrenaline pumping into full panic.

I yanked with my entire body weight and spun toward Rory.

I smashed him in the face with a loose fist, making contact before I could tighten it. I connected with his nose and he grabbed for his face as I cupped my sore hand. As blood ran from his nose, I kneed him in the ribs, right on his festering wound. He buckled over in pain.

I pulled from his weakened grip and ran.

I looked back at the boulder and watched the warrior swirl into a cyclone of mangled shades of red and violent screams. I flew ahead, but as the mist cleared, there he stood again, in my path. Sword drawn, eyes homed on me like a missile.

I darted to the right and was blinded by black gusts of violent winds hitting me square on. The wind swirled and sliced, focusing in on one point and taking the form of the wrathful Gráinne Ní Mháille.

She whirled all around me creating a protective force against the warrior.

I ran without looking back.

Over the hills and high roads, I retraced our direction to the abbey and begged for its familiar sanctuary to come into view. Grace's shadow blew around me, sheltering me from every side, building my courage with each stride.

I searched for her face in the gusts.

A wave of unconditional love blanketed me. It was Grace's protection that warmed me, just like the feeling of my own mother's love. I burst with my newfound inner strength and power, knowing I had Gráinne surrounding me.

Over the last rise, the cemetery came into view, then the abbey.

I bolted the final distance and darted between the gravestones, forging my way to the back of the abbey. I hid around the corner of the ancient structure and looked back to see if anything or anyone was following.

As Gráinne's mist settled around me, I had a better view back over the rise. At first, the gravestones were all I saw, but then, in a shocking instant, the angry cyclone exploded over the ridge.

It was the savage warrior. His hate and rage filled the torrents and shot red through the squalls. The violent storm moved toward the abbey... and Rory led the way.

He charged forward with all his effort toward the ruin, gaining strength from the warrior and searching for me with a focused hunt in his eyes.

The skies darkened and filled my soul with terror.

I had nowhere to hide.

Chapter Sixteen

Sanctuary

Grace whirled around me and the force of her current threw me to the door of the abbey.

I searched all around for alternatives, and as my eyes darted across the cemetery, the red blasting tornado tore through the gravestones, coming straight for me.

I pushed open the door and burst into the dark space seeking shelter. I slammed the door behind me and the fury of Gráinne settled in the silence of the ancient walls.

I stepped into the echoing darkness and took my first breath, brushing my clothing and searching for any injury. My shaking hands were scratched and my shoulders were sore, but other than that, I was okay. For now.

I hurried toward the faint light at the front of the abbey, lit by the narrow windows letting in the dull gray skies. Small pebbles and shrapnel hit off the glass, reminding me of what searched for me just outside.

As I followed the echo of my own footsteps, the door behind me burst open with the fury of a stampede and the air in the abbey churned to life.

Rory filled the doorway in an aggressive posture of broadened chest and snarled features, backed by the imposing figure of the warrior, teeth bared and larger than life. They pushed through the opening as one and the dark red gusts surrounded them and reached into the space, searching for me.

Run!

Grace's voice filled my mind.

Hide!

I tore into the front of the abbey and darted around the corner where I had found Rory earlier. The open space offered no shelter or crevice to crawl into. Nowhere to hide.

I turned and ran in the other direction, looking back through the doorway into the rear section where all I could see was a fury storm of red.

I ran toward Gráinne's crypt but stopped short as I caught a glimpse of the O'Malley crest. Just before the crest plaque was the opening in the wall. The ornate space that looked like it once held a coffin.

Hide!

Gráinne's voice forced me forward toward the spooky visage, nudging me into it.

Without hesitation, I climbed onto the surface and lay down on my back, hands crossed over my heart, still as a corpse.

The red wind burst into the front abbey hall and whirled around every corner and into every crevice, everywhere but on me. Rory's silhouette blurred in the wind as he searched along with the warrior and they pushed through the room together with guided-missile determination.

I held my breath and remained frozen in place. Still as death.

As I lay silent, Gráinne's soul blanketed me and connected to my soul.

My eyes closed and bright light filled the inside of my lids.

She'd spent over a hundred years in this same spot, not resting… but waiting. Waiting to be reunited with her lost love. Waiting for her lost daughter.

My eyes flickered with the enlightenment of Gráinne's being. The torment of her soul bore down on me.

The light in my eyelids burned bright. Flashing memories of the O'Malley boneyard and my last time seeing her there, grief-stricken and broken.

The O'Malley boneyard flashed again. Then again.

The O'Malley boneyard!

Every nerve in my body tightened and tingled. I stiffened like a board at the realization.

It was all there. All this time. In the O'Malley boneyard.

My impatient eyes popped open and glanced to the side.

The red wind slowed with dwindling power and began retreating. It wiped the walls in a final effort to find me and then melted to the floors and flowed out of the abbey like thick, heavy fog.

I gasped for life-saving breath and remained frozen in place for longer than I wanted, just to be safe. Finally, my body awareness returned and I moved my feet. I wiggled my fingers and toes and blinked my eyes.

I was alive. More alive than ever before.

Gráinne was here. She was laid to rest here.

But then she was moved.

Most likely by the O'Malleys. Moved closer to them and her roots… and her lost love.

My body quaked as a massive shiver moved through me.

I inched out of the close space and stood. I glanced back at the alcove and smiled. I smiled at the fact that I actually had lain there, as in a coffin, and it had worked.

Though it seemed out of place, I couldn't wait to tell Michelle.

I peeked around the corner before walking into the back part of the abbey, toward the door to the outside. I scanned the walls in the darkness, making sure Rory didn't lurk there or some other form of evil, ready to attack me, and saw no ominous shadows. No creepy forms.

I snuck to the door.

I hesitated, unwilling to leave the safety of the abbey, but worried about Rory. I wondered if he was okay. If the warrior harmed him.

I shook my head in frustration. How could I worry about Rory after he just attacked me?

But it wasn't his fault. It was the warrior.

I dug my nails into my palm, disgusted at making more excuses for him.

I pulled the door open and was met with a wash of fresh air and calm bright skies.

My senses settled and absorbed the tranquility of the quiet cemetery and the rolling green Irish landscape. I inhaled the salty brine and earthy air, bringing new life to my spirit.

As I emerged from my dark cocoon, I jumped back into my defensive armor as I saw Rory come out from behind a tall gravestone. His hands were up in surrender and he moved toward me with slow, cautious steps.

"Stay away from me." My voice was firm and unfriendly, but the quiver exposed my true composition. "Not another step."

My hand shot up to stop him.

I turned and ran toward the road at the front of the abbey. I looked back and stumbled.

Rory was following with his gaze fixed on me.

"Stop! I told you to stay away." Tears constricted my voice. "Don't come near me. I knew you were my enemy," I yelled at him.

"Maeve! It wasn't me. I don't even know what really happened. Stop. Please." His voice cracked as he begged.

I made it to the road and shot a glance back at Rory.

He fell to his knees watching me leave. His shoulders slumped as he curled into himself. His expression twisted with regret.

I turned back to the road and looked toward the direction of the docks. My immediate journey home waited for me just over the bend.

One last look back at Rory and I saw his tortured form, kneeling in the grass. His hands had fallen to his sides and his head fell back with his eyes closed. He leaned back on his heels in the dirt.

The gentle rain began to fall and wet my face, softening everything around me.

My feet slowed on the road and stopped. I clenched my teeth and resisted my natural instinct to go to him.

He restrained me and looked at me like he didn't know me.

I turned around.

He betrayed me. He handed me over to the savage warrior.

I walked back to him.

"Rory, you're hurt."

I stroked his hair and checked for his injury.

He opened his eyes and straightened his posture.

"I'm hurt," he said with a broken voice.

"I know. I just said that." My eyebrows scrunched.

"*You* hurt me." His gaze met mine as he held his side and winced. "Every day."

"What are you talking about?" I pulled on his hand and helped him stand.

He reached for me and I flinched. I pulled away from him by defensive instinct.

"I love you, Maeve." He held my gaze with sadness in his heavy eyes. "From the first time I saw you. Even when you spilled my pint all over me." He huffed. "I'm in love with you."

He looked at the ground, as if he were too ashamed to look at me.

"But we're destined to be enemies. I know that now," he said.

His eyes met mine again.

"I never want to hurt you." His voice broke and his lower lip quivered.

He looked at me, waiting for me to say something.

Words were lost on my tongue, but my fist had no problem speaking. I punched his arm and then smacked his head.

"You bastard!"

The seething anger that spewed from my mouth was unrecognizable.

"What are you doing to me?" My mind scrambled into a mess. "You tried to kill me, you lunatic. You have no idea what you are talking about!"

I panted and stepped back.

My hands went to my knees as I bent over, feeling sick. Sick about Rory. And sick about Paul.

"I know. I'm sorry." He raised his hands in defense. "I can't blame you for wanting nothin' to do with me. But I had no control, Maeve. I swear. That's never happened to me before."

I didn't know if I should believe him, but I was pretty sure that *was* his first encounter with the warrior. And he was definitely shaken up by it.

But he'd had sinister intent, before the warrior showed up. It was probably what conjured the warrior in the first place. I had to hold on to that knowledge.

I glanced into his misted eyes. They were red around the edges.

My guard softened. It always did with Rory.

"Well, now you can tell your elders you know a bit about the mystical ways of being chieftain." I half-smiled. "That's something, I guess."

He huffed and reached for my elbow.

"Come on. At least let me take you to the ferry. I'll leave you alone after that. For good. I promise" He sighed. "It's for the best."

***

I stood with my back to Rory and looked out to sea as the ferry bounced in the rising swells. My vision in the abbey replayed in my mind, on endless repeat, and it was all I could focus on.

Gráinne had been moved from her resting place, around four hundred years ago, to the O'Malley cemetery in Claremorris. It made sense. That was where she had attacked Paul and me with such vengeance, protecting Hugh chained at the burial mound... until she'd recognized Paul as Hugh's blood.

I hitched my backpack up my shoulder in response to my thoughts on the tomb key that hid inside it.

The burial mound in the O'Malley cemetery held secrets beyond my imagination. Had Grace been moved there, to be with the rest of her family?

I was sure the tomb key glowed in the darkness of my pack, just from my thoughts alone.

"So, chieftain to chieftain...," Rory interrupted my thoughts, "I think we need to hash out a few details. Not to be a downer or anything," he mumbled as he stepped closer to the rail with me.

"What sort of details?" I looked at him from the corner of my eye.

"You know. Territory stuff. This entire region—Clare Island, the land surrounding Rockfleet Castle and all of Clew Bay, basically. It's MacMahon land, Maeve. The O'Malleys have been making trouble about it for generations and I need you, as O'Malley chieftain, to put an end to it." He returned my glance through the corner of his eye.

I pondered his words and felt my temperature rise, likely from boiling blood.

"Actually, it's my understanding this is *O'Malley* land. Always has been." I turned my body to face him directly.

"Was. That's the word yer looking fer." He nodded his head for emphasis. "Then the English came. Shook things up for Grace and her clan. She had an enemy in Sir Bingham. The MacMahons moved in then." He pressed his lips together in finality.

Visions of the MacMahon leader slaughtering Hugh filled my mind with loathing. I pushed the anger aside and unleashed my feelings all over Rory.

"The MacMahons didn't *move in*! They stole the land. Stole it after Grace was gone. And only through Brehon Law have they been able to keep their hands on it. Temporarily. Until proven otherwise."

My hands balled into fists, thinking of generations of O'Malleys struggling to find the proof of their rights to the territory.

"And I can prove the land is O'Malley land," I added. "A deed! Signed and sealed by Queen Elizabeth herself!"

The words left my lips without proper censorship. My hand flew to my mouth to stop it.

Should I have said that? Should I have held that information close to my vest for longer?

"What are you talkin' about?" Rory's voice pierced into me through his squinted eyes.

"I have the deed to the land, Rory. It's the signed document I told you about before. The one with the map. I just need to present it to the clan council in a few days and all will be settled, once and for all."

"Show me." He stuck his palm out.

"I already told you. I don't have it with me." My eyes darted to the floor.

He reached for my pack and I pulled away.

"I know ya have it, Maeve."

"Get outta here," I commanded, as I squirmed my pack out of his reach.

He stepped closer, pressing me against the rail of the ferry.

"Maeve. Show me the deed." His steady monotone sent chills

through me. "It's not a game anymore. I have a duty to my clan."

Fear coursed through my veins as the certainty of my big mouth became clear. I'd said too much. With no escape and no protection.

The old burn on my chest awakened and my ring from Gráinne pulsed with energy.

Danger was near. And this time, it was Rory.

"When we get back. We can…."

My words were cut short as I was knocked off balance by the shifting ferry, hit by an angry wave.

I fell forward, right into Rory.

He caught me and held tight, with his arms around my backpack. He smiled a wicked grin into my face as he yanked on the pack.

I squared my shoulders and pushed him off me with a force I didn't know I had in me. He stumbled back several steps and looked at me in shock.

The strength that surged through me was incredible. Like I'd been bitten by a radioactive spider and the tingling energy ran through me, building my muscles from within. I stood taller.

"Rory MacMahon. Don't you betray the laws of the clans. Ancient Brehon Law dictates our every move. Who are you to break that sanctity?" My finger pointed straight at him as I imagined smoke swirling from my nostrils. "Chieftain of the MacMahons, you will keep your distance. You will respect the laws of the governance. If you tread near me again, I will view it as a hostile threat, a call to war, and you will regret it."

My voice pierced through him and he slumped like he'd been shot.

My words weren't my own. I'd never spoken like that in my life.

This was bigger than me. Bigger than him. And his eyes revealed knowledge of the same.

Rory stepped back, standing strong once again. He nodded and backed away.

"Rory. You need to start doing what's right. Not just right for your own clan. But right for Gaelic Ireland. Its history is sacred. It is your responsibility to honor that."

Accusation of misguided leadership rang true in my voice and caused Rory to flinch.

He turned and I watched his back as he sauntered into the cabin.

My eyes closed as I felt the sting of sadness hit my chest.

Rory may have duty to his clan, but so did I. The O'Malley clan was my priority. But letting Rory walk away from me felt like a huge sacrifice for it.

And there he goes again! Distracting me from my duty and weakening my fight.

That was the final straw. I would build a high wall against him for now on. Keep him out. It was the only way to move forward and succeed. If he refused to work together with me, with our clans, then we had nothing.

We would be at odds forever.

A tear rolled down my cheek as a small sob escaped my throat. My lips pressed into a frown as I fought my feelings for Rory.

I gathered the tear on my palm and with a snap of my wrist, flicked it out to sea.

***

Time was immeasurable as the ferry slowed and settled at the docks of the mainland. I stepped away from the planks onto dry land and watched Rory pull away, without looking back. His tires spit up pebbles and dust as he left the scene without delay.

So that was it.

That was how things were going to be left between us.

A twang of guilt filled my gut—a sour sadness.

I stood as my eyes followed the road he took until he was out of sight.

My exhale left my lips and blew out my cheeks. I pursed my mouth to the side and thought about my next issue—how to get home. A taxi or bus would be ideal. But what would I do at home? There was still so much more to do here in Mayo.

Like visit the O'Malley cemetery.

The thought pulled a wicked smile across my face like the Grinch.

I checked the time on my phone. Four hours on Clare Island felt like a full day, but it was only two in the afternoon.

I had the information I needed for my next moves— Gráinne's *final* final resting place at the O'Malley boneyard. Paul and I had always wondered if the tomb could be hers, but the cryptic engravings left us unsure. We leaned more toward its being Hugh's grave. And every history book led us to Clare Island instead.

But all along it was right under our noses.

I had the tomb key. And was certain it would be a match for the burial mound. I would finally have the chance to bring peace to my pirate queen's soul. Centuries of torment settled through reuniting her with her lost love.

And I had the deed to the O'Malley territory. Vast amounts of land and hidden secrets.

Now I just needed to finish this by pulling all the pieces together and presenting them to Clan Council before it was too late.

Chapter Seventeen

Boneyard

The taxi pulled away before the driver even checked to see where I was going.

I stood alone at the crossroad, inhaling fermented silage and fresh air into my lungs to generate a fresh perspective on the already-insane day. I turned down the long, narrow lane toward the O'Malley cemetery and gave in to the draw that pulled me to it.

Hazy cloud cover stretched across the sky, filtering the afternoon sun into heavenly rays across the fields on either side. I kept my head down and passed Ol' Man Rooney's place without detection from Jack the Bitch, the unfriendly terrier who'd nipped at my heels my first trip here.

A few moments later, the ruins of the O'Malley family cottage came into my view. I shuddered from the memory of when I first saw it, expecting a warm family reunion and finding a caved-in, rotted ruin. Its carcass fought a brave fight against the elements but its injuries were prevalent and fatal.

Beyond the O'Malley ruin lay the thick gathering of spruce—the shroud of boughs that insulated and protected the O'Malley boneyard.

My phone chimed in my pocket.

Paul: Where are you?

My heart rate spiked to high gear, nearly flattening me.

What the hell? *Now* he's texting me?

My head spun like a top.

Forget it. Too late.

I stared at the letters on my phone and didn't know where to begin typing. My fingers shook like rustling leaves. I'd show him.

Me: boneyard

I thought for a second and typed more.

Me: alone

That'd freak him out, for sure. He deserved it.

His response would be something like, *What! That's too dangerous. Get out of there.* Or maybe something like, *Maeve, don't do this. I didn't mean to cut you off.*

Whatever. Let him suffer.

I stopped walking and watched my phone. Waiting for the dialog dots to appear as he typed his crazed reply.

Nothing.

I refreshed, closed out previous screens, and opened my text messages again.

Still nothing.

That asshole! My temper raged.

Now *he's* mad. So, silence. I hated that! *Grrrrr!*

I squeezed my phone as if it were his head and quickened my pace into the cemetery.

My teeth unclenched and my shoulders slackened as I entered the solemn space. I glanced around the perimeter, looking for brown cloaks, and assured myself all was clear. No one knew I was coming. Well, except Paul now. But he was almost an hour away in Galway, so whatever.

I kicked my feet through the ivy to double-check for the sword. Fergal had his grimy hands on it last time, but I checked anyway.

A sickening pain shot through me as I thought of Fergal with

Gráinne's sword. It wasn't right. I had to wonder if he would have the ability to draw her power from it, much like I was hoping to do.

I moved closer to the burial mound, careful to not step on fallen gravestones or markers, and dropped to my knees at the front of the chamber.

The solid stone door was sealed tight by a wall of smaller, intricately set stones all around it. The plaque at the top was still visible after Paul had pulled the weeds and moss away from it. It read, "G R A," and numbers, a date likely, starting with 15 and then fading out. 1500-something. I rubbed the letters and numbers with my palm.

I ran my fingers around the stone slab door, along its edges and felt for any obstacles or locks—anything that might seal it from time or intruders.

I crawled to the side of the tomb and pulled carpets of moss away from the edge, feeling the stonework for indentations or keyholes, hoping with every ounce of my being that the tomb key would be a match.

I sprang to the other side and pushed the ivy and moss away from the outer wall of the doorway to the tomb. I gathered the loose ivy into a clump and brushed the stonework with it. It swept small bits of debris and dirt away from divots in the stone.

My eyes widened as I revealed two identical square holes.

I dug my fingers into the dirt-filled holes and picked the earth out with my nails. The two openings were stacked, one above the other, about the size of a square matchbook each. My breath stopped as I stared at the keyholes.

I whipped off my backpack and spilled its contents around me, digging for the leather satchel that protected the ancient tomb key. My heart rate soared and burned my ears with excess blood. My hand pushed past the tube with the scrolls that held value beyond my original thoughts, and grabbed the leather package.

If I could open this tomb, and confirm Grace was safe in there, I would be able to take steps to reunite her with Hugh and hopefully find out what I was supposed to do next. If she wasn't in there, well, I'd be back to square one. Again.

The weight of the contents of the leather pouch made me pause and sit back. It wasn't heavy in actual weight, but in the centuries of truths that it held. It was the key to Gráinne and everything she had been. And everything she was.

The leather string resisted with stiffness as I untied it from the folds of cracked, aged leather. The string fell and I slowly unrolled the wrapping in my lap. The final turn revealed the long metal handle with four prongs on the end. The corroded key resembled the shape of an old toothbrush, but bent at the midsection.

When Paul first examined it, he explained to me the prongs would line up with stone pins inside the keyhole and move them upward, out of their locked position. The pins could be put back when the key was moved to the top hole and pressed downward.

My eyes widened at the hope of it working after all this time.

Scrambling onto my knees, I shimmied right up to the edge of the tomb. I blew into the bottom hole to remove any residual dirt and picked away the loose bits.

As I adjusted my positioning of the key, and readied to place it in, my head shot around at the sound of a snapping twig.

My body froze, listening.

I turned my head in the opposite direction and held still.

Blackbirds flew high above in the tree branches, creating movement I had ignored, lost in my sleuthing. I exhaled my nervous tension and looked back at the hole and lifted the key again.

"Maeve!"

I shook my head in disbelief as Paul's voice shattered the sanctity of the grounds and made me question my sanity.

There was no way he could be here.

"Maeve!"

His voice scratched out of him with excessive effort and weakness, but still commanded my attention, causing me to jump.

He was here? But how?

I flew to my feet, alarmed by the sound of his broken voice and panicked by the impossibility of his being there. My eyes followed the sound and focused on him at the edge of the graveyard by the heavy line of spruce.

"Run, Maeve!"

His voice trailed off as Fergal pounded him to the ground.

Oh my god! Fergal was here too!

I went blind for a second as terror consumed my every sense.

Paul's body crumbled from Fergal's blow and he fell like a weakened rag doll. Red and blue marks on his face revealed bruising and blood as he struggled to see me through swollen eyes.

"Don't bother, Maeve. Running won't get ya far. And will only cost this poor sod more pain, maybe his life."

Fergal's voice was steady with arrogance as he sauntered over to me, dragging Gráinne's sword unceremoniously through the weeds behind him.

He stood by the tomb and observed the contents of my bag on the ground and then the key in my hand, as he rubbed his chin.

I stood, motionless, without blinking as despair rose in me.

Scenes from my alley flooded me as I relived his rancid hand crushing my breath and his blank stare stealing my life.

"Yer text message was very helpful, Maeve. Told me exactly where to find yeh." He laughed at my foolishness. "And luckily, or you might say smartly, I never stray too far from here."

He circled my items on the ground, eyeballing them like quarry.

"Seems you have a few things I want."

He kicked at my backpack and nodded at the tomb key still in my hand.

"All these... bits and pieces, you might say." He wiped his nose with the back of his hand and sniffed. "You thought it was all yers, didn't cha?"

Fergal's seedy smile and blackened teeth made my skin crawl.

Paul's shoulders moved in the grass as he pushed himself up. I locked my eyes back on Fergal to keep him from looking Paul's way, a millisecond too late.

"Yeah, my prisoner, you see. I needed him. As collateral. Basically him... for all of this." He waved his hand at my possessions. "Is he worth it to ya?"

His decadent words whirled through my skull and stuck in hidden crevices in my brain, stored for future use. He was threatening to take everything. Threatening my very existence. But all I could focus on was Paul.

He hadn't left me.

Fergal had held him against his will this whole time.

My knees nearly went out from under me as I yearned to run to him.

"Gimme that!" Fergal swiped the key from my hand while pointing the sword up at my throat.

I pressed back through the ivy out of his reach and watched him fumble with the orientation of the key to the holes I'd uncovered.

Brushing his grimy hair out of his eyes, the greasy strands blocked his view with precision. Curses spewed from his lips as he slipped on the incline of dirt at the side of the burial mound and missed the key hole with every attempt.

Through his distracted efforts, I crept further back through the ivy and snuck away. Hunched over, I raced to Paul and helped him to stand.

"My god! What happened to you?" My voice cracked and choked me as the words squeezed out. I pushed his hair away from his face. "Why did he do this?"

With a hoarse, low whisper, Paul said, "To get to you," He winced as he held his side. "To use me against you."

My eyes widened.

"Well it worked!" I brushed the twigs off him and put his arm over my shoulders. "Can you walk?"

Paul limped a few paces and then hurried along with me.

"You can't leave Grace to his evil mitts." Paul looked back. "He plans to take everything for his clan. Her territory, her treasures. He'll erase her existence from history by stripping her of everything she built and fought for." He hesitated. "We need to fight him."

I pulled him along, out of the shelter of the cemetery and onto the dirt lane.

"We're in no shape to fight him right now. Look at us! We need to hide." I looked back to be sure Fergal wasn't following.

We ran together toward the ruins of the O'Malley farm.

"Where is Gráinne when we need her? Where is she?" I called into the open air.

"And you," I shot Paul with my poorly timed judgment. "I thought you left me!"

Paul stumbled on a rock and gritted his teeth with pain.

"I never left you, Maeve."

"I saw you with Patricia again. Then you went away. Silent." I looked back again.

"Jesus Maeve. Ya have ta trust me." He winced. "I had no idea what Patricia wanted. Until she asked me to meet a colleague of hers. To view his ancient relics." He shook his head as if to shed the memory of his gullibility.

We shuffled along the road toward the ruin, looking back every second.

"I thought it might help her, in her job and to, you know, move on. When I got to the location, she wasn't there. It was Fergal and his men." He gestured his head back to Fergal. "He tricked her into luring me there."

"*She* took you to Fergal?" My voice oozed with judgment as my eyes popped out of my head.

The decrepit cottage welcomed us as the warmth and safety of home washed through me.

"She had no idea what she was doing," he said in her defense. "Still doesn't know what she's done."

We staggered into the yard and headed toward the back of the ruin, searching for a place to hide.

A seething anger rose in me.

Fergal was a madman who wouldn't stop until he stole everything from us— Gráinne's treasures, the land, her history.

And now, he'd stolen my faith in Paul. I would take *that* back first.

My brain shattered with the shriek of Fergal's voice.

"It's bloody empty!"

His snarled screams pierced through the sanctity of the graveyard and shot into our brains.

"Where the fook is the gold? Fookin' wild goose chase!"

His voice grew closer. His rants pursued us like dogs on a hunt.

Blind with fury, he slashed at nettles and weeds with her sword, as he barreled toward the cottage.

My grip tightened on Paul's hand as we rounded into the backyard of the ruin.

"How can that be?" I looked into Paul's eyes. "She's here. I'm sure of it. She told me."

Paul spun me and pushed me toward a mound of stones at the far end of the yard.

The rocks waited, for what looked like hundreds of years, to be built into a stone wall. Moss grew out of every crevice and lichens stained each surface of the pile. Rusty farm equipment littered the surrounding ground like decomposing carcasses with reddish-brown metal for bones.

Just as he gave me a final shove to the top of the stone pile, Fergal pounced on him.

I scrambled up to safety, knocking loose stones on my way up. My foot slipped, again and again, casting stones off the pile, cascading them down onto Paul and Fergal.

As I crouched and found my balance at the top, I was shocked to see the corner of an ornate chest or a crate, exposed in the stone pile from the fallen rocks.

My eyes widened farther when the glint of the sword blinded me as Fergal raised it against Paul.

Before the scream left my mouth, the wind blasted from all directions. The darkened fury filled the yard but Fergal was only fueled by it. He swung the sword at Paul, missing him by hairs.

"Where is she? Where are her treasures?" He yelled like a wild person as the wind spun into a black funnel.

He raised his sword again and I chucked stones at him hoping to connect with his head. He flinched to avoid being hit and swung at Paul. Just as the blade made contact, I flew off the stone pile at Fergal and was whisked into the black funnel.

It was Gráinne. And all her strength and fury wrapped me and whipped me into a goddess of revenge, hell-bent on avenging my love. Just as she was.

Like two ghostly banshees from a mystical realm, we tore at Fergal with blazing eyes and scowls of destruction.

He dropped the sword by Paul as a cowardly whimper spewed

from his quivering lips. He shrank from us and raised his arms to shield himself. The look of terror on his face proved the force we had created against him.

My vision tracked Paul with the focus of a hawk as I squinting through the dizzying squall. I reeled back in my assault on Fergal as I stared in horror, as Paul dropped to his knees holding a gaping wound in his shoulder—the exact location Hugh took the hit from the aggressive leader of the MacMahons five hundred years earlier. And died.

My terror at the sight of Paul keeling over sent screams of panic from my lips. Gráinne's agitation became wild again as the torrent raged and she took full human form in the funnel.

Her blue cloaked and long black hair flapped around us as she held my shoulder and bored her eyes into mine. Wasting no time, she pushed her way into my mind, connecting to my history and knowledge while adding missing links and a new clarity that brightened my vision.

A piece of the sequence she layered into my being reminded me of the scene on her galley when Hugh was murdered. It was part of the ancient truths she past along to me.

It wasn't the MacMahon warrior who slain Hugh. The warrior was the evil one who gave the command. To a fellow clansman—with the same tattoo on his arm as Fergal.

I shuddered at the memory.

She was right. It was another man who turned on Hugh, under the warrior's command. And now, that other man stood before us. He had turned on Paul and hit him with the sword, in the exact same way. Fergal was the warrior's minion.

Gráinne stormed toward Fergal with the war cry of a banshee. The sound of her screech shattered my mind and scarred my ears with unearthly sounds of crushing metal, exploding bombs, and mangled cries of pain. The sickening wave of desperate assault forced my legs into a sprint as I raced along with her.

Fergal scrambled back, eyes wide with shock but still baring his teeth as he spat at the ground in our direction.

In a flash of light, we rolled over him like a steam engine and he fell, arms flailing like a child warding off evil spirits. He jumped to his feet and ran across the yard, weaving through rotting farm equipment, slipping on cow splats.

Gráinne came around to my side again and we raged toward him. This time, he turned and held his ground, shooting us with a condescending glare through squinted eyes.

Gráinne lowered her shoulders and I did the same. We bowled him over with the force of our strike and his heels kicked up as he went flying.

His head struck the stony base of a water pump and his face went white. A rusty shod of steel poked through his shoulder as he lay impaled by the thin rib of a hay cutter's carcass.

He lifted his head enough to find the source of his pain and grimaced as he absorbed the notion of a metal spike protruding from his body. He whimpered like a child and looked to us for help. His eye lids fluttered and his head wobbled. Like a drunkard, his eyes went in and out of focus as his head fell, hitting off the stone a second time. He was out cold.

Gráinne swirled into the black funnel again and moved higher, spreading out across the yard. The gray and black haze darkened the yard adding new levels of fear and sorrow to the area—the moment in time.

The shroud of mist opened near Paul, allowing the low light of the dull skies to shine upon him and I inhaled sharply as the original murderous scene tried to replay itself right before my very eyes.

I raced to his side, imagining the worst, as he lay bleeding. His shirt oozed with thick, dark red blood. Terror ravaged through me as I struggled for a better look.

"Paul. Oh my god."

He was alive.

It didn't appear to be a lethal wound.

My shaking fingers searched around the site of the injury. A shudder of relief buckled through me, unhinging every joint, as I assured myself he wouldn't die.

He lifted his head to me.

"It's okay. Just a scratch. No arteries hit." He squinted his eyes and bared his teeth. "We just need to cover it to stop the bleeding."

I looked all around me for a solution, praying for a first aid kit to materialize.

"I don't know what to do. Paul!" My voice choked with tears as my fingers trembled at the bloody tear in his shirt.

My eyes searched around the yard again and focused on Fergal's still form.

I stroked Paul's cheek with the back of my hand. "Wait. I know."

I raced over to Fergal and nudged his leg with my foot, checking for signs of wakefulness. He remained motionless, still unconscious.

I pulled his jacket open to expose his waist and saw what I'd hoped for—a belt. Fumbling with the buckle, I cringed and dry-heaved from the foul stench that rose off him. I'd never smelled a corpse before but was pretty sure that was what it would be like.

Once the buckle was open, I pulled and the belt slid out from under him. I fell back as it flapped into freedom and then ran to Paul.

The wound needed to be covered first.

I pulled off my jacket and unbuttoned my blouse, popping the last buttons free in my haste. Paul winced as I wrapped the pulpy mess with the soft cotton and tied it. I worked the belt around his shoulder, just above the wound and laced the buckle. "Okay, on three. One. Two…." And I pulled the belt tight.

Paul tossed his head back and arched his spine.

"Ach!" The cry of pain filled the yard and echoed through the air as he clenched his teeth to stifle any more sound from escaping. His breath huffed in and out of his nose as he worked through the pain.

I stood back with my hands covering my mouth, eyes wide.

The stain of blood on the white fabric stopped growing and the blood all around the area darkened. Nothing fresh came through.

"Can you move?" I looked back at Fergal to be sure he was still down.

The dark mist and wind calmed into a subtle hover.

"Yeah. I think so." Paul sat up and shook his head. The color returned to his face and he swallowed. "I'm okay. Couple stitches and I'll be good."

The sight of his injury flashed in my eyes as I considered more than a couple stitches as the solution.

"We need to get out of here," I said as I flinched toward the sound of movement behind us.

"I don't think so."

Fergal's voice filled my soul with another flash of terror. He held his hand over his impaled wound by his collarbone as small amounts of blood dripped from the site. His other hand gripped her sword.

His face blanched as he looked at the blood on Paul's shirt and the sword wobbled in his trembling hands.

"Fergal! Stop!" A commanding voice sailed from around the side of the ruined cottage.

My eyes grew wide as I stared, waiting for him to reveal himself.

It wasn't possible.

He'd left me. He'd abandoned any hope of an alliance when he drove off.

Rory stormed around the corner and stopped, frozen, as he took in the sight of Paul and me, covered in blood. He launched at Fergal and slammed into his body with the force of a wrecking ball.

Fergal flew off his feet and landed with a heavy thud.

Gráinne's sword spun in the air and fell to the ground.

Cringing through the added trauma to his already-battered body, Fergal turned to Rory and shouted, "Defector! Yer scum!"

Rory was on him in an instant and connected his boot to Fergal's ribs. He grabbed Gráinne's sword out of the grass and held it at Fergal's throat.

My breath sucked in as time froze.

Rory postured over Fergal like a battle-seasoned soldier. His black boot held Fergal down as the outstretched sword shot out like an extension of his own arm. His comfort with the weapon took me aback as his confidence oozed out of his stance and his control over the situation.

Desire rose in me.

Rory made everything rise in me—anger, shame, passion—and that is what drove me crazy.

Paul was my heart, yet Rory had a control over me I couldn't shake.

And he came back.

To stop Fergal.

But maybe more. Maybe to work together, as an ally.

My eyes opened wider with hope.

I bit my lip and looked back at Paul as he pushed through his discomfort. I bit harder to punish myself for my distraction by Rory. I tasted blood and pulled back into Paul's world.

My misconstrued abandonment by Paul had taken such a deep hold that it left me spinning, and my heart needed a chance to realign to its original intent.

"Howya, Maeve?" Rory's light, arrogant tone echoed in the back of my already-brimming mind.

Chapter Eighteen

Tomb Raider

The blood gutter ran down the middle of the heavy blade and pointed straight at Fergal's throat as Rory stared down its length with keen focus on the jugular.

Fergal fidgeted under the pressure of the threat but Rory turned away with boredom drooping his eyes, as he targeted Paul and me with sharp interest.

"What the hell happened here?" His mouth fell open.

Fergal flinched and Rory wobbled the sword at his neck without hesitation.

"Don't you move," he grumbled through clenched teeth and a backward glance.

Rory stepped closer to us and reached to the ground for my jacket. He passed it to me and turned away as I wiggled into it. Shame burned my cheeks as I took a second to care enough that I'd been standing there in my bra.

He turned back around and searched me up and down for wounds or damage of any kind. Once satisfied I was unharmed, he dropped to his knees to check Paul's condition.

Anger brewed in my veins as my temperature rose to boiling.

Instead of feeling gratitude for his assistance, I was pissed. I couldn't get my head around why he kept showing up and getting involved.

"I thought I told you to stay away from me!" I blasted at Rory.

"Or it would be *seen as a hostile threat*?" he mimicked me. "I think you *need* me right about now. The rules must bend in times of war, ya know."

Paul pushed himself upright, masking his pain with a hardened jaw and steely eyes, but his battered condition betrayed his efforts.

Rory poked around my blouse-tourniquet, nodding at his understanding of what became of my shirt, and inspected the wound.

"We have ta get you ta hospital," he said to Paul.

"I'm okay." Paul pushed himself up to standing. "It can wait. It's superficial."

Rory raised his eyebrows at him. "Yeah, *right*."

"We're so close to finishing this." He winced as he tried to move his arm. "We need to finish this. *Now*."

Rory looked back at Fergal sulking by the rock pile.

I glanced at his pathetic form and silently thanked god Rory came when he did. Even if he *did* defy my order.

I wondered if he'd decided to work together as allied clans. The thought made my eyes open wider as I considered the possibilities. It was actually a little surprising to me how intriguing the concept was.

"What made you come back, Rory?" My arms hung by my sides as I looked at him with a slight tilt to my head.

"Ach. Ya get ta me, Maeve. All up in my head." He swirled his hand around his head and squinted his eyes at me in annoyance. "I figured I had to do what was right. Not just for me clan. Right for Ireland and the generations ta come. It's not up to me to decide." He pressed his lips to the side. "It's up ta the Tribal Council. Like you said."

I stared at Rory in shock.

He'd taken on a bigger view of our roles. Bigger than I'd even seen.

My breathing slowed and went deeper as I gazed at him. He appeared different to me now. But I wasn't sure how.

I pulled my eyes away and stared at the ground.

Then on to Fergal, to be sure he wasn't moving or hatching any sinister plans.

My eyes moved from Fergal's slump to the rock pile where I'd exposed the corner of a decorated crate.

"There!" I pointed to intricate designs peeking out from the rock pile—hand-carved Celtic swirls and knots.

It was the small edge of something much bigger, like the tip of an iceberg.

"In the rock pile. Look at that!" I moved closer.

I scrambled up the stones and tossed rocks away, exposing the corner further. Stone after stone, I uncovered medieval history, hidden in plain sight.

Working along the edge, I pushed away the rocks that concealed the length of the enormous decorated box. Masterful craftsmanship etched the symbol I'd seen at the abbey monolith onto the front end of the container. My eyes went wide as my heart beat out of my chest.

The more stones I moved, the more I knew what I'd discovered.

The stone pile revealed to me the answer to the ancient mystery of Gráinne Ní Mháille's final resting place.

Protected among family, for generations. In the backyard of the O'Malley home. Safe from grave robbers or any other threats. Gráinne Ní Mháille lay hidden in the stone pile for hundreds of years.

The air swirled and churned with gray and black haze. The briny mist filled my senses with fresh awareness of the discovery.

The three men stared at me, each processing the find in their own way, but all mouths agape.

Fergal wriggled in for a better look.

"Don't you move!" Rory commanded, stopping Fergal short, and he stepped to the stone pile himself for closer inspection.

Paul ambled over, supporting his injured arm by the elbow and stood taller as he gazed upon the crate. Each new breath brought more color to his face and light to his eyes.

"We need to move it." I spoke to the stone pile. "We've got to bring it to the tomb. It's her proper resting place with Hugh."

Rising angst quickened my breath with the thought of completing our quest. I'd dreamed of this moment but never actually believed I would lay eyes on her sarcophagus.

It was up to me now. To take care of her with honor and respect. I prayed I could do this.

Fergal's foul voice permeated the air, making my lip curl.

"There's nothing in the fookin' crypt. You're all fools." He spat at the ground.

Ignoring him, I turned to Paul and Rory.

"Can we move it? Is there *any* way?" I pressed on it to feel its unforgiving heft.

Rory walked through the yard with his hand on his chin, thinking. He paced and wove around the rusted farm equipment.

"Over there." Paul pointed and moved to Rory. "In the tall grass. It's got wheels."

The cart appeared content in staying put in its own final resting place, with its wheels worn down to bare metal and its flatbed barely able to hold its beams.

Rory nodded with a twinkle of hope in his eye.

He ran back to Fergal.

"Move." And he shoved him over to the hidden cart.

Pulling overgrowth away and running his hand along the side rail with optimism, Rory coaxed it back to work, clearing a path for its resurrection. He kicked dirt and debris away from the wheels and instructed Fergal to pull.

I hopped off the stone pile with a thrill of anticipation and joined Rory.

Rory and I pushed as Fergal pulled with his good arm, cursing under his breath, and the cart came free from its resting place. We moved it all the way up to the stone pile and nestled it as close as possible to the base of the rocks.

I flew around the yard looking for a hoist or a lever of some kind to help move the coffin onto the cart. A pile of rusty clothesline poles tripped me and I stumbled as my feet rolled across them.

And then I got an idea.

We set the poles horizontally up the stone mound toward the coffin. Rory got behind the heavy crate and pushed. At first it didn't budge but as he shimmied back and forth, it creaked from its position and moved out of its four-hundred-year hiding place.

Rory pushed more and the heavy coffin rolled on the poles, gaining speed as it moved from pole to pole and smashed onto the edge of the flatbed.

Paul used a pole to prop the end of the coffin up to the exact level of the platform and Rory and Fergal pushed it the rest of the way.

Our busy activity halted without a word as we stared at the sarcophagus in its full glory. Fantastic tribal detail and ancient Celtic designs—beasts and swirls, knots and Gaelic words, adorned the stone coffin, sealed tight by time.

It was the casket of a queen.

The stunning beauty of the encasement caused my breath to suck in and my chest heaved. Pure joy overflowed through the tears that blurred my vision.

We stared. Our silent stillness speaking volumes.

Without a single spoken word, we pushed the cart through the yard and out onto the dirt road. The swirling gusts offered strength and assistance to ease the operation, which fueled our spirits— knowing Gráinne was near.

As a makeshift funeral procession, we entered the graveyard like beaten soldiers with steadfast hearts. Fergal dragged his feet at the back, grumbling and resisting every step.

The path we carved toward the tomb was well-traveled by us and we followed the familiar route in solemn silence. We pushed and heaved as the cart groaned in weary resistance through the tangled ivy and thick moss and then we lightened our efforts as we approached the front of the burial mound.

The tomb door remained open by several inches, after being abandoned by Fergal's unsuccessful looting attempt. Stone on stone scratches, like tiger claw marks, streaked the jam where the door partially separated from its tight, centuries-old installation.

Fergal's relentless probing had worked, and the key stuck out from the hole, panting from the effort of performing its intended task after hundreds of years of inactivity.

We stood stock-still, staring into the narrow opening to the dark cavern of the tomb, wondering what secrets either escaped on the wind or hid with stealth in the shadows within.

I couldn't believe it was open.

I'd waited so long for the answers I prayed it held.

My narrowed eyes flashed a glare at Fergal as I reeled with resentment of him stealing the moment from me and turning it to something evil.

I never actually thought we'd get this far, though.

A shiver ran through me as I thought about the simple fact of what we were doing—opening a crypt like grave robbers. It seemed wrong, on so many levels. But the silence in my settled gut assured me it was right.

"Sure, I told ya," Fergal said from behind, leaning for a better look. "There's nothin' in there."

I moved closer and wrapped my fingers around the stone slab door and pulled. Inch by inch, stone scraping on stone, I heaved it farther open.

Golden rays from the sinking sun eagerly reached in, attempting to gain access to a space that was hidden from its reach for centuries. The gentle glow illuminated the empty blackness of the tomb, exposing tightly packed fist-sized rocks in the sidewalls and a stone slab bottom.

My heart sank.

Fergal was right.

I looked back at Rory and Paul who were waiting with bated breath, watching my every move and I shook my head.

"Rory, help me pull it all the way open," I urged him. "So Gráinne's coffin can slide in."

He stepped closer and pulled from the outside of the door as I pushed from its inside.

The polished stone interior of the door was liquid-like, reflecting light in every direction. Like a magic mirror, it cast my reflection back at me in a blur of whirling haze. The one fixed feature was a masterful engraving right in the center. The same as the one on her coffin. And on her original grave marker on Clare Island. I smiled to myself.

I reached for the marker and traced the outline with my finger, then pulled back as if being shocked. The low light of twilight bounced off the inside of the door and lit the interior of the tomb enough for me to see all the way to the back through the reflection on the door.

My head snapped around for a clear look into the depths of the tomb.

The hazy reflection could have been playing tricks on me.

As I leaned in farther, my hair stood on end as my eyes zoomed in on objects resting against the rear wall.

"Paul! There's something in there!" I shouted.

The three of them crowded in for a better look.

Rory shoved Fergal back and sealed off his access by shimmying in close to Paul.

I crawled in and reached as far as I could with my arm, wiggling my fingers in hopes of connecting with something. The length of the tomb ran at least six or eight feet to the back and I gulped back the dread rising in my throat—the dread of having to go farther in.

I inched my knees along the rock slab bottom and stretched again, reaching only half the way. I swallowed a mouthful of air and looked back.

"Go on," Rory said. "You got this."

Paul pressed his lips together in agreement.

"I have to go all the way to the back," I said to myself loud enough for anyone else to hear, hoping for resistance or some other excuse to stall.

Paul and Rory's eyes widened as they bared their teeth and grimaced, sending clear signals of how they felt about my predicament, but understanding the necessity of moving forward.

Fergal jockeyed for a better view, tapping his fingers off one another in eager anticipation. His lips moved, exposing his rotted teeth, as he jabbered to himself as if counting his share of the booty.

I crouched into a compact form, with my knees tucked under me and my elbows in tight, and shuffled along the rough bottom of the tomb. Claustrophobia threatened my already-shaky confidence as the side walls closed in as I moved deeper into the crypt.

My elbows touched both sides at the very back and my subconscious suddenly had the need to stretch and move about, egging on my claustrophobia like a teasing sibling. Ignoring my inner turmoil, I reached to the back wall and felt around blindly, patting down the area, to see with my hands.

My fingers moved around a wooden box, maybe the size of a milk crate, and then a leather sack, like a large garbage bag filled with loose pieces. I pulled at the leather parcel and dragged it along the length of the tomb back to the open air.

Everyone stepped away as I crawled out with the ancient, dust-covered sack. They stared in disbelief as I knelt at the leather bag and allowed the tension to shudder out of me without shame, in jolts of pent up fear and phobias.

I glanced up at Paul and then to Rory. Looking for agreement of what to do next. They nodded and nudged at me to open it.

I ran my hands over my face and through my hair as I took a deep breath.

Leaves rustled and then lifted up from the ground and the ivy fluttered in the rising breeze. The mist of the boneyard swirled in agitation as the wind picked up and gusted all around us.

She was awakening again, responding.

She was here.

If she wanted to stop me, she would have by now. Without any trouble she could've sealed me in that tomb and annihilated everyone else. A clever plan if I'd maybe misunderstood her intentions all along. I paused as the possibility sunk in.

My hand went to my mouth to stop the idea from forming any further. My own thoughts might have more power than I knew, so keeping focus was key.

My eyes darted around for any sign of her taking form and then focused back on the leather wrappings. I unfolded thick flaps of the weathered hide, revealing the opening. Cracked leather cordage sealed the bag but crumbled in my hands from the ravages of time as I fumbled with it. A clang of metal on stone rattled from within the parcel, raising everyone's eyebrows with anxious curiosity.

I reached in to the unknown with a shaking, cautious hand, careful not to damage the fragile, aged contents. My fingers glided over a smooth round object, like clay pottery, and then a cold metal plate of some kind. I grasped onto the heavy metal object and pulled it out for its first breath of fresh air in over four hundred years.

My mouth fell open as I looked up at Paul and Rory.

The ancient family crest was the size of a dinner plate. Raised features in the metal depicted a fire-breathing mythical lion-beast. The crest of the DeLacy Clan.

I dropped it into the moss and pulled my hand away, as if I'd touched something I shouldn't have. Tears misted my eyes in anticipation of what else might be hiding in the satchel.

I reached back into the bag for the pottery. My hand pushed past rods or solid tubes of some form and found the pot. My fingers went into grooves almost like a bowling ball and I grabbed one and pulled it out.

As it emerged from the bag, the wind came in whipping gusts all around us—swirling debris and shaking the boughs of every tree along the perimeter of the graveyard. The space around us went wild as I pulled the solemn skull from the bag.

My hand froze with my fingers in the eye sockets as terror quaked through me. The urge to throw it consumed my every nerve but I held on, protecting it from harm. Tears ran down my cheeks without shame.

"Hugh." Paul's voice broke through the roar of the wind around us.

My arm trembled, shaking the skull in my hand, making it look as if it were struggling to come back to life. I pushed it back into the bag and rested it within the rods and tubes, his bones I assumed.

My knuckles hit off another metal plate and I pulled it out as I withdrew my hand from the bag, shaking off the heebie-jeebies from whatever else could be lurking in there.

The boar and galley of the O'Maille family crest stood proud upon the plate. I inhaled and filled my lungs, hearing the clan motto play over in my mind. *Terra Marique Potens. Powerful by Land and Sea.* I placed it next to the DeLacy crest in the moss, feeling closer than ever to reconnecting Grace to Hugh.

I rewrapped the leather bundle of Hugh's remains with careful efficiency and lifted it back into the tomb.

He fought for Grace. He defended her honor and her territory. She was his captain. His queen. With deep respect, I handled his remains like those of a brave and honorable soldier.

I inched deeper and deeper, scooching along on my knees, until his remains rested in their original place. I pressed on the bag with my hands, as if to assure him that he wouldn't be alone any longer. His time for eternal peace was soon to come.

As my eyes adjusted to the darkness more, I reached over and felt around at the box, searching for something to grab onto. The potential contents couldn't be ignored and my burning curiosity kept me moving.

A metal ring hung from the center of one side. I pulled on it and dragged the heavy wooden crate, shimmying it across the slab floor to the opening of the tomb. I crawled out and then reached back for it. Rory squeezed in closer and found another ring on the opposite side and we heaved it out and onto the ivy.

The wind whipped into a violent frenzy casting twigs and leaves through the air like explosive shrapnel. I shielded my eyes in response but felt none of it as our spot remained calm and unaffected, like a safe dome. The churning blasts came right to the edge of the burial mound and the surrounding gravestones but spread up and over us, leaving us untouched.

In the blur of the gusts and debris, a figure emerged at the side of the mound, crouched and struggling with his chains. His muscles strained from the effort of centuries, trying to free himself. His leather pants and vest moved with him like his own skin as strands of hair broke free from the cord that tied it back as he struggled.

It was Hugh.

Bound by time and grief.

I jerked my gaze over to Paul in terror, begging him with my tear-filled eyes for him to be seeing the same thing. His eyes locked on Hugh as his jaw hung open and his head nodded in astonishment.

Rory and Fergal froze in disbelief and stared. Fergal stepped back to distance himself from the ghostly apparition, his head shaking as if wishing it away.

I moved faster as my hands shook and fiddled with the latch that sealed the crate. The rusted metal flap pressed over a protruding metal piece. I pried the time-seized latch with my fingers and forced it off the peg, bending my nails to the quick in my haste. Pressing my palms along the line of the lid, I pushed the top open and it fell back on its stiff leather hinges.

We all leaned at the same time and peered in, holding our breath with wide eyes.

I blinked into the crate to clear my vision and be sure what I was seeing wasn't a hallucination. The shaking of my body twitched through every awakened nerve as I shook my head in disbelief.

I'd just opened a pirate's treasure chest from the 1500s.

My hands ran back through my hair in disbelief.

The weight of our actions through my mind into overload. We were traveling back in time by touching these things, breathing the same air as them, and bringing a new level of life to their once-lost existence.

The contents of the chest shone out from their dark, ancient imprisonment, begging to be touched. Scrolls and fabric, metal wrist plates—like battle armor cuffs adorned with clan symbols—and Celtic broaches for fastening cloaks.

I reached in and lifted a handkerchief, yellowed and stiff from time but still holding onto its lace edges, and placed it on my lap safely. I removed the wrist cuffs and their embedded gemstones glistened in every direction, widening Fergal's eyes and stretching his sinister grin.

The scrolls reached out from within, as if hoping to be picked next. I pulled the engraved metal tubes out of the crate, one at a time, and laid them side by side in the ivy. Weathered parchment poked out of one and I gently eased it from its protective shell.

The three men hovered over me while the winds whipped into a frenzy as I touched the concealed sheets, closing in for a better look. Unrolling just a small bit, images of hand drawn maps, old English scrawl, and royal seals jumped out at us. More treaties and land deeds.

Everything we needed.

My eyes darted to Paul's, wide with astonishment.

"It's all here. Grace's treasures." I peered back into the box to see what was hidden under the scrolls.

I gasped and reeled back with my hand covering my mouth.

Coins. Hundreds of them. And more jewels. Rings. A crown.

"Oh my god." I spoke into the chest.

"Real pirate's booty," Rory chuffed, shaking his head.

Thunder roared around us as the sky darkened to heavy black and the sound of a stampede rumbled from every direction. Gráinne took form in the swirling squall and stood tall at the top of the burial mound, staring down on us.

My captain. The pirate queen.

Her thick locks of long hair flew in the powerful gusts as the fabric of her white blouse flapped across her arms in ivory waves. The leather of her vest laced tight under her chest wrapped her waist with a thick sash that held the empty sword scabbard.

Gráinne's penetrating eyes held me slave to her every command and my fierce loyalty guided each move without question.

Her arm jolted up as she pointed at me and then at the crate, leading my line of vision with her finger straight back to the tomb. I nodded in understanding and lowered my head in shame wondering if I'd made a huge mistake.

My face reddened as I gathered the contents back into the crate, imagining violating the pirate queen, instead of helping. I didn't dare look at her again.

My muscles acted like they belonged to someone else and the task became increasingly difficult under her close scrutiny. I readied the scrolls for last, planning to place the handkerchief delicately across the top.

As I lifted them up to the chest, a burst of agitated wind blasted them out of my hands. In a rattling splash of clanking metal, they landed by her sword on the cart.

Rory startled at first but then stepped closer to the cart and with hands on his hips, set a protective barrier between the items and Fergal.

I twisted back toward Grace with wide eyes.

She gave us the scrolls.

Relief washed over me. I hadn't upset her.

And she allowed the scrolls into Rory's protection.

My eyebrows scrunched as my head tipped in thought.

As I gazed back into her eyes, her voice filled my mind with her ancient language that permeated our sheltered space.

Rory moved closer, hearing it too.

"Taoiseach na clans O'Maille agus Mac Mathúna. Ní mór duit troid go Gaedhealach chur ar ais go dtí a ghlóir bunaidh. Beidh an Druids tú a threorú. Filleadh ar an talamh ar an rhythms ársa an aois Ceilteach."

Rory repeated the words as they flowed from her.

"Chieftains of the clans O'Maille and MacMathuna. You must fight to restore Gaelic Ireland to her, her original glory." He stumbled on some words but continued in monotone. "The Druids will guide you. Return this land to the ancient rhythms of the Celtic age."

I looked at him and he gazed back at me, pressing his lips together. He nodded and looked back at Grace. He nodded at her, too.

She was pleased and gave a half-smile, confirming in my gut she knew I would do the right thing with the scrolls.

I stood taller and stronger, accepting my responsibility to Grace without hesitation. I gazed into her eyes and was pulled into the magic of the universe swirling in her pupils. But then my line of vision was drawn away by the motion at the side of the tomb.

Hugh.

Gráinne's eyes followed mine, only so slightly. She was aware of his presence but remained focused on what needed to get done first.

She waved her arm from the chest to the tomb, guiding me to return it to its place of eternal rest.

After placing the handkerchief on the ancient treasures, I sealed the crate and scrambled to my feet. Paul reached for a handle with his good arm and helped me lift it to the opening of the vault.

I pushed it in and shimmied it to the back of the crypt to its original location. Panic sent quakes through me as I prayed the stone door wouldn't slam shut and seal me in there for all of time.

It was just a feeling I couldn't get used to.

I backed out clumsily, scraping my knees in my haste—happy to never have to go in there again but knowing too well that its haunting darkness would revisit me in my nightmares or future panic attacks.

"Let's slide her in!" I commanded.

We backed the cart up to the tomb and heaved the sarcophagus into the opening. Struggling with the minute adjustments of lining it up, we set it straight and pushed. The stone coffin slid into place, a perfect fit.

Before closing the door, I took the two family crests and placed them, overlapping each other, at the inner entrance to the tomb.

Rory and Paul pushed on the stone slab door until it crunched its way back into its tight seal. I jumped up the side of the mound where the key stuck out and pulled it from the hole. I wiggled it into the hole above and pushed the key in, prongs down. With a steady movement of my wrist, I lifted the key shaft, pressing the prongs downward, relocking the internal pins.

Together again. Forever.

With key in hand, I ran back to Paul's side as we watched the swirling dark storm settle into a calm stream of white and gray gusts, moving around us like a whirlpool of light.

Gráinne's form glided to Hugh as he burst from his crumbling shackles. The chains and cuffs fell to his feet in a clanging heap, freeing him from centuries of separation from his true love, as his powerful arms embraced her.

He lifted her onto his chest and she held him around his neck. Her head fell back and tears streamed from her eyes as she rejoiced in their reunion. He spun her in the glowing white mist as his heavy black boots sent quakes through the ground.

He stopped then and lowered her in front of him and kissed her with a passion that had grown for over five hundred years.

Their contact blew my mind with a blast of light that blinded me. When the flash cleared from my eyes, they were gone.

The wind and mist seeped into the earth and air and out into the world around us.

A final clang rang out and I jumped to the mound where they had stood together.

The scabbard lay at the top of the stony tomb and I reached for it. Closing my fingers around it, I knew it to be a gift.

The four of us stood silent, staring at the sacred ground where Grace O'Malley and Hugh DeLacy reunited after centuries of grief and searching.

Together now.
For eternity.

Chapter Nineteen
Defector

"Don't move!"

Fergal's command cut through the blissful calm like a fire-breathing dragon.

His hands grasped the hilt of her sword and he pointed it at my face, addressing me with it. The weight of the blade made it wobble in his hands as he tried to focus it on me.

My eyes darted to the cart where the sword had been.

He'd crept around us and swiped it off the unguarded cart as we stared into the realm of the other side. His lack of respect and humility fueled him to continue his vile thieving and plotting.

Paul jumped in reaction to the threat and placed himself between the sword and me in one swift motion.

Fergal aimed the sword square at his chest with a jerk. His eyes bounced from each of us, as if trying to predict our next moves.

"All this was meant to be mine!" He turned to Rory. "Ours!" He spat at him. "Defector!"

"No, Fergal. You're wrong." Rory shot down his rant. "You've been wrong all along."

He took a step closer to Fergal.

"We will honor whatever is written in those documents, Fergal. It's our rightful duty." Rory's tone left no room for negotiating.

His chest pushed out as his shoulders squared up against Fergal.

Stepping back from Rory's advances with a lost look of what to do next, Fergal turned the sword on *him*.

"You! You're the weak link. Turnin' yer back on five hundred years of clan history." Fergal spat at him again. "Yer a buncha fools, leavin' the treasure in there to rot!"

"Drop the sword, Fergal. We're done here." Rory's voice remained calm and steady as he held his hands up to settle Fergal's rising angst.

Paul dropped his hands to his knees, losing strength, and looked up at him.

"What? Are ya gonna kill us all, Fergal? Is that your plan?" Paul shook his head, looking up through his brow.

Fergal snarled with a laugh.

"No. Not *my* chieftain." He huffed, glancing at Rory. "But if I have to do his dirty work for 'im, then so be it. I know my role in my tribe."

He pointed the sword at Paul's chest and took a step closer to him.

Paul held his ground, remaining between Fergal and me.

Panic widened my eyes as Fergal's pupils shrank to pinpricks as he zoomed in on his target.

"Fergal stop!" My voice shattered the tension in the air. "It's me you want. You've caused enough harm to him."

Paul's broken condition spoke for itself as he slumped and propped himself up on his knees.

"That's right. Tis you I want. To stop," he spat.

He stared Rory down, as if annoyed that he had to take care of everything himself. Then he set his attention back to me, with a piercing glare of disdain. He took a quick step to the side and turned the sword on me.

"Careful now, Fergal." Rory grew tense in response to Fergal's move on me. "The consequences to a traitor are steep. Make another move on her and I'll have to stop you m'self. For good." His hand went up, to redirect Fergal. "Understand?"

"You already think I'm nothin'. Go ahead and try to stop me." He turned the sword back on Paul. "This is my rightful duty and I will not yield!"

He strained, spitting the words out through clenched teeth.

Rory took a step closer to Fergal.

"Stay back, Taoiseach. Don't try to change what's meant to be." Fergal blasted at Rory, referring to him as chieftain with loathing judgment oozing from his tone.

He held the sword against Rory and then back to Paul.

"She'll watch her lover die by my hand," Fergal threatened. "It's what history intended. To finish what I started, long ago." He growled at me like an angry animal. "I. Will. Stop. Her."

My heart plummeted as I considered his words. "Finish what he started?"

Was he Hugh's killer?

It was impossible. But the deeper the notion sank into me, the more possible it became.

Terror rose in me and pounded in my head as I understood Fergal's motivation and I gazed into Paul's eyes, seeing death and carnage deep within him. He held my gaze, unblinking, as if I were the last thing he wanted to ever see.

In a burst of force, Fergal lunged at Paul with the sword aimed at his heart.

"For my warrior captain! The true MacMahon chieftain!" he proclaimed as he sailed at him.

My exploding mind slowed every movement to a slow-motion pace.

Rory glided across the ivy to block Fergal's attack on Paul and launched himself at him.

Fergal side-stepped to avoid Rory as Paul put his arm up in defense while reaching back for me with his wounded arm.

Without hesitation, I pushed around Paul and with my head down, bulldozed at Fergal and knocked him off his path with a blow that hollowed out my ears, making them ring.

My strength was that of a bull. Or that of a pirate queen.

The sword flew from Fergal's hands as he stumbled off course from my hit and Paul dove out of range.

Rory ran through the air where Fergal had stood and regained his balance while spinning back around.

The sword spun through the air then landed with a twanging *whap* on its hilt, wedged at the base of an O'Maille gravestone, pointing straight into the air like a beacon.

Fergal stumbled from my blow, off his murderous course, and caught my eye just before falling onto the gravestone.

The surprised look in his eye, just before he fell, haunted me. Like he knew in that moment, I'd beat him. Or worse.

The three of us squared up together in solidarity against him. He held the top of the monument, bracing himself, and snarled back at us in seething defiance.

"Ya foo…." Fergal hesitated and hacked, glaring at us with murderous intent. "Ya'll nev…." He stopped again, struggling to pull in a full breath.

He pushed with his arms to prop himself up on the stone but winced in pain, unable to move. He dropped his gaze down and met the sword's hilt, jammed into the base of the gravestone, and followed the length of the blade as it went out of sight up into his chest.

He coughed out blood. It gurgled down his chin as his lips curled in revolt.

I turned my face into Paul's chest to hide from the gruesome image.

Rory ran to Fergal and held him by the shoulders. "Hang on, man. We'll get help."

With no regard for his own predicament, Fergal reached up and grabbed Rory's neck and squeezed, revealing the insidious tribal tattoo on his forearm.

"Scum. Defec…." and his voice trailed off into oblivion as his hand fell from Rory's neck.

Paul collapsed as the final ounce of energy left his body in the same moment Fergal's soul left *his*.

"'Paul!" I cushioned his head in my lap, looking anywhere but at Fergal's propped up body.

My body shivered beneath him, releasing the terror of Fergal from my being.

He was gone.

And we would be safe now.

Tears fell from my eyes in relief of it being over.

"Come on." Rory encouraged me up. "We need to get out of here. Before anyone else, or any*thing* else, shows up." He looked back at Fergal. "Sure, and we'll need be callin' the gards, I s'pose."

Rory pushed Paul upright, to help him to stand. His limp body fell back into the ivy. He'd half-passed out, either from blood loss or dehydration. Rory crouched down and pulled Paul up over his shoulder and hoisted him up as a firefighter would.

"Get the scrolls and the scabbard," Rory directed me. "We'll get the sword later." He pursed his lips and winced at the thought. "You know, after the Garda have a look."

I grabbed my pack and stuffed it with all my things and added the new scrolls into it.

The nagging desire to get my hands on the sword pestered me to the point where I could think of nothing else. It had been held just out of my reach for so long. I ground my teeth in frustration and craved it.

Rory was right, though. It was part of a crime scene. A gruesome one. And I had to be patient.

I scratched my head and looked back over my shoulder. I hated being patient.

Rory leapt over the low wall of the cemetery, carving a shortcut to the car. The extra weight on his shoulders didn't slow him or cause him to falter in any way.

He lay Paul in the backseat and I positioned myself under Paul's head to keep him comfortable while we waited for the police.

My head tilted as I stared into Paul's peaceful face. It was like being home. His face was all I wanted to see, ever.

Rory's voice filled the car but didn't break my gaze.

"We'll bring the scrolls to the Elder Council. We'll tell our story and see what their ruling is. I can't... I just can't believe all of this." His head shook at the night sky.

Rory seemed to have the same plan as me.

Even now. Even after everything.

I smiled to myself, hoping for a peaceful resolution. One that worked for both clans.

I pulled my pack closer, keeping the scrolls connected to me. This gift from Gráinne was the final piece needed to put her soul completely to rest and end the centuries-old curse on my clan.

She was finally reunited with Hugh. After centuries of sorrow and searching.

My haunting visions would end. And the next generation of O'Malley women would be spared. I inhaled deeper than I ever had and blew it out through pursed lips as contentment settled into my bones.

And now, her territory could be reinstated to its rightful holders— the O'Malleys. Peace and prosperity would return to the clan and it would become strong again.

A giddy smile pressed on my lips as I imagined the possibilities.

I would have to figure out my role as chieftain and what to do next from here. The myths and legends of generations tugged on me as impatience gnawed on my nails.

The vast responsibility and the mystical unknown didn't bother me though.

I was home.

I was finally home.

**

Oncoming headlights filled the car with streams of blue and white light.

My head bobbed to avoid the assault of flashing lights on my weary eyes. Buzz from walkie-talkies filled the road along with pacing uniformed-men asking questions.

"You stay here, Maeve. I'll take them into the boneyard." Rory leaned into the backseat to check if I was okay. "There's a gard in the car, keepin' watch. So, you'll be fine."

I listened to the gravel-grinding footsteps and fading voices as Rory brought three officers with him into the cemetery.

Paul twisted and then jolted to wakefulness after the searing pain from his shoulder woke him.

"Ach. Jeez." He sucked air through clenched teeth and looked around. "Where's Rory?"

"The police are here. Rory took them to Fergal's body."

He reached for me. "Are you okay? Holy Jesus. I don't know what I'd do if that fooker hurt you."

His lost eyes searched me.

"It's over now." I rubbed the back of my fingers along his cheekbone. "He's gone."

"He's gone!" Rory's voice filled the car with new alarm.

"What! Who?" I stared at him as my face awakened with horror.

"Fergal. He's gone," Rory repeated.

My eyes shot open in terror.

There was no way. He was dead.

Fergal's revolting stink awakened in my nostrils, causing me to retch, reminding me of his decaying condition. Nothing had a stench like that, except… a rotting corpse.

A shudder of pure disgust ran through me.

The police came to the car and looked in at Paul and me.

"Sorry, miss. No body. No crime." He took a better look at Paul through squinted eyes. "However, you might want to press some charges, sir. You look at bit under the weather."

"It was Fergal." He hid his injured shoulder and put on a strong face to avoid interrogation. "They'll take me to the ER now. No worries."

"Ach, sure. Your call." He nodded at Paul, then turned his gaze to me. "Well, I understand this belongs to you, miss."

The officer held the sword out in full view. Without any traces of blood or malpractice, it glinted bright light into my eyes.

"No law against wieldin' swords, sure, odd enough." He smirked at the loophole in the law.

Rory brought him around back and they placed the sword in the trunk like a fragile relic, though we knew better of its practical use.

Rory pulled away slowly from the scene, leaving the flashing squad cars and buzzing radios to headquarters, behind us.

"No bleedin' on me mum's backseat now, McGratt," Rory poked.

I pulled my gaze from Paul's face to verbally smack Rory for the sarcasm but my eyes were drawn out the window behind us instead, back toward the cemetery.

Over the flashing blue and white lights of the gards, my eyes widened as a haze of red and black gusts swirled above the cemetery, gaining strength and fury within itself. The whirling streaks grew stronger in intensity and pulled into a tight funnel of red rage.

My jaw fell open as I stared at the violent force that could be only one thing.

The warrior.

He'd come for Fergal. He'd taken him back.

I dropped my face into my hands and rubbed my forehead with enough pressure to redden the skin.

No.

It couldn't be.

I dragged my fingers down my face as I looked up at the crimson night sky again.

As words of caution prepared to leave my lips, they stuck on my tongue as the red cyclone dispelled and spread across the night sky.

And into oblivion.

Epilogue

"It's yours now," Paul said as we left the assembly. "Officially granted to you by the Elder Council of the Chieftain Tribes. Kinda makes it official." He squeezed my hand. "No pressure. Particularly since it's been deemed priceless."

I looked around with exaggerated surveillance, pretending to search for lurking brown cloaks, then gripped the hilt through its protective wrap. I swung the sword with precision and leaped in the air like a panther attacking its prey. A final swirl and slash then finished with a graceful curtsy.

Paul tipped his head. "So, you're a pro. Where'd you learn to wield a sword like that?"

I looked down at my adept sword-slinger stance and said, "Actually, I have no idea."

I considered the idea of Grace training her daughter in stealth swordsmanship. The lost daughter. Maybe the skill had been passed down somehow.

I shook my head to set the thought aside. But I'd be sure to practice my form to perfection. I knew that much.

"Looks a little strange to the unsuspecting eye, Taoiseach." Rory's voice came up from behind me. "You realize you're in public, right?" He pressed his lips together and tipped his head.

Paul stood up straight and lost his playfulness. His primal response to Rory hadn't changed a bit, even after all we'd been through together.

Rory nodded at Paul and walked up to me.

"Now that the official business is taken care of," he started, "I aim to find out your plans on returnin' stolen lands to the MacMahons." His original pleasant tone dropped a few octaves to something more serious.

My eyebrows shot up in curiosity as I watched the look in his eyes change from jovial to sinister. My eyes narrowed trying to recognize him through his unfamiliar stare.

"I don't mean to rush you," he added, "but sure, you and I both know there's unfinished business to all this. Castles and land, taken by force." He stepped closer and leaned in to me, glaring into my eyes. "I aim ta get back what's mine."

Paul stepped forward with an arm out, creating space between Rory and me.

I held Rory's stare, feeling his aggressive posturing as a direct threat. Grace's ring sizzled on my finger as it awoke with the sensation of molten lava.

"Back off, Rory." I held my palm up at his chest to stop his pressuring. "Negotiations are still to come. But now that I've been appointed O'Malley Chieftain by my kinsmen, it's my lineage-based duty to act as custodian to my clan."

"Ya think yer royalty now or somethin'?" His eyebrows pressed together and he shifted his weight from one foot to the other.

His classic insecurity seeped through his nervous fidgeting.

He knew my clan held more power over his. Through war and politics of medieval times, the status of the O'Malley clan grew powerful. It was time now for me to restore it.

"I'm Chieftain of the O'Malley Clan, Rory. It's who I am."

"So it is." He pressed his lips together in a tight line.

He reached for the hilt of my sword and I swatted his hand away with a solid chop of my wrist.

Rory pulled his arm back and held it to his ribs protectively.

"Well, ya'd be needin' ta watch your back then." He looked from me to Paul, then back at me.

"Seems our friend from Clare Island, you know, the freaky warrior… He's none too pleased with the proceedings. I thought ya should know. In case you get a visit from 'im."

He looked at Paul with raised eyebrows, as if passing responsibility of my well-being to him.

My eyes shot wide open. "What do you mean?"

Rory pulled his sleeve up and exposed his inner forearm. A festering burn covered the majority of the area. It was fresh and raw, nearly still smoking.

"Oh my god, Rory!" I bent in and looked closer at the burn.

As the image took form in my mind, I shot upright and stepped back.

The same tribal marking had been tattooed on Fergal's arm. It was an exact match.

Paul turned pale and stared at Rory in surprise and then looked back at the mark.

"He branded you," Paul stated.

Rory lifted his chin once, in a subtle nod and covered his arm.

"Keep your sword by ya at all times, Maeve," Rory directed me. "He may be holdin' ya accountable for Fergal's death. Don't want to take any chances."

He shook his head at the unfortunate possibilities.

I swallowed hard and looked around at the clouds and searched for any sign of a breeze or red haze. I stole a glimpse of Rory from the corner of my eye and searched him for clues.

I wondered if the warrior had turned him against me. Were we truly destined to be enemies?

And who else might be against me?

Patricia flashed in my mind in the same moment and I turned to Paul instinctively. He'd dismissed her involvement so easily. Yet she'd had direct contact with Fergal and his rogue tribe. She'd put Paul in harm's way.

All of us, really.

My eyes narrowed as my fear of her turned from jealousy to that of a true foe.

Rory squinted his eyes and shot me a sideways glance.

"On the brighter side," he interjected, "I heard from some inner council members—there was more than just maps and deeds in the scrolls, ya know."

He looked straight into my eyes waiting for me to take the bait.

"What do you mean?"

What else could there be, besides maps and deeds?

My mind raced.

Rory pressed his lips together and smiled.

"Love letters." He lifted his eyebrows at me.

My eyes darted to Paul's.

We never actually saw the full contents. The scrolls were taken to a museum for proper opening and preservation, then stored there in the name of the O'Malley Clan.

"Love letters?" I looked back to Rory.

"Yup. Loads of 'em." He smirked a half smile. "In Hugh's handwritin', and the written word of Gráinne Ní Mháille, herself. Controversial, too, I hear." He winked and he walked away with familiar arrogance in his stride.

I followed his confident gait as he sauntered toward the city center as if he didn't have a care in the world. His black boots dragged at the back with each step. I pictured the high laces that hid under his jeans. My eyes moved higher and I forced myself to look away.

I turned with a guilty smile and fell right into Paul's watchful gaze. His tilted head and pinched eyebrows slapped the smile off my face and I laughed.

"Warriors and love letters. Sheesh," I huffed. And my eyes glued themselves to the sidewalk as we headed to McSwiggan's for pints.

"Told ya he couldn't be trusted," Paul said through clenched teeth.

***

My fingers clung to the envelope in my lap as we pulled up to St. Mary's House of Tears. They were expecting us but didn't know the extent of the news we had for them or the value of the investment funds in the envelope.

It didn't take me a split second to know what I would do with the trust fund. The deeds led to a fortune of land, castles, and valuable historical documents beyond measure. All granted to the O'Malley Clan and placed in my guardianship.

Aside from securing professional restoration and preservation of the Clare Island Abbey and the castle ruin, as well as Rockfleet, I had a bigger plan, and the O'Malley Clan Tribal Council members—the 'Original Three' from Ballynahinch—supported it unanimously, with agreement from the entire Clan Council of Elders.

I still had to wonder though, what the true intentions of the 'Original Three' were. I had broken the wax seal on their letter and read it the night before Clan Council. I kept the contents secret because they made no sense to me.

Why would they send me details of a marriage to O'Flaherty? As if it had anything to do with me.

But the nag it created in the back of my mind wouldn't stop. They called me "the lost daughter" and seemed hell-bent on making more out of it. And they had said the ring held the secret.

What secret?

I looked down at the ring on my hand and examined the bulky design and mythical details. It held a million secrets, across the centuries and through Grace and Hugh's love story.

I rubbed the top gemstone and ran my finger along the far side of the setting. It moved across a straight line of metal, like a thick wire, and I rubbed back and forth on it, feeling minute bumps and ridges that I hadn't noticed before.

I turned my hand to see the far side of the ring and stared at the small seam of metal, camouflaged among the intricate Celtic artwork. My eyes widened as I gasped and covered my mouth with my other hand.

I was staring at a hinge. The ring was a locket of some kind.

The door flew open and Mary welcomed us in with warm embrace.

"Brigid is inside awaitin' yer arrival. Come in out of the chill."

She ushered us in to the kitchen where the kettle was set to boil and my mind quickly moved back to the visit.

"How's Brigid been these days? Is she okay?" I remembered her crazed state last time I visited and worried she was still frenzied to that level.

"She's well. The letter you sent was helpful. It explained everything to her in a way she could grasp. On her own time." Mary nodded with pleasure. "She read it over and over, for days, until she came to believe every word."

Mary poured the tea.

"She's more grounded since. Like a reckonin' or a comin' home," she added.

"Can I see her?" My knees bounced out my jitters.

"Go on." She swooshed at me with her tea towel. "She's in the sittin' room. I'll entertain Paul here. No worries."

She passed him the milk for his tea and gave him an encouraging tap on the shoulder to drink up.

Brigid sat facing the fire with her head tipped to the side. She stared into the flickering light as if in a trance. I swallowed and moved closer, feeling my optimism wane.

"Hello, Brigid."

She flinched, like being woken from a dream, and turned to me with a bright smile.

"Hello, Maeve." She bounced up and came to me. "Thanks for comin'."

Her arms reached out to embrace me. My inner micro-muscles flexed in preparation for the flight response, but I concealed the natural reaction with my returned hug.

She smiled as sincerity shone from her eyes.

"Won't ya sit down?" She gestured to the upholstered chair next to hers.

We sat in silence for a moment and my spine stiffened as I searched for words. I had no idea what to say at a time like this.

"So, you got my letter…?" I mumbled.

"Maeve. Everything's different now." She leaned closer and gazed directly into my eyes. "I have a clarity I haven't felt since I was a teen. I know meself again." Her eyes filled with tears. "I'm no longer lost."

She reached for my hand and squeezed it.

"You saved m' life, Maeve."

My eyes widened and I gulped on the tightening tickle in my throat. Her words were unexpected and my response to them even more so. My eyes filled with heavy tears and they poured over my lids in thick wet streams while I kept my gaze fixed on hers, never blinking, certain to not miss a word.

She continued.

"Grace had been comin' to me for years. I thought to kill me. Or at least to drive me mad. But she needed me. She needed me to do what you have done. I just didn't know." She shook her head. "I was too frightened."

Her face fell as she stared at her wringing hands in her lap.

"You just needed someone to believe you." I leaned forward. "To understand."

"Yes. That *has* made all the difference." Her lips curled up in a gentle smile and her eyes twinkled as she took a slow, deep inhale and let it flow out of her like years of isolation and fear draining from every pore.

Mary bounced into the room with a clanging tray of tea.

"How're me ladies?" she sang and brightened the room. "Brid?"

Brigid held eye contact with me, as if fighting to keep the dream going.

"Good, Mary. T'anks."

Mary's eyebrows scrunched as her head pulled back in surprise. She blinked at Brigid as if she didn't recognize her.

"Well, okay then. Shan't keep Mr. McGratt waitin' in the kitchen."

She left the tray for us and headed back toward the door, keeping a curious watchful eye over her shoulder on Brigid.

Brigid passed me a tea cup and pushed the milk jug closer.

"So now what?" She shook her head in bewilderment. "I feel like I have a new life to live."

I bit my lip to suppress the huge smile that pushed its way out.

"I have an idea for you, Brigid. And for Mary." My eyebrows shot up in anticipation of her response.

Brigid's eyes widened and her back straightened.

I continued, "And for St. Mary's."

"What is it?" she whispered, moving in closer to me with twinkling eyes.

***

"Mary! Mary! Mary! Mary!" Brigid's voice filled the house and burst into the kitchen.

I followed her racing form, feeling as giddy as a schoolgirl.

Paul's chair screeched against the floor as he stood in alarm.

The last time he heard Brigid yelling Mary's name that way was a complete disaster and he jumped to defensive attention.

"Mary!" Brigid embraced her in a powerful hold that nearly lifted Mary off her feet. "It's all going to be okay. We can stay!"

"What?" Mary's face fell in disbelief. "Whatcha mean, Brid? Are ya jokin' me, now?"

"No, there's money, Mary. A trust fund to keep St. Mary's. To turn her into a learning institute. For archaeology. And Celtic history. Like a retreat for students to come do research and, and…." Brigid's feet danced as she spoke.

Mary's hands flew to her mouth with a gasp. Her drawn look of fear and apprehension pulled up and brightened into a look of belief and hope.

"Really…?" Mary turned to me for assurance.

I nodded and smiled as Brigid went on.

"We can run it, Mary. Like fine Irish hospitality. And I'll be the one to tell everyone about Grace O'Malley. Sure, I'm an expert." She burst out laughing as the words flew out of her.

Mary looked at me again with eyebrows raised.

I nodded at her.

"We'll call it, 'The Gráinne Ní Mháille Historical Institute of Higher Learning,'" I confirmed.

Mary's hands flew to her mouth again.

"NUIG has already agreed to back it," Paul added, with a hint of pride in his tone.

NUIG's offer to Paul went beyond his wildest dreams and his path to tenure unfolded in front of him with every step closer to the GMH Institute.

He continued, "And they want to create a national memorial. To the mothers and babies whose souls passed through here."

His lips pressed together as we all held a moment of silence.

Mary picked her head up, eyes misted.

She moved to the table and flopped onto a chair.

"Well, I'll be."

THE END

Thank you for reading! Find book three of the *Pirate Queen* series coming soon.

And catch the prequel, ROCKFLEET, in the Other Worlds: A Limited Edition Collection of Paranormal Romance and Science Fiction Romance box set, coming this October.

For more from Jennifer Rose McMahon, check out her website at www.jenniferrosemcmahon.com and join her mailing list.

Please sign up for the City Owl Press newsletter for chances to win special subscriber-only contests and giveaways as well as receiving information on upcoming releases and special excerpts.

www.jenniferrosemcmahon.com

www.facebook.com/jenniferrosemcmahon/

www.twitter.com/BohermoreSeries/

www.instagram.com/bohermore_series/

All reviews are welcome and appreciated. Please consider leaving one on your favorite social media and book buying sites.

For books in the world of romance and speculative fiction that embody Innovation, Creativity, and Affordability, check out City Owl Press at www.cityowlpress.com.

Acknowledgments

A huge thank you to City Owl Press for the hard work and dedication to this series.

I want to thank Amanda Roberts, Associate editor, for her incredible guidance and fine tuning. And a special thank you to Tina Moss, Executive Editor and Chief Operations Officer, for her mentoring and professionalism and to Yelena Casale, Executive Editor and Chief Marketing Officer, for her marketing support and expertise. I am so happy and honored to be a part of the City Owl Team.

Special thanks to Naomi Hughes for being an amazing writing coach and mentor.

I also want to thank Sarah Kelley, Chieftain of the O'Malley Clan, for her support of this project and for inviting me to perform a reading from the Pirate Queen Series in a medieval castle at the O'Malley Clan Rally in Claregalway, Ireland, 2017.

And especially, enormous gratitude, to my family and friends who have believed in me all along the way and encouraged me through this journey with love, laughter and friendship.

About the Author

JENNIFER ROSE McMAHON has been creating her Pirate Queen Series since her college days abroad in Ireland. Her passion for Irish legends, ancient cemeteries, and medieval ghost stories has fueled her adventurous storytelling, while her husband's decadent brogue carries her imagination through the centuries. When she's not in her own world writing about castles and curses, she can be found near Boston in the local coffee shop, yoga studio, or at the beach...most often answering to the name 'Mom' by her fab children four.

www.jenniferrosemcmahon.com

About the Publisher

CITY OWL PRESS is a cutting edge indie publishing company, bringing the world of romance and speculative fiction to discerning readers.

www.cityowlpress.com